Darling Rae

The Little Sister

with ~~lots~~ of love,

Tracey xxx

THE LITTLE SISTER

TRACEY WAPLES

LUME BOOKS
A JOFFE BOOKS COMPANY

Lume Books, London
A Joffe Books Company
www.lumebooks.co.uk

This book is a work of fiction. Names, characters, businesses, organisations, places and events are either the product of the author's imagination or are used fictitiously. Any resemblance to actual persons, living or dead, events or locales is entirely coincidental. The spelling used is British English except where fidelity to the author's rendering of accent or dialect supersedes this.

We love to hear from our readers!
Please email any feedback you have to: feedback@joffebooks.com

Cover design by Imogen Buchanan

ISBN: 978-1-83901-541-0

For John, William and Charles, with love,
as everything always is.

PART ONE

PROLOGUE

The car is stifling. It is thirty-five degrees outside and the air con clearly isn't up to it. I can feel the sweat trickling down my back and my thighs sticking together. My eyes sting but that's because I've barely slept. By the time Elisa came to collect me this morning I'd been up and dressed for hours.

We drive quickly. Unfamiliar sights, trees and signposts whizz by in a blur as the heat shimmers on the road. We travel for about half an hour before traffic builds and we are forced to slow.

"There will be an interpreter," Elisa says, not glancing my way. I nod, although I'm not sure why I would need one. Elisa has been more than adequate up to now.

"It's a formality," she says, as if reading my thoughts. "They have to be assured you understand everything."

The jam clears and we move forward again. Elisa indicates and pulls the car off the main highway. A large sign announcing Centro de la Ciudad appears. I recognise this area and my stomach lurches as I realise we are just minutes away. I squeeze my eyes tight shut and say a silent prayer.

As the police station comes into view the car seems to get hotter still. It's like an oven now and my face is burning. I wipe my clammy hands on my thighs.

Elisa drives round to the side and pulls up under a line of trees. "Ok, here," she says matter- of-factly, as if she was dropping me off at the airport. She leans into the back seat and pulls out her briefcase.

"Let's go," she says.

I follow her lead across the cobbled stones towards the large, imposing building. It seems too quiet. I look from left to right, expecting photographers to appear. Elisa strides forward purposefully. I wonder how many times she's been in this situation and realise I've never asked. In fact, I know so little about her, other than her track record as a criminal lawyer.

She pushes the door open. Fear simmers inside of me and bile rises in my throat. I swallow hard. I have imagined this scene so many times. The harrowing library of mental images I have curated, usually during the dark, small hours, are replaced as I take in my surroundings.

I'm not sure why I was expecting an old building, with lots of dark wood but it's bright and modern with whitewashed walls. There are lots of windows, too high to see out of, but they flood the place with light. What is the same as I had imagined is the noise and the smell. The place is packed. Several conversations are going on at once, some louder than others as voices compete to be heard.

Elisa indicates I should wait while she makes her way to the front desk. There is a line of men to my right, some sitting, some leaning against the wall. One holds his arm; his sleeve soaked in blood. Another sits with his head in his hands. Two armed police officers stand next to them, chattering in rapid Spanish. The rancid stench of sweat and tobacco pervades the air.

Every now and again a number is called and there is a flurry of activity. People come and go, doors open and close, there seems to be some semblance of order amongst the chaos. I remain exactly where Elisa left me, staring at my feet, trying my hardest not to cry.

Suddenly the main door bursts open and a young woman is escorted in by a female officer. She has a cut on her forehead, dried blood in a line down her cheek and the beginning of a black eye. Her hands are cuffed and she's yelling and wriggling, trying to shrug off her escort. I can't understand a word but the unmistakable smell of alcohol hangs over her like a cloud. I take a step backwards and jump as I bump into a harassed-looking man. His huge, tattooed arms bulge out of a grubby, tight T-shirt. "Sorry, erm, lo siento," I mumble but he doesn't seem to notice. He's arguing with the man next to him, jabbing his finger at a printed sheet.

The woman in handcuffs starts screaming; she yanks her shoulders from side to side, knocking into me. Another officer rushes to help and the pair drag her away, bundling her through a side door.

Finally, Elisa beckons me over. Relieved, I go to her and we follow a policewoman through what looks like an airport security scanner and along a corridor lined with identical doors. In front of the last one, the policewoman punches numbers into a keypad and we are led into a smaller room. A long, high desk divides the space. Uniformed officers stand behind the desk and a man in a dark suit greets Elisa. They seem to know each other. He glances at me without acknowledgement.

One of the officers is standing in front of a monitor. He taps away at his keyboard before asking my name. He speaks clearly, allowing Elisa to translate while the man in the suit, who I'm guessing is the interpreter, stands by. I've picked up enough Spanish by now to have a fair grasp of proceedings but it is comforting to listen to Elisa's familiar voice.

The comfort is short-lived. As soon as I hear the words "homicidio involuntario" my anxiety levels soar. Adrenaline courses through my body and the blood pounds so loudly in my ears that I'm sure everyone can hear it. My heart races and I'm struggling to take a proper breath. I don't need Elisa to translate. I'm familiar with the Spanish for manslaughter.

CHAPTER 1

She lay cocooned, listening contentedly to the rain smacking against the window, wind rattling the trees. She stretched out her hand to touch him, to feel his thick, dark hair that would contrast so starkly against the white linen. All she hit was the perfectly laundered pillowcase, and all she could feel was the smooth, cold sheet. She blinked as her eyes adjusted to the bedroom's dim light and then remembered. The sadness descended. Its weight crushing her, as it always did, and she rolled onto her side, drawing her knees to her chest, forcing herself to breathe slowly. It had always been a big bed, but it felt vastly oversized these days.

Struggling to pull the duvet around her for comfort, she realised Percy was on the bed behind her. He'd managed to push the bedroom door open again. She tugged hard, trying to dislodge him and caught the full force of his disapproving glare.

"Come on, Perce, move."

The large black cat still didn't budge. She yanked at the duvet again, and he let out an indignant little squeak. He was clever enough to know that if he held his stance she might leave him alone.

Sighing, she gave up and got out of bed, carefully clambering over Percy. It would have been easier to get out on the other side and avoid the cat, but the his-and-her side of the bed habit wasn't one she was ready to break. Wrapped in *his* dressing gown, she breathed deeply, catching the dwindling scent of *him.*

In the kitchen, she forced herself to sit at the table and eat something. She'd been skipping breakfast too often recently. She scrolled through the *Times* headlines. Putin, Brexit and a high-profile divorce took up most of the front page. A photograph of a cross-channel swimmer, beaming as she came out of the water, lightened the tone. She skimmed through the rest of the paper, pausing if something caught her eye.

Loading the single bowl and mug next to last night's plate, she turned the dishwasher on. It was time to get ready. She put on a plain navy dress teamed with a pale pink cashmere cardigan. A two-second smile hit her as she remembered how he used to tease her, calling it her uniform.

She tied back her long dark hair and applied natural-look makeup, catching sight of the misshapen wooden beams behind her in the mirror. She loved her little dressing room. Phil had suggested converting this dark corner into something useful. He'd always had great vision and had immediately seen the potential of Saffron Cottage, which they had made unrecognisable from the three-hundred-year-old dilapidated building they'd bought.

"See you later," she said, giving Percy one last cuddle.

Her commute was an easy twenty-five minute drive from the village into Cambridge, and the rain had stopped by the time she got to the surgery. She took the last remaining staff parking space next to her boss's shiny red Mercedes and opened the car door tentatively, making sure she didn't knock his paintwork.

Inside was the usual Monday morning mayhem. Phones ringing, a child crying loudly and a queue of people at the front desk. She slipped behind the reception area, head down to avoid eye contact with anyone. She wanted to go through her usual routine before seeing any patients. Coffee, emails, today's list. Always in that order.

Joanna, the practice manager, was in the galley kitchen and beamed when she saw her.

"Good morning, Helen. How are you? Nice weekend? Coffee?" she dropped a pod into the Nespresso machine without waiting for a reply. It was the same series of questions most Mondays. "I'll bring it to your room."

Helen went to collect her paperwork in the office behind reception. A handwritten Post-it note saying "*GYM CLASS TODAY*" was stuck to a computer screen. She wondered if this was someone's self-encouragement or bragging for colleagues' benefit.

The practice was one GP short, and the locum wasn't due until next week. Inevitable delays and cancellations had increased the number of disgruntled patients. Each passing day brought more. She could hear the calls at the front desk.

"As I said, I'm sorry, he can't see you today. I can offer you next Friday?"

"I am trying to help you, Mrs Black, but your results aren't back yet. As soon as they're in, someone will contact you."

One of the receptionists raised her eyes at Helen, and they exchanged a smile. On the other side of the desk, an elderly man leant against the wall for support, breathing heavily. Helen moved towards him to offer assistance just as a young woman came bustling through the front doors and steered him towards a seat.

In the sanctuary of her consultation room, Helen closed the door and opened the blinds before powering up her computer. Waiting for it to leap into life, she noticed the branches swaying on the large oak tree outside. The wind was still strong.

She had started to look through her list when a gentle knock at the door signalled the arrival of her coffee. Joanna placed a steaming mug in front of her.

"Thanks so much."

"Pleasure. It's going to be a busy one today."

"Mmm, so I see," Helen said, nodding towards her screen.

Joanna smiled and closed the door softly behind her. Helen's colleagues had been good to her. Supportive but never too intrusive. Thank God for her job. She might be in the business of making other people well, but in reality, her patients had helped her through some of her own darkest times. It was hard to believe it had been almost two years. Despite the heartache, she must have made progress. She wasn't waking in the middle of the night quite so much anymore, and she hadn't caught her mother side-eyeing her, checking she was ok, for quite a while. Weekends were still the worst, but she was getting better at planning ahead, making sure she wasn't on her own for long periods of time. She happily volunteered to cover when they needed extra work at the practice.

There was another knock, and before she could answer, Stephen walked in. "Ready for another week at the madhouse, Dr Nash?" He looked tired. At fifty-two, he was fighting to keep the advancing years at bay while trying to keep up with a wife who was considerably younger than him. A keen golfer, he struggled to accept being outplayed more and more by some of the younger members at his club and had recently employed a personal trainer to "up his cardio" and lower his handicap.

"I've got four extra emergencies already, and surgery hasn't even started," she replied.

"I know, which is why I thought I'd come and see you early to ask if we can book some time for a chat on Thursday. To go through the patient participation stuff amongst other things."

"Er… yes, sure. What time?" She hoped it wouldn't interfere with her plans. Her sister was taking her out for dinner.

"After afternoon surgery, if you don't mind? But I need to get away on time. I'm off to the theatre that night, so will need to be prompt."

"Of course," Helen suppressed a smile. Stephen had the worst record for timekeeping. His patients were always complaining about it.

"Did you have a nice weekend anyway?" he asked.

"Yes, great thanks," she lied. Her sister had been in Paris shopping, her parents weren't back from holiday until tomorrow and her friends, great though they were, had been doing what most couples or families do at weekends – hanging out, taking their children to various weekend activities, catching up on the previous week and preparing for the week ahead. She'd gone for a walk, done some shopping, visited the gym, read the papers. She had mastered lying as an automatic defence mechanism as well as shifting the focus of conversations. "What did you get up to?" she asked before he had a chance to ask her the same.

"Oh, the usual… stress. Kids, wife, *ex*-wife, golf. You know." She smiled as if she understood perfectly about kids, golf and ex-wives.

"It's good to come back to work for a rest," he added. She nodded knowingly. "And on that note, we'd better make a start. Don't forget Thursday."

She checked the name of her first patient before following him out.

"Mrs Clarkson?" she said to the room of expectant faces in the waiting room, smiling back at a toddler who beamed at her from his mother's lap.

A woman followed her to her room.

"How can I help?" Helen asked.

CHAPTER 2

Just as she had predicted, the surgery was particularly busy all week, and Thursday had come around before she knew it. She'd worked late every evening, but today she needed to finish in time to get home and change before Mia collected her.

There were still a couple of calls to make, and she dialled the first number. She didn't hear it ring before a worried voice sounded at the other end, "Hello?"

"Mrs Page?" Helen asked.

"Hello, Doctor Nash." Helen knew Mrs Page must have been waiting phone in hand for this call all day.

"Ok, I've got your results. They only came back this afternoon, and you'll be pleased to hear there's nothing to worry about. The scan showed that there was no increase in size, and the blood tests didn't throw out anything suspicious either. It's a benign cyst, and I very much doubt it'll cause you any problems." The woman made no attempt to disguise a loud sigh, as if she'd been holding her breath until Helen's call.

"The consultant and his team are happy for us to continue monitoring it so we will repeat the checks when necessary."

"Oh, thank you doctor, thank you so much" Her relief was clear, gratitude seeping through the receiver.

"My pleasure – now, if you have no other questions, I'll see you again in three months."

She dialled the next number. This time the news she had to deliver wasn't as good but she presented it as clearly as possible. There was no point in giving false reassurances. When she hung up, she sat back in her chair and let her shoulders fall. She doubted she'd ever get to a stage where she wouldn't feel sympathy for her patients.

Her internal phone lit up, snapping her out of her thoughts. Nicki, the practice nurse, wanted her to look over an emergency patient. Seventy-five-year-old Harry had slipped at home, knocking and cutting his head. She'd stitched it to save him a trip to A&E but wanted Helen to double-check that there were no signs of concussion.

"Why is it that when we're younger we 'fall over', but then once you're my age it's called 'having a fall'?" Harry asked as Helen performed a battery of checks on his pupils, reflexes and coordination.

She smiled. He certainly didn't seem to have suffered any additional side effects. "How did you get to the surgery, Harry?" she asked.

"My son. He was staying with me tonight anyway."

"Perfect. So you're not on your own. I'm sure you'll be fine, but symptoms can come on later. Any sign of a headache, nausea, just not feeling quite right, you'll have to let us know."

"Yes, of course," he said, "and thanks so much for seeing me. I couldn't face the drive and the long wait in hospital. I know you don't normally do A&E but Nicki here was very kind." He beamed at the nurse who returned his smile.

Glancing at the clock, Helen left Nicki to finish up. She still had the patient participation group meeting. There was no way she'd be able to squeeze that in and get home on time now. Should she tell Stephen she had run out of time or risk facing Mia's wrath? It was an easy decision. Stephen would be more likely to understand. She logged off the computer and grabbed her bag.

"I'm so sorry, but can I possibly push our meeting back?" she asked him. "I'm already running late, and I've got an appointment this evening. I wouldn't normally, but I—"

"It's absolutely fine. We can sort it tomorrow," Stephen assured her." So what are you up to this evening that's so pressing?"

"Just a longstanding thing I've had booked for ages, and I… er…" She wouldn't mention her birthday. She didn't want a fuss.

"Sure. Well, I'll see you later, erm, tomorrow," he said. "Have a good evening."

"Thanks, Stephen."

By the time she got home, her sister's car was already parked outside. Knowing Mia would be calling demanding to know where she was, Helen had left her phone off since leaving the surgery. She pulled alongside the gleaming Range Rover, smiling at the driver. Mia was invisible behind the security glass in the back. She was halfway through a driving ban and had employed a chauffeur, Mickey, to get around.

Helen got out at the same time as her sister and raised her arms above her head. "I'm so, so sorry. No point giving you the gory details, but I got stuck. Nothing I could do. I got here as quickly as I could."

"You've got five minutes to turn it around," Mia made no effort to disguise her annoyance. "*Literally* five minutes!" she added, following Helen into the house.

Percy met them at the door.

"Would you feed Percy for me please, Mia? His stuff is in the second cupboard on the—"

"Absolutely not! I won't touch that stinking cat food. You know I can't stomach it," Mia replied. Percy started to wind himself around Mia's legs. She kicked her leg out, making him jump away. Helen bent down and scooped him up, carrying him into the kitchen. Mia perched on the edge of the table, tapping her foot impatiently.

Upstairs, Helen reapplied her makeup. There was no time to shower, so she spritzed herself with Jo Malone's Nutmeg and Ginger before changing into a pale-blue chiffon dress.

"How's Chris?" she called down to Mia as she rearranged her hair into a bun at the nape of her neck.

"Fine, I haven't seen much of the old codger recently. I was in Paris until yesterday. I met with a fabulous plastic surgeon and did a bit of shopping." Helen sighed. She'd given up trying to talk her out of unnecessary surgeries. Once Mia made up her mind, it was futile. Her marriage to a wealthy businessman almost fifteen years her senior had given her access to an extravagant lifestyle, which Helen didn't think was always in her sister's best interests.

After pulling down some loose strands at the sides of her face, Helen abandoned the look altogether, leaving her hair long. As she turned to check her reflection, she caught sight of Mia in the doorway.

"That dress looks good on you, where did you get it?" Mia said.

Helen gave a half-smile. Mia had given her this dress, one of many designer items she'd passed on, which she did frequently when she'd tired of them. They'd hardly ever been worn, and Helen had them altered to fit, although she didn't have many occasions to wear them now.

"I'd change your shoes though. Maybe more of a heel? But hurry up! The table is booked for 7.30, and the restaurant gets very busy."

Obediently, Helen changed her shoes.

"Perfect!" Mia nodded her approval. "Now, let's go."

Helen checked the contents of her bag. Mia was already downstairs.

"*Finally*! Let's go." Mia strode to the car, turning to make sure Helen was close behind her.

El Donne was a thirty-minute drive away. Mia checked her watch repeatedly, asking Mickey for reassurance that they'd get there in time. Helen knew to give her space when she was like this and turned to look out the window as the quiet country lanes gave way to busier roads. The lights of Cambridge city centre loomed ahead of them, their growing, sparkling display a distraction as she tried to blot out the thought of Phil not being here for another birthday.

"We're here," Mia called, jolting Helen back to the car. Mia sat towards the front of her seat before the car had come to a halt.

"Thank you," Helen said to the driver while climbing out of the car. Mia was already at the restaurant door furiously beckoning her sister with a whizzing hand.

"I'm coming as fast as I can," Helen said under her breath and met the driver's eyes. He winked at her, and Helen smiled conspiratorially. She smoothed down the front of her dress and followed her sister into the restaurant.

"Good evening, Mrs Carlyle." A smartly dressed young woman met them at the door. "How lovely to see you again." She turned to the man next to her, "My colleague will show you to your table."

Mia stepped aside, opening her arm wide to encourage Helen to follow the waiter and walk in. Helen felt self-conscious as they were led across the dimly lit restaurant while some customers looked up from their tables. She hadn't realised the place was so big. At the end of a short corridor, the waiter stood aside in front of a panelled door.

Helen turned to look behind her but could barely see Mia in the dim light. She was confused.

"Through there," Mia said, and before Helen had a chance to reply, Mia moved ahead of her to push open the door with one hand and propel Helen through it with the other.

"*Surprise*!"

Helen gasped as she took in the sight before her. The small private dining room was packed. Her parents, Meghan and Roger, Mia's husband, Chris, friends and work colleagues – including Stephen and his wife, Susie – had been waiting for her. Bunting hung from the ceiling, and a beautiful floral arrangement stretched along the centre of the main table. Someone broke into *Happy Birthday*, and they all joined in as Helen blushed, laughed and turned to Mia, "I should have known when you were extra stressy about getting here on time."

"No, Helen, you were just late as usual," Mia replied, but she was smiling, finally, and she planted a kiss on her sister's cheek. "Happy birthday! Now, go and enjoy yourself."

CHAPTER 3

The evening passed so quickly, Helen thought as they said goodbye to the last guests outside the restaurant. Mia pressed an envelope into her hands.

"This is just from me. Open it tomorrow, when you have time to appreciate it properly."

Helen smiled, promising she would. "I'll look forward to it, and thanks so much again for tonight. It was really good fun, and it was wonderful to catch up with everyone."

"This can be the start of the new you. Your relaunch back into society. Single and ready to mingle," Mia laughed and then, under her breath, out of earshot of Chris who was talking to their parents, "and I'll be more than happy to be your wing woman."

Helen shook her head, "Mia, you are a shocker."

Mia just smiled and ushered her sister into the waiting car. Chris had taken a taxi earlier so the trio could travel back together.

Back home, Chris and Mia helped Helen carry her gifts into the house, and after she'd waved them off, took a closer look at the envelope – "*Hels*" and a large "*X*" was written in Mia's childish scrawl. She placed it next to the other cards and presents, deciding to deal with them all in the morning.

As she got into bed, Helen reflected on the evening. It had given her such a lift, and it wasn't just the champagne. Mia was right, she really did need to get out more. She promised herself to make more of an effort.

The next morning, she felt a glimmer of excitement as she caught sight of her gifts, a sensation she thought she'd lost forever. The sun was already spilling through a gap in the curtains, lighting up Percy's shiny black fur as he snored softly next to her. Stretching, she recalled previous present-opening times and tried to push the image of Phil standing in the bedroom doorway from her mind. He'd always hold a tray with a beautifully wrapped little box and a cup of coffee. Christmas, birthdays, Easter, he loved any excuse for a celebration.

"Oh, Phil…" she said quietly and got out of bed.

She opened her parents' gift first before tearing into Mia's envelope. She recognised the British Airways logo immediately. Return flights to Ibiza, leaving in ten days.

Helen frowned, scanning the ticket again and double-checked the dates. It clashed with her annual GP appraisal. How typically silly of Mia to book the ticket without checking first. True to form, she'd expected Helen to fit in with her plans. And why Ibiza of all places? The party island had never really appealed to her, not even when she was younger. Now, she couldn't think of anything worse. Heaving nightclubs and illegal drugs weren't exactly calling her name. Normally, she dreaded her GP appraisal but was grateful it would give her a bona fide excuse not to get drawn into a hedonistic wilderness with her sister.

She was still opening cards when the phone rang. Helen smiled as she heard Meghan sing *Happy Birthday*. Not only tuneless, she was out of time too. No one could massacre the song in quite the same way as her mother. Helen used to feel embarrassed when she was younger – now, it just made her laugh.

"Thanks, Mum. And thanks to you and Dad for the gorgeous sweater. I love it."

"Oh, good! I thought it was a great colour for you."

"Absolutely. And thanks for coming last night. How long had you known about the party?"

"Not long, darling, you know Mia, she wouldn't want to give me too much notice."

"Did she invite Caroline?" Helen asked.

"I wondered the same," replied her mother. "Although I very much doubt it. Mia wouldn't have wanted to share you." An explanation wasn't needed. Helen knew exactly what she meant. Caroline was Helen's closest friend, but Mia had never warmed to her and her mother had always said that Mia was envious of the friends' bond.

"Naughty of her not to invite her if that is the case," Meghan continued.

"Yes, and slightly embarrassing as I'd told Caroline that I didn't want a big celebration and was just having a quiet supper. That's just Mia, I guess. Her heart is in the right place."

A sigh came down the phone from her mother, as if she was about to speak but thought better of it. "Did you get some lovely gifts?"

"I haven't opened everything yet. I was just looking at what Mia gave me."

"Hmm… and?"

"Do you know what it was?"

"I don't, no."

"Why do you sound suspicious then?"

"Do I?" her mother laughed. "Darling, when I saw Mia pass you an envelope with a wink, telling you that it was just from her, my imagination went wild. What is it?"

"Tickets to Ibiza."

Silence. And then, "Oh!"

"Erm, yes, *'oh'* is one word for it. And I'm supposed to be leaving in under two weeks."

"I wonder why Ibiza?"

"Exactly what I thought, and to be honest, Mum, I can't go. That week just won't work. I've got my annual appraisal meeting."

"Well, I suggest you tell her sooner rather than later. It's not your fault, she will understand that."

"Of course she won't, Mum, you know her."

Meghan didn't reply and passed the phone to Roger who also wanted to wish his daughter happy birthday. They chatted happily until Helen realised that she was already late, ended the call and rushed to make her way to work.

"Please say yes, Helen. It'll be great fun. Pleee-ass-sseee." Mia's voice boomed around the car as Helen drove to the surgery. "Come on, it's just a few days. The weather will be amazing, the villa is fantastic and—"

"Mia, it's not that I don't *want* to go," Helen persisted. "I can't. It's an extremely generous gesture, and I know how much thought you will have put into it, booking the villa, arranging the flights and everything, but I can't take the time off. I've been working up to my appraisal. Also, we're so short-staffed at the moment. We're a doctor down for a couple more weeks before the new one starts, and I've promised to do the induction when they—"

"Well, that's a real shame." It was Mia's turn to interrupt now. "I thought we could have a fun time together. I was thinking it would be really good for you since…you know… It would be just lovely for you to have a little holiday."

"I know, Mia, and it's really kind of you. I appreciate it, I do, but I simply can't make it. Look, I'm just pulling up at work now. Can we talk later, and please, get these tickets refunded. I noticed they are business class."

"I'm not refunding anything," Mia snapped. "The villa belongs to a friend of mine, and he's lending it to us."

Helen sighed inwardly. She's so used to getting her own way. She'll start piling on the guilt next.

"This was all for you, Helen."

"I know, love. Look, let's talk later. Thanks again for last night, Mia. It was fabulous."

"Think about the sunshine," Mia replied, ignoring her.

"Bye, Mia, got to go. Love you." Helen hung up.

Inside, the surgery was already a hive of activity. Stephen looked up from behind the front desk as she walked in. "Ah… there she is, the birthday girl." He smiled as the practice manager and nurse said "Happy Birthday" in unison.

"Thanks everyone," she replied, making her way to her room, embarrassed by the attention.

"Could I have a quick word before you start, please?" Stephen asked.

"Sure," she replied, already slipping off her coat as she made her way to her room.

"That was a fun party last night."

"Yes, a lovely surprise, and it was kind of you to come. I hope my sister didn't put any pressure on you. I know it was a work night."

"Don't be silly, we loved it. Your sister's a great organiser, isn't she? Has she always been like that? She got me involved a few weeks ago, that's why I told you I was going out last night so I could get home and collect Susie in time."

"Ah, now it makes sense why you made such a fuss about leaving on time," she said as he nodded. "But I'm sorry I didn't manage to speak to you about the patient participation stuff yesterday."

"Don't worry. I knew we weren't going to get it done. I just needed to make sure you wrapped up your surgery on time. That was half of my birthday duties from your demanding sister."

"Oh, dear, I hope she wasn't overly bossy."

"Not at all." His tone was gentle, but Helen still felt embarrassed. She knew what Mia could be like.

"She can be a bit, erm… overbearing sometimes."

"Don't you worry about that. If you knew my ex-wife, you'd know what overbearing really looked like. At least Mia asks nicely." Stephen sipped his coffee. "She's right though, Helen. You could do with a break."

"Oh, God, she hasn't mentioned Ibiza, has she?"

Stephen smiled. "I know all about the holiday, which brings me to the second half of my birthday duties." He took another sip, this time with a slurp. "I've rearranged your appraisal meeting."

Helen began to protest, but Stephen held up his hand. "I've simply pushed it back a couple of weeks. And before you say anything, I know for a fact you've already prepared your PDP, so you'll be fine. I've got a locum covering for you, and your diary has been sorted for the days you're away."

"But—" Helen began.

"No ifs or buts! Mia said you would listen to me. I liked that. I've never felt so powerful." He winked. "So, you can't say no. For one, I'm your boss; and two, I'm not letting your sister realise my power isn't as great as she thinks. If I were you, I'd get on with your surgery and start looking forward to a break in sunny Spain. Good God, look at the time."

He left the room before she could answer. Noticing that she was running late, Helen sat down quickly and logged on to her computer.

CHAPTER 4

As their plane taxied at London City airport, Helen tried not to show her sister how nervous she felt.

"Do you still get spooked about flying?" Mia asked.

"No," Helen lied.

"I wouldn't be surprised if you did. I read somewhere that most aircraft problems occur during take-off and landing." Mia's voice grew louder as she spoke. "And did you know, the odds that your aircraft will crash are one in one point two million?" Catching the admonishing eye of another passenger across the aisle, Helen urged her sister to lower the volume. "Ssshh, please."

Undeterred, Mia continued, "I read some study just the other day. It said the odds of dying from a plane crash are about one in eleven million but the chances of dying in a car accident are just one in five thousand." Helen pretended to look for something in the seat pocket in front of her. "Though the way you drive it's more likely to be those having to overtake that will get hurt." She nudged her playfully in the ribs.

Helen closed her eyes, balling her hands into fists as the plane soared. If she engaged with her, Mia would take it as encouragement to expand further on the statistics of aircraft mishaps and fatalities. Anxiety bubbled in her stomach before the *ping* of the bell signalled they could unbuckle their seatbelts. She opened her eyes, and the nervousness abated as she saw the cabin crew moving around.

Next to her, Mia was looking out of the window, craning to see if she could recognise any landmark below. The roar of the engines settled into a gentle hum, accompanied by the low chatter of passengers. Soothed by the reassuring sounds, Helen settled back into her seat.

"Wait until you see where we're staying!" Mia said. "Remember my friend, Victor? The photographer? He takes the most amazing pics. He's done loads of famous people. You met him at our house, with his partner Pedro." Helen didn't think she did remember. "Anyway," Mia continued, "he spilt with his partner eighteen months ago, and the poor thing just can't face the villa – says it's too painful. But he doesn't want to sell it either, so he's delighted that we'll make use of it. Staff keep an eye on everything, it's in a little hamlet called Balafia and it's just gorgeous. Look at these photos." She held out her phone. Helen glanced at the screen but started to feel herself nodding off. It had been very early start.

She woke up just as they were coming in for landing. From the corner of her eye, she spied Mia reading a magazine and quickly closed her eyes again. It was only when they had safely touched down that she spoke to her sister.

"We need to look for the concierge desk," Mia said once they were through the arrivals hall. "Victor always leaves a car here and said we should use it. If you wouldn't mind driving, please, Helen. My driving ban applies abroad too, unfortunately."

"Of course I don't mind," Helen replied. It never failed to amaze her how Mia refused culpability for anything. She'd accumulated points on her licence not only for speeding but for driving without due care and attention when she had clipped another car as she left a car park. Her justification was that she had been running late for a hair appointment.

True to his word, Victor had left the keys. They stepped out of the terminal and were greeted by a wall of warm air and a cloudless blue sky.

"Fabulous," Mia said with a broad grin when linking her arm through her sister's. She was practically bouncing as they made their way to the car park.

As they approached a gleaming white jeep, Mia pressed the key fob and the car leapt into life, indicator lights flashing.

"It's cute, isn't it? Like a mini Land Rover, and part of the roof slides off. I'm beginning to wish I hadn't worn quite so many clothes," Mia said, peeling off her wrap and putting on her sunglasses.

Helen followed her lead and removed her sweater. They loaded their bags into the boot, and Mia entered the address of the villa into her phone.

"It says it will take us about thirty-five minutes."

Helen nodded, before walking to the passenger side of the car.

"Where are you going?" Mia asked "Maybe I should be driving if you don't even know which side of the car the driver sits on in this country."

"Whoops, good start" Helen smiled and returned to the driver's side, acquainting herself with the layout of the unfamiliar car. They laughed as she tried three times before managing to put it into reverse. Mia found the switch to roll back part of the roof, and they pulled out of the car park, a breeze ruffling their hair.

"We'll never get there at this rate," Mia said sinking back into her seat and sighing as a camper van overtook them. "You drive slowly at home, but this is just ridiculous!"

"We won't get there if you don't keep us on the right road. Just make sure we see the turning. It can't be much further," replied Helen.

"I remember this bit." Mia sat up straight again, pointing at a building in the distance. "I remember stopping near there once when Chris and I came." Helen looked to where she was pointing when Mia made her jump with her cries, "Here, here, this one, now!" Helen had just enough time to turn as they pulled onto a much quieter road.

"Now it's just a few miles before we get to the camino," Mia added.

Helen was dreading the last part of the journey. Mia had told her they needed to be extra careful on the little track that led to the villa. Ibiza's narrow dirt lanes, or caminos, were notorious for being difficult to navigate, and the one leading to Casa Miguino was particularly bad.

Mia was the first to spot the sea glittering beneath them as the road climbed upwards. The tiny, horseshoe-shaped bay of Cala Xuclar was dotted with simple fishing huts and crystal-clear water, nestled like a jewel surrounded by green hills and a rocky coastline.

"Every bit as magical as I remember," said Mia. "Look at the old fishing huts, Helen. Look, down by the water – there's a really lovely restaurant down there. We could go for lunch one day."

Much as she wanted to look, Helen had her eyes fixed firmly ahead. She didn't feel overly confident on this narrow, winding road with only a small barrier between them and the edge of the cliff. Parts of it had been damaged, and the numerous paint scrapings betrayed many a close call. In a couple of areas the barrier was missing altogether, and she wondered if someone had actually veered over the cliff face.

"How much further before we turn off?" Helen asked, shaking the thought from her head.

"Should be the next right, about half a mile ahead," Mia said, glancing down at her phone. "I bet the people behind us will be delighted," she added, and Helen glanced into her rear-view mirror. A line of cars snaked around the bends behind her.

"Mia, I can't go any faster, this road is treacherous, and it's too narrow for anyone to overtake. I'm not used to this car and—"

"There it is!" Mia shouted excitedly, pointing at a turning up ahead. Helen slowed, fumbling for the indicator. They turned off onto an even rougher road and bounced along between potholes and loose stones. The jeep seemed to groan as Helen navigated her way along the track, setting the wheels into grooves made by numerous other vehicles before them, the long, scorched grass in between them grazing the underside of the car with a rustling sound.

They drove like this for about ten minutes, with Mia providing excited commentary about her plans for the trip. Despite her assurances to Helen that it was to be primarily a rest and relaxation jaunt, she clearly wanted to try the nightlife that Ibiza was famous for.

"On Thursday night, there's this brilliant DJ at Morgans, I'd really like to see him, and of course, we can't come all this way without visiting Pacha and then on our last night, we just have to do the Closing Party. It's the big end-of-season one."

Helen stayed tight-lipped. She had no intention of going clubbing every night but didn't have the appetite for an argument with Mia now. The thought of fresh seafood and delicious wine in a coastal restaurant was definitely a priority, while squeezing into a pounding nightclub with a crowd high on coke and ecstasy left her cold. She gripped the wheel even tighter at the thought.

Finally, the road began to snake downwards, the track winding its way through a dense pine forest until the gates of the villa came into view. Mia was already pulling off her seatbelt as Helen drew up alongside the security panel.

"Oh God, I've forgotten the bloody code again. Shit! Try 2432." When nothing happened, she told Helen to try swapping the last two digits which didn't work either.

Helen leant out the window, hoping to spot someone behind the gates. When nothing happened, Mia leant over and pressed the horn repeatedly.

"Wow, give them a chance. It's literally been..." Helen's voice trailed off as but the gates suddenly swung open.

"Bloody housekeeper," Mia muttered. "Hurry up, the gates will close on us if you're not quick enough!" They rolled forward onto a driveway that was framed by oleander and lavender. The scent drifted into the car, and Helen took a deep breath, soaking it in as they stopped at the front of the house with its u-shaped drive and pretty stone fountain. Helen stretched and took a good look around. The photographs hadn't done the place justice. The house, surrounded by extensive gardens, all looked so beautiful. As she took it all in, Mia walked towards the house. She was just a few steps away when the front door burst open and a petite woman rushed out to greet them.

"Buenos días. Hello. Good afternoon, Mrs Carlyle," she smiled broadly.

"Hi, Victor said you'd be here," Mia replied. "Our bags are in the boot."

At first, Helen thought Mia was going to add a comment about bringing them in later when she realised, to her acute embarrassment, that Mia was expecting the woman to unload the car for her. Helen rushed to lift the bags out herself as the woman approached.

"Please," the small woman said to Helen, taking a case from her. "Welcome, I am Valentina. I look after things for Mr Victor."

"Thank you," Helen replied as she pulled another bag from the boot and followed Valentina into the house.

Mia was already inside, and as they walked through a pair of thick wooden doors into a large hallway, Helen was instantly struck by how cool it felt. On a large glass table in the hall was a magnificent floral arrangement.

"Wow, are those real?" Helen asked, marvelling at the elegant birds of paradise and other exotic lilies amongst the display.

"Yes, for you," Valentina replied. "Mr Victor asked me to. He always loves my flowers."

Valentina wasted no time in showing them around and telling them how everything worked. She explained the pool temperature sometimes dropped unexpectedly.

"It is a good idea to use the cover at night. I know it's not so nice to swim in a very cold pool. Now, can I show you your rooms?"

"No, no, all ok, I remember from last time. I'm hoping I'm in the pale pink room again?" Mia said quickly.

"Yes," said Valentina, "and I have arranged the tour you asked for. The details are in your room." When Mia nodded without replying, Valentina turned towards Helen. "I have prepared a room overlooking the rear garden for you. Are you sure I can't show you?"

"No. That's all we need," Mia interjected, positioning herself to one side as if urging her to leave.

Helen felt uncomfortable at the curtness of her words. "Thank you so much for your help. It was very kind of you to meet us," Helen said, walking Valentina to the door.

"There's only one way to find out if the pool's ok," said Mia, unzipping her case on the hall floor and pulling out a bikini. "Let's go and try it out."

"Shall we unpack first and freshen up?" Helen asked. Mia was already walking towards the kitchen, so Helen lifted her suitcase and climbed the honey-coloured stone staircase. The place was vast. Five doors led off a wide landing, two of which were open. Helen popped her head around the first one, which she guessed was meant for her. It overlooked the rear garden, which was every bit as beautiful as the front, with sweeping views across distant pine forests She gazed in wonder. She couldn't see another building anywhere. Although the property was a short drive to the nearest village and only half an hour or so to the thriving hub of the island, it felt isolated. What a shame that poor Victor didn't feel up to coming out here.

As she started to unpack, she heard a loud splash and looked out the window to see Mia in the pool. She hadn't even bothered putting on her bikini and was gently moving through the water, attempting a half-hearted breaststroke, before turning over and floating on her back, eyes closed, face turned towards the sun, her hands making gentle sculling movements to keep herself afloat. Her blonde hair floated behind her, like a long golden veil.

"The gardener is having a lovely time watching you," Helen called from the window, smiling broadly as Mia opened her eyes immediately and dropped her legs beneath the water so only her head was visible. She looked around, her eyes scanning the garden for the spectator.

Helen couldn't help herself and burst out laughing which made Mia do the same.

"Liar!" She shouted to Helen, before adding, "I wouldn't care anyway!"

Helen knew she meant it, she was hardly the shy type. Mia was used to attention, with her neat figure, big boobs and brash personality, all of which she used to maximum effect. Dark brown eyes set off her pale blonde hair which seemed to be getting lighter every year. When she was younger, their mother was always telling her to get her hair cut and "sort out those split ends", but she resisted, loving the way the end of her hair grazed her bottom when she tipped her head backwards.

Helen changed into her bikini and tied a sarong around her waist before going downstairs. She saw a basket on the kitchen table laden with a variety of fruit, next to eggs and delicious-looking bread. Opening the double doors of an enormous larder fridge, there was fresh milk, butter, orange juice and a whole shelf stacked with champagne and white and rosé wine. How kind, she thought.

She found her way to the pool, perched on the edge of a wooden lounger and took out her laptop and a bottle of sun lotion from her bag.

"Aren't you coming in?" Mia asked, swimming over to the side and watching her lazily from the water, chin resting on her forearms.

"I thought I'd do a bit of catching up first."

"Catching up? Not with work, right? We've just got here!"

"I know, and I will, but in a bit," Helen replied firmly. She shifted focus to the sun cream, offering the bottle to Mia. "Don't suppose you've put any on?"

"Nope. Maybe in a bit," she replied, mimicking Helen's voice. Helen smiled at the imitation but knew Mia was annoyed. She was used to getting her own way and could be remarkably childish if she didn't. More often than not, Helen gave in just to keep the peace, though right now she needed to send a couple of emails. Then she could put work behind her for the duration of their stay.

She noticed the towels Mia must have taken from the little cabana by the side of the pool and spread one over a lounger, opening a large sun umbrella above her. It's like a first-class hotel, she thought as she opened her laptop. Everything had been thought of. It was good to be here.

CHAPTER 5

"I've arranged a little surprise for you." Mia climbed out of the pool and stood by Helen, wringing out her hair, narrowly missing Helen's laptop.

"Just give me a few minutes, I need to focus on this right now," Helen said, not looking up.

"I need you to focus on *me* right now," Mia retorted. Helen smiled and started to compose her reply.

Mia gave an exaggerated sigh. "I didn't think I'd come all this way to play second fiddle to a laptop."

Helen looked up from her screen mid-typing. Had it been anyone else, she'd have presumed they were joking, but Mia had a petulant look about her that Helen recognised all too well.

"Hang on, please. Just a bit longer, I promise, then I'm all yours."

"*Charming.*" Mia dropped onto a lounger. She lay there for a few moments before turning over onto her front.

"What is it you're doing anyway? Stephen said the practice would survive without you. He used those exact words. In fact—"

"Mia!" Helen interrupted. She'd keyed in the same sentence twice.

"Fine. Let me know when you're free." Mia got up and started to walk towards the villa.

"Ok, ok." Helen shut down the laptop. She'd have to try and find some time later.

Mia beamed, and skipped back over. "So do you want to know what surprise I have for you?"

"As if this trip wasn't enough. What now?"

"I've arranged an island food and wine tour."

"Oh, Mia, what a lovely idea."

"Yes, I thought you'd like it! It's a bit of a foodies' favourite. We're going to see Ibiza's oldest bakery, which is famous worldwide, and we'll visit a local market and see how those delicious Iberian hams are made. Last stop is a wine tasting at a vineyard not too far from here."

"That all sounds amazing." Helen stood up and hugged her sister. Mia grinned; her mood transformed now she had Helen's undivided attention.

"My pleasure. It'll be good to do something special for you."

By nine the next morning, the two women were ready and waiting when their tour guide buzzed on the intercom. He had arrived in a smart cabriolet with the roof down.

"Good morning, my name is Manon," he smiled, holding the car door open. Helen introduced herself and Mia, and they shook his hand before sliding into the back seat.

First stop was a tour of Sant Joan de Labritja. They explored the eighteenth-century church and listened as Manon told them tales of the village's patron saint. Helen was entranced with the church's majestic interior.

"It's so beautiful," she said, breathing it all in looking up at the ornate ceiling towering above them.

"It was all painted by hand." Manon smiled. "It is even more remarkable when we remember that the painters didn't have modern aids that we take for granted like scaffold towers or even paint rollers."

"Incredible, isn't it?" Helen asked Mia. When she didn't get a reply, she turned around and realised her sister wasn't even listening. She was too busy smiling into her phone. Her attention shifted back to the paintings and Manon's teachings. After leaving the church, they walked up to the cobbled village square surrounded by whitewashed buildings. Helen marvelled at the simple beauty of the place as they arrived at a small café and sat down outside. Immediately, Mia's attention returned to her phone.

"Is that Chris?" Helen asked.

"Huh?" Mia replied, not looking up. She used both hands to text, thumbs and fingers moving with lightning speed.

"On the phone? Is that who you're texting?"

Still, Mia didn't reply, and Helen bit down a remark that *she* didn't want to play second fiddle to a mobile phone when Manon joined them with a waitress bearing a large tray laden with coffee, water and four slices of delicious-looking cake.

"This is Flao. A traditional dish and one of our oldest recipes," Manon, told them.

Finally, Mia looked up and picked up a cake fork.

"Historically, it was a special treat eaten on Easter Sunday because that was the time of year when farm fresh cheese was abundantly available and—"

"Urgh! I'm not having that," Mia exclaimed. "It's got mint in it!" She pushed her plate away.

Manon's eyes widened. "Erm… yes, it does contain mint. It is cheesecake with spearmint. It dates back to the thirteenth century when Ibiza was conquered by Catalan Christian forces, but it also has Moorish influences, hence the exotic addition of spearmint."

"Spearmint… exotic?" Mia quipped sarcastically.

"Well, I think it's delicious," Helen said, truthfully. "It reminds me of a dessert I once had in Morocco."

"Exactly," replied Manon. "The Moors left us some wonderful culinary legacies."

"And what about architecture? Do you have anything like the Alhambra Palace?" Helen asked.

"Not quite as grand as that, but we do have some beautiful old city walls which protected the island from the Moors for so long," Manon recounted proudly.

"Oh, here we go…" Mia said, raising her eyebrows.

Helen and Manon turned towards her.

"What?" Helen asked.

"We're not here for a history lesson!"

Helen flushed. "My sister likes to tease me, Manon."

Manon looked bemused. "I'm not teasing," Mia began. "I'm genuinely—"

Helen was too embarrassed to let her continue. "Mia's been to this part of Ibiza before, but it's my first time. It is a very pretty area. Do you live around here, Manon?"

The guide told them a little about himself, to which Helen listened with interest, asking questions for him to elaborate. Mia sat impatiently, jigging her knee, huffing and checking her phone. As soon as they'd finished their coffee, they returned to the car for the next leg of the tour, the market at Forada.

"Forada is one of the most well-attended local markets on the island. It has a wonderful selection of artisan goods, but there is so much more to it than just the shopping. What I suggest is starting off at—"

"We'll just have a wander around ourselves and come back in about an hour," Mia said.

Manon hesitated as if he was about to object but thought better of it. "Of course. I will be parked here when you are ready."

The sisters moved amongst the crowds, browsing the stalls, stopping occasionally to make a purchase. "How about this for Chris?" she asked, holding up a brown leather wallet. Mia shook her head and wrinkled her nose, despite the stall-holder watching them. Embarrassed, Helen smiled at him as they moved on, pausing a little further ahead to listen to some live music.

"What's that over there?" Helen asked, pointing towards a low building. A small crowd was funnelling through its doors. "It says *Art Café*," she added, squinting to read the sign. "Come on, let's go and have a look."

"I'm beginning to wish we'd brought Manon now," Mia said.

"I did wonder why you told him to stay in the car. He would know all of the best bits to see. Helen replied.

"No, I meant so he could take some of this stuff back to the car. These weigh a tonne." Mia laid her bags down with an exaggerated sigh.

Helen looked down at the bulging bags. "I hardly think that's what Manon's here for. He's supposed to be taking us on a tour."

"He's getting paid, isn't he? He can do whatever we ask." Mia retorted.

"Here, let me help. I haven't got quite as much as you," Helen offered.

"No, it's fine, but could we just go back now? I wouldn't mind a glass of wine and something to eat."

"Did you like it?" Manon asked as they drove away from Forada.

"There was plenty to see," Helen replied.

"Did you visit the art café?"

"No," Helen replied. "We were running a bit short of time."

"What about the Greenheart-Greenhouse?" Manon asked. Helen shook her head.

"That's a shame," he replied. "It's an Ibizan cooperative project and very interesting. Next time?" He smiled at Helen in his rear-view mirror.

Helen glanced sideways at Mia. She was on her phone again. "Gosh, you're popular," she said, leaning towards her sister. Mia put the phone down immediately.

"Just catching up on a couple of messages," she smiled. "Now, how far is this wine-tasting place, Macron?"

"Manon," Helen corrected her.

"How much longer? I'm dying for a drink."

"Not far," Manon replied, and they pulled up at Can Sol Winery ten minutes later.

The sisters sampled a number of delicious white and rosé wines, as well as traditional Ibizan dishes. When they'd finished, Mia sat back, her face towards the sun, and stretched out her legs. "Wow, that was good, wasn't it?" she sighed.

"It really was. Such a treat, thank you, Mia. The frita de pulpo was excellent with that dry white. I've made a note of the name. I'm definitely going to take some back home. I might get Stephen a bottle or two."

"I'm glad, Hellie. So… we've done something for you today, can we do something for me tomorrow?" Mia cocked her head to one side and gave Helen the look she always used when she wanted something.

"Well, I hope you've enjoyed today too?" Helen asked.

"Yes, yes but it's more your thing – the churches, artisan market, foodie stuff, you know…" Helen nodded, despite not feeling fully satisfied with the day by Mia cutting short the sightseeing. She didn't want to spoil the evening though so she didn't say anything.

"I'd like to sample a bit of the nightlife," Mia said.

"Surprise, surprise," Helen replied, relaxed, thankful for the wine.

"Honestly, it'll be so much fun. You'll love it."

I doubt that very much, Helen thought as she returned Mia's smile.

"Por favor, Macron," Mia said, slightly flushed. "Another two glasses of white! Then you can drive us home."

"Not for me," Helen protested. "I'll fall asleep if I have another one."

Mia would have none of it. "Relax. We're here to unwind, loosen up a bit!"

CHAPTER 6

The next morning, Mia began her badgering in earnest until Helen agreed to venture into Ibiza Town.

"We can go and have some dinner and then visit Morgan's to see this amazing DJ. He's an absolute legend." Mia promised her that it wouldn't be a late night and that she'd leave without protest when Helen wanted to go. She also said she wouldn't ask to go out again if they could just do it this once, although they both knew that was highly unlikely.

Helen acquiesced, thinking it was only fair to indulge Mia. She'd had a lovely couple of days and was feeling the benefits of the holiday already. After yesterday's tour they'd spent the rest of the afternoon by the pool. Helen had risen early this morning after a good night's sleep and read for hours, finishing her book before her sister was even awake. She couldn't remember the last time she'd indulged herself with such an uninterrupted period of reading.

The pair had spent the day gently pottering around in anticipation for a long night. They enjoyed a leisurely walk, time by the pool, and agreed to drive for Ibiza Town early enough to wander around the shops and grab a spot of dinner before going to Morgans.

"I'm sure we will find a little tapas bar and enjoy a cocktail or two… or at least, I can," Mia added quickly before Helen had a chance to make a remark about drinking and driving.

That evening, Helen waited patiently for Mia to get dressed, which took an age as she chatted animatedly – at this rate she realised they wouldn't arrive into town in time to visit the shops. Finally, Mia stood up and admired her reflection in a full-length mirror.

"You look amazing," Helen enthusiastically volunteered as Mia turned from side to side and then back to the front, adjusting her top and rearranging her bra to maximise her cleavage.

"Ah, thanks. So do you," Mia replied, looking at Helen's reflection behind her in the mirror. "I love that dress."

"You can always have it back. This is the first time I've had a chance to wear it, to be honest."

Mia laughed. "Don't be silly. It looks so much better on you than me. You need to be *really* slim for that. I was being far too optimistic when I bought it."

Outside, Helen glanced up at Mia's bedroom. "You've left your window open."

"It doesn't matter – it's not as if it's going to rain."

"I didn't mean that, I meant for security."

"Oh, Helen, you really are so Sally Sensible at times, aren't you? Don't worry, burglars don't come all the way out here," she whispered, exaggerating a furtive look around her. "It'll be fine."

Helen started to protest, but Mia was already making her way to the car. The sun had gone down, and the heady, musky scent of nicotiana sylvestris was unmistakable as they walked through the garden, accompanied by a chorus of cicadas.

Unable to let it slide, Helen caught up to her sister. "Surely you'd feel responsible if anything happened though. While we were staying here?"

"No!" Mia snapped back. "That's what the housekeeper is for."

"But she isn't on site."

"No, but I don't think she misses a bloody trick. She doesn't live far away, and Victor says she's his eyes and ears. He's so worried about his privacy. He had a bit of a run in with the press when Pedro decided to sell his story about their breakup to some Spanish rag. Paparazzi camping outside the gates apparently. She was like a Rottweiler keeping them at bay."

"Really?" Helen's eyes widened. "Is Victor that well-known?"

"Clearly not in your world, granny," Mia smirked. "Maybe if you read a bit more of the popular press you'd know." Helen shook her head at the jibe. Mia was fond of teasing her about their age difference.

"This is quite a nice little motor, isn't it?" Mia said, leaning back in her seat as they drove along the rutted track.

"Maybe I should get one of these once I've got my licence back."

"*If* you get it back," Helen replied and shrank away as Mia reached over to hit her playfully.

Despite two speed awareness courses, which seemed to have done little to improve either her speed or her awareness, Mia had accumulated too many points to escape a driving ban.

Leaning forward to turn on the radio, a large aquamarine and diamond ring on Mia's right hand caught the moonlight.

"Wow, that's pretty," said Helen. "I haven't seen that before."

"It's new," Mia replied. "We only picked it up last weekend. A late birthday present."

"It's stunning. Oh, but where's your wedding ring?" she asked, suddenly noticing that her other hand was bare.

"I hate wearing rings on both hands," replied Mia. "It feels too clunky."

Helen frowned and nodded.

"This DJ we're going to see really is a coup, you know." Mia changed the conversation. "It's really hard to get to see him. Friends of mine will be so envious that I'm going to one of his nights."

Helen wasn't in the least bit interested in the DJ, but made the right noises, wondering if Mia's friends really would be so envious, or like her, could not have cared less. She pushed the thought of a couple of glasses of wine and an early night from her mind. She knew she should take advantage of the chance to spend time with her sister. It wasn't as if they had many opportunities like this.

Before long they could see the glittering lights of Ibiza Town in front of them, moonlight shining on white buildings and rippled reflections in the sea.

"Oh, it looks amazing!" said Mia excitedly. "You could almost forget this busy part of the island exists after being in the villa on our own."

As she spoke, a little moped came round the corner in front of them, its beam dazzling Helen. "Bloody hell," she muttered, "he's overtaking on a blind corner."

"I wouldn't worry, Helen, you're driving so slowly that you've got plenty of time to avoid him." Mia shot her a look that they both knew said *touché*.

They parked in a quiet spot on the outskirts of the town centre, and Helen dropped a pin with their location on Google Maps.

At least we know we are on the right side of town for an easy drive home, Helen thought but kept it to herself. She was still a little stung from Mia's Sally Sensible comment earlier and didn't want to give her more ammunition. As they got out, Mia checked her reflection in a nearby window.

Mia linked her arm through Helen's. They walked a few hundred yards along the residential street before turning a corner, and the atmosphere instantly transformed.

"Oh, look at this, Hels, it's buzzing!"

The area was packed, and as they progressed towards the centre of town it became busier still. Crowds bustled along wide pavements, some out for an evening stroll, others drinking outside of bars, some seated at tables. Greeters called out above the laughter and chatter, trying to tempt passers-by into their restaurants. There were bright signs advertising happy-hour cocktails and all types of seafood and tapas. Helen noticed how much white there seemed to be everywhere: men in tight white shirts and women in tight white dresses mirroring the white walls of the town. Helen watched as one young woman tottered in front of them on perilously high heels. She was wearing a particularly short, diaphanous dress that left little to the imagination. Every now and again, there would be a loud blast of music as they passed a bar. The restaurants looked enticing, and as waiters called them to take a table, Helen was keen to take them up and veered towards a large display menu. "I'm hungry," she pleaded, but Mia didn't want to stop.

"Not yet," she protested, pulling Helen back into the street. "Let's at least walk to the end of this strip and see what's what." Reluctantly, Helen walked beside her, and they continued to push their way through the crowd. Narrow, cobbled side streets led off the main drag, with yet more tempting bars and restaurants.

"That looks pretty," Helen nodded towards a café to their left. Tables sat under white parasols with fairy lights strung in the trees around them. It looked busy, but a waiter caught Helen's eye and moved towards them.

"No, not there," Mia said quickly. "I like the look of that one over there," and she tugged Helen back.

"Which one?" Helen asked, throwing the waiter an apologetic look.

"That one – up there." Mia pointed somewhere ahead of her.

"They will all be the same, Mia. Let's just eat."

"No, just a bit further – up there. I've heard it's good."

They walked past another five or six restaurants before Mia settled on one that looked exactly like all the previous restaurants. She gestured to the waiter.

"We'd like a table for two."

"Yes, of course, ladies. Would you like inside or out?"

"That table just there would be fine," Mia said.

Helen, delighted that a decision at last had been made, nodded eagerly and moved towards the table. "I'm starving!" Helen was almost salivating as she saw the lists of tapas. "What do you think Arroz de Matanzas is? Mum always used to choose some lovely fish dish when we went to Majorca, but I can't remember what it's called. Bullet something, I think…"

Helen glanced up but Mia wasn't listening, instead was almost staring through her. Mia was occupied with something behind Helen. Helen started to follow her gaze and turn her head desperate to see what the fuss was about.

"Don't turn around," Mia said under her breath, lowering her eyes to the menu.

"Why? What is it?" Helen replied discreetly.

"Just some guys. Didn't you see them as we came in?"

"No?" Helen sighed, her curiosity abating. She might have guessed it would be a man that had captured her sister's attention.

"Hellie, you're hopeless," Mia smiled. "They were staring as we walked in. You brushed past one of them. He practically had his tongue hanging out."

"Shut up, Mia, and—"

"Well, lovely ladies, would you like some wine while you are deciding what to eat?" Their waiter reappeared. He leant over and lit a little votive candle on the table between them and set down a small basket of bread.

"We definitely want some wine," Mia answered quickly and glanced at the wine menu.

"I will leave you for a few minutes to decide," the waiter replied.

"No, don't you go anywhere. We'll have a bottle of the white Rioja," she said, pointing at an entry in the list.

Helen was horrified at how demanding Mia had become. She had been embarrassed when they'd arrived at the villa and expected Valentina to unload their bags from the car. She'd been very offhand with Manon, and now her curtness with the waiter made her feel more than a little uncomfortable. Mia seemed to have forgotten basic pleasantries. Since she'd married Chris, Mia had embraced the trappings of his wealth a little too readily, without a backward glance.

When the waiter brought their wine over, Helen took the lead eager to start. "I think we are ready to order now, please, when you're ready. Can you just tell me what these are?" She pointed to an entry on the menu. The waiter explained in detail a few of the dishes, and in the end, Helen decided on the Bullit de Peix, which she thought was the fish stew her mother had introduced her to years ago. She looked up from the menu and felt a twinge of exasperation when she saw Mia staring past her again at whoever had captured her attention.

"Mia, have you decided?" she said firmly, shifting slightly to one side so that she blocked Mia's line of vision.

"Ages ago, thank you very much," Mia said, pushing the closed menu away from her. "I'm going to stick to my trusted favourite, the grilled red prawns." She remained expressionless as the waiter told them they had both made "excellent choices, madams".

Mia dropped her head to one side and smiled broadly at someone behind Helen.

"For God's sake, Mia!"

"What?" Mia shot back, still gazing behind her sister.

"You. And them, or him, or whomever it is I'm not supposed to turn around and see."

"Mrs Hangry," Mia said, taunting Helen, who freely admitted she could be irascible when she was hungry.

"I'm not!" she said defensively. "It's just…" she paused.

"Just what?" Mia said mischievously, tilting her head to one side and grinning. She was tossing her hair like a teenager now.

"Well, you know… Chris for a start."

"Good for the goose… good for the gander," Mia replied, a smile still playing on her lips. At that point, the waiter arrived with their wine, showed them the bottle and poured a little into Mia's glass.

"That's fine, just pour it. I'll soon know if it's corked," Mia said, not bothering to thank him.

"What do you mean?" Helen was still puzzling over the goose and the gander.

"Oh, come on, Hellie, you don't honestly think Chris has given up all of his old ways just to be faithful to me, do you?" Helen faltered, wondering if this was a trick question.

"Well… yes, of course! I hadn't ever thought otherwise. Are you saying he isn't?" Her mind was working overtime. "Is he having an affair?"

"I don't think it's an affair exactly. There hasn't been anyone special, but he's had a couple of…" she hesitated, looking down at her hands, "well, let's call them 'dalliances'," she said, using air quotes to punctuate her point.

"Oh, God, Mia, I had no idea."

Mia took a gulp of wine. "This is delicious, Hels. You should try it."

"I will, in a minute, tell me about Chris."

"Looks like he's been shagging an old flame from the tennis club. I found out about it from a private investigator. The same guy I employed when I suspected him of seeing a girl he used to work with."

"Wow." Helen took a sip of her wine and a long hard look at Mia. There didn't appear to be any sadness, more a resigned acceptance. She seemed to be recounting her own husband's infidelity as if she were reading a paragraph in a newspaper about someone she'd never met.

"Mum was right," Mia said solemnly. "But I don't think I could ever admit that to her."

"Sorry?"

"Remember when I told her I was getting married and she made some reference to the fact that I should wait because Chris was still married? What she was trying to say was that if he'd had an affair and left his wife once, he would do it again."

Helen dropped her gaze. Her parents had been more concerned that Mia, blinded by Chris's wealth, had been hell bent on having her share of it, and made it her mission to get him to walk out on his wife and two young children.

"Anyway, we're not here to talk about bloody Chris," Mia interrupted Helen's train of thought. "We're here to have a lovely time, and there's no harm in a little window shopping," she said, smiling broadly at the table of men behind her sister before bringing her gaze back to meet hers.

CHAPTER 7

As quickly as Mia had opened up about the state of her marriage, she abruptly changed the subject. They chatted about old times and previous holidays with their parents, reminiscing about a disastrous camping trip from their childhood. Helen was dipping another piece of bread into some olive oil when she looked up to see Mia flash a dazzling smile at someone behind her.

"Hi, sorry to bother you both," an approaching voice said. "I just thought I'd come over and introduce myself. I'm Adam."

"Hi. I'm Mia, and this is Helen." Adam nodded and smiled at Helen. He was so typical of the kind of guy Mia went for, or at least had done before she married Chris. Tall, clearly a fan of the gym, with a fitted shirt that showed off broad shoulders and well-developed biceps. His fair hair was cut in a classic public-school style, and he smelled expensive.

"Are you—"

"Where are—"

Mia and Adam spoke at the same time, and Mia giggled as Adam grinned. He had a wide smile that showed off white, even teeth.

"Please…" Adam offered an up-stretched palm, indicating Mia should speak first.

"I just wondered if you were over here on holiday?" Mia asked.

Helen was beginning to feel like a gooseberry already. She tried to look nonchalant and glanced around her. A group of men, who she presumed were with Adam, were standing by the entrance to the restaurant, chatting and looking over at them. Every now and again they'd laugh out loud at something one of them had said.

"Yep, for my friend's stag night. Well, not a stag *night* exactly, just a short break with the boys before the wedding. We've been playing some golf, hanging out by the pool."

"Clearly," said Mia, referencing his tan and smiling again, holding his gaze. Helen felt even worse now. She lifted her glass to take a sip and felt a prickle of embarrassment when she realised it was empty.

"What about you two?"

"We're on holiday too," said Mia. "A bit of R&R."

"Well, I just thought I'd say hello. And if you don't have plans tonight, there's a really good DJ playing at Heart and—"

"Luther Sway," Mia cut in and Adam beamed.

"That's the one."

"We're already going," Mia continued. "He's the main reason we're in town tonight."

"Brilliant, we may see you in there then. Assuming we can get in, a group of chaps on their own and all."

"Come with us then," Mia answered quickly without even glancing at Helen. "We can all go together."

"Oh, if you don't mind, that would be great." Finally, Adam turned his gaze to Helen. "If *you're* sure?" Helen tried to look enthusiastic, though wasn't sure if she managed it. The whole interaction was making her uncomfortable. Nevertheless, she said, "Of course, but we were going to go quite early because I've got to—"

"Shall we meet up with you in say, an hour?" Mia interjected. "That bar over the road would be good, it's just a short walk from here."

"Perfect. Looking forward to it." Adam flashed another smile and turned back to his friends. Helen saw Mia's face flush with excitement.

"Bloody hell, Mia! We haven't been in Ibiza for two minutes."

"And… what?" Mia laughed now. "I can't help it if they're like moths to a flame. It's good to know I've still got it. I've been a bit out of practice."

"But remember, I'm driving tonight, so no mad late night with me having to nag you to leave. We agreed."

"Yeah, of course." Mia rolled her eyes. "You were about to tell him we couldn't stay late before we'd even got in there! Going in with them won't make any difference. We're just being kind, doing them a favour. Groups of lads always get pushed to the back of the queue at clubs, remember?"

"Of course I remember," Helen replied, but she couldn't. In fact, she couldn't remember the last time she'd been to a club. She also couldn't remember feeling so out of place anywhere as she did now and was beginning to wish she'd never agreed to come. This trip seemed as if it was more about Mia escaping her home life rather than lifting Helen's spirits.

As the waiter approached, asking them if they'd like more drinks, Helen politely refused and asked for the bill. "We agreed we'd go for a walk," she said firmly to Mia, who looked ready to order another bottle.

They walked down to the marina. Mia had protested, saying they should go onto a bar for cocktails, promising her sister that some of the mocktails were fabulous, but Helen stood firm. She knew it might be the last chance she'd get to have a look around. Once Mia met up with Adam again, there would be no chance for her to have any influence on what they were going to do.

The sisters marvelled at the floating palaces moored at Botafoch Marina. Some were hosting drinks parties where glamorous guests could be seen mingling with uniformed staff on wide, teak decks. One gorgeous-looking boat, with the name *Corpo Santo* in elegant calligraphy across its transom, had its uppermost deck festooned with fairy lights and candles flickered in glass hurricane lamps. A table was laid for what looked like a special dinner.

"It looks magical," Helen said.

"Yes," said Mia, "but we've seen enough, don't you think? We need to get back to meet the others before we head to Heart." She tugged Helen in the direction of the main drag.

"I think you need to put your head before your heart," Helen said quickly, just loud enough for Mia to hear.

"Oh, very funny," Mia replied. "Don't worry, Helen, I'm not going to do anything silly. But you've got to admit, Adam is cute."

Helen smiled and nodded. "Yes, he is cute, but don't forget I'm driving us back tonight. In fact, don't forget I'm here, full stop!"

"Of course not! Look, there they are," Mia said excitedly, and Helen followed her gaze across the road to where Adam and his friends waited at the bar. Adam had already spotted them and offered a wave. Helen forced herself to smile, feeling awkward. She wished Mia hadn't dragged her into this; it was bad enough having to spend the evening in a club without having to make small talk with strangers.

Adam introduced them to his friends. Ian, the groom, already looked slightly worse for wear; Henry and Oliver stood either side of him, laughing as their friend swayed unsteadily; Xander, who was raving about the whisky cocktail he was drinking and Simon, who hid behind the others and seemed about as happy to be there as Helen did. She nodded politely while Mia did most of the talking, and after the men had finished and paid their bill, the group made their way to the club.

Outside Heart, a queue had already formed. Two burly bouncers stood on the door, tattooed biceps bulging from short-sleeved white shirts. They wore earpieces and ushered women-only parties in without inspection, while turning several male-only groups away– just as Mia had predicted. Some put up a fight, but the bouncers weren't up for negotiation.

"With any luck, we might not get in," one of Adam's friends muttered as they joined the end of the line.

Helen glanced sideways. It was Simon who had spoken. These were the first words she'd heard him say aloud, though from what she had gathered in the bar, he was an old uni friend of Ian.

"Take no notice of Simon – he's only joking… aren't you?" Adam pulled him into a mock headlock as the others laughed.

Simon was smiling but shaking his head.

"It's way past his bedtime," Ian said as Simon pulled away. "You'll love it when you're in there. You'll get a second wind."

"Whatever you say, Ian," Simon replied as the queue of people inched its way forward.

"Helen doesn't really want to go either. She's just doing me a favour," Mia said, linking her arm through her sister's.

"No, I do. It's just I don't… erm…" Helen felt her face flush as all eyes turned to her.

Mia laughed. "Hey, it doesn't matter, we're here now. Let's see if we can all get in."

As they approached the bouncers, Mia dialled up the charm, beaming at them and explaining, before they had even opened their mouths, that it was her friend's wedding in a few weeks' time and that they had two doctors in their party.

They were waved through without question.

"*Two* doctors?" Helen said into Mia's ear as they made their way up the dramatically curved staircase, following the thump of the music.

"You and Simon. Didn't you hear him say so? He works in a London hospital."

Helen shook her head. She hadn't heard him say anything until a few seconds ago… then again, she hadn't heard much of the conversation when they were in the bar. It had been difficult to with so much background noise. Mia had been so engrossed in conversation with Adam that she hadn't exactly noticed her sister's discomfort or lack of interaction with the others.

The men paid for the tickets, refusing to let Helen and Mia dip into their purses in return for helping them gain entry.

Inside the club, the noise was deafening. They managed to find a table away from the dance floor where the music wasn't as loud.

Adam insisted on buying drinks for everyone. "It's the least I can do," he said, and Mia beamed at him, offering to help carry the glasses. Helen watched them disappear into the crowd.

"Is this your first time in Ibiza?" Ian asked.

As Helen strained her voice and told him about Victor's house, Simon joined the conversation, saying he knew that area of the island.

"He runs and goes wild swimming over that way," Ian said. "He loves all of that, don't you? A bit of an action man!" Ian looked proud as he patted his friend on the back.

Simon shrugged him off and continued chatting about the northern part of the island. "Have you seen the little church of Sant Llorenc in Balafia? They have an amazing celebration there in August where the whole village turns out. It's all to do with the Catalan invasion apparently, and the locals celebrate the feast day of the saint. I was there for it a few years ago."

"I read something about it," Helen replied. "And how lovely it's so well attended. A traditional community event."

"A very different Ibiza to this," Simon nodded towards the vast sea of people next to them, hands and bottles held high in the air, some jumping to the beat of the music.

"Yes," Helen agreed. "We did a food and drink tour yesterday – more my sort of thing. We started off at Sant Joan de Labritja, then went to a traditional market and ended up at a vineyard for lunch, not far from where we are staying. It was great. It's hard to believe that all of this," she nodded towards the heaving crowd, "is going on just a few miles away."

She paused, realising Simon was leaning in closely due to the noise and studying her, which suddenly made her feel a little self-conscious so she pulled back.

"It sounds wonderful," he answered quickly, pulling back himself as if sensing her discomfort. "Did your sister not enjoy it?"

"Let's just say she's much more at home with this aspect of Ibiza," Helen smiled at him.

"I should have come with you instead," Simon held Helen's gaze, and for a second, she felt a fluttering sensation in the pit of her stomach.

"Where do you do your wild swimming? I've always wanted to try it," she asked, changing the subject.

"You can do it everywhere these days," he replied. "There are quite a few places in London actually."

"Oh, really—"

An announcement boomed over the club's sound system, "Here he is, the ONE AND ONLY…MR. LUTHER. SWAY!"

"Mia has been looking forward to seeing this DJ for ages," Helen said, raising her voice above the noise and wondering where her sister was as Luther Sway whipped up the crowd from his DJ podium several feet above the dance floor. "To be fair, I quite like this music," she added, as a familiar tune started to play.

"Just wish he'd turn it down a bit," Simon said, and Ian rolled his eyes. Helen tried to suppress a smirk.

"What?" He looked from Ian to Helen and then back again.

"You sound like my granddad," Ian said and did an impersonation of an old man, bent over his walking stick, pretending to hold his lower back in pain. The others laughed, and Helen giggled.

"Hang on a minute, I don't think *you* were desperate to come to Heart by the sounds of things," Simon looked at Helen with an earnest expression.

She didn't know whether he was teasing her or not. "You're right, I wasn't. It's just the thought of you asking them to turn the music down."

They all laughed again at this, and Simon raised his hands. "It's really not my thing, but I guess it's a small price to pay for a few days in the sunshine with friends. This time next week, I'll be back at work, wishing I was off my head with Luther."

"What happened to those drinks, then?" Ian asked, looking around. He nodded towards Mia and Adam, who were engrossed in conversation near the bar. Mia was holding a large glass with bright red liquid, an umbrella and vast quantities of fruit on skewers. It didn't look like they were coming back this way any time soon.

"Helen, what can I get you?" he asked.

"Something soft, please." She mimicked driving to no one in particular.

The others gave Ian their orders.

"Coke for me, thanks," Simon said, and once again, Ian raised his eyebrows.

"I might have guessed. Ok, gramps, I'll be back in a minute."

"Granddad…" Simon smiled at Helen. "Cheeky git."

Helen returned the smile, and the pair continued their conversation about outdoor swimming venues before Ian returned, this time with Mia and Adam in tow, a waiter following them carrying a large tray.

"They were just having a little sharpener while our drinks were being sorted," Ian said, raising an eyebrow.

"I ordered champagne for the girls, and it wasn't cold enough. They had to go off and get some more," Adam explained.

Helen held up her hand. "Oh, not for me—"

"What do you think of Luther?" Mia shouted, trying to make herself heard above the music.

"Yeah, he's great," Helen assured her sister.

"Just a bit loud," Ian added quickly, winking at her and then smiling at Simon.

"Exactly as I'd imagined he'd be," Simon shot back at him. "I'm just so glad Adam made us come here. It was well worth the extortionate entry fee for this lovely, relaxed vibe," he quipped as the heavy beat reached a crescendo, forcing any conversation to be raised to a full-blown yell.

An hour and a half later, Helen was delighted when the DJ finished his set. As he left the stage, shouts went up from the crowd wanting more, but another DJ had already entered the booth and started their set. Keen to leave, Helen looked at Mia, who was doing her utmost to avoid eye contact with her. She'd done her bit, driven them to the club, spent the evening listening to Luther Sway, been left with strangers while her sister got to know Adam and, now, she wanted to leave. To be fair, the evening hadn't been too bad. Simon was interesting to talk to, but it was an effort just to hear him properly, and anyway, she'd had enough.

"Who'd like another drink?" Adam asked loudly, above the music, directing his question at Helen.

"Oh, no thanks – I think we're going to—"

Before she could finish, Mia cut in, "Yes please, same again for me."

"Er, Mia, I thought we said we'd be leaving after he'd finished?"

"One for the road," Mia replied moving towards her sister and draping an arm around her shoulders imploringly. "*Plee-ase*?"

"Mia, I, er…" Helen felt awkward insisting they leave. She was tired, her feet were beginning to pinch in the heels, and she'd had enough of the deafening beat, but she felt embarrassed admitting it. It was hardly the attitude for a club in Ibiza, and she didn't want to be the one to break up the party.

But she steeled herself, not ready to cave in for once. "I'm sorry, Mia. I want to head back."

"Ok, ok," Mia said. "Let's go home, Cinderella."

Helen smiled weakly and said goodbye to the others. Mia leant in and whispered something to Adam before the pair made their way towards the exit.

Outside, the crowded pavements did nothing to suggest it was late. The party vibe was still in full swing as they made their way back to the car. Mia chatted animatedly as Helen concentrated on remembering where they had parked. The streets all seemed to look the same, and she scanned the area, desperately looking for a familiar landmark.

"I thought you'd dropped a pin when you parked up?" Mia said as Helen studied her phone.

"I thought I had too, but I'm not sure I did it properly," she replied, looking at her phone and then up at the buildings, as if something she recognised would magically appear.

"Let me have a look," Mia said, taking the phone from her sister's hand and inspecting it. "We've come too far down from the main drag. The car is back there. It was a much quieter street," Mia said, pointing behind her. "Remember that furniture shop was near where we parked? That's back there."

Without anything better to suggest, Helen let Mia lead them back along the street they'd just come from, monitoring their movements on her phone.

"It should literally be the next right and then at the end of the road on the left after that," Mia said, and Helen felt hopeful. This was starting to look a little more familiar now.

As they approached the end of the road, sure enough, there was the furniture shop Mia had mentioned. Relieved, Helen quickened her pace, and Mia matched it. She could see the car ahead of her.

Turning into the road directly ahead of them were Adam, Simon, Ian and the others.

"Hey! You two again. Are you following us?" Adam said. "You're following *us*, more like," Mia laughed bounding up to them. "Helen took a wrong turn. She hasn't quite mastered this Google Maps lark."

Helen felt a flush of irritation as the boys laughed and carried on towards the car. She wasn't prepared to go through another round of persuading Mia to leave. "See you tomorrow," she heard Adam call as Mia joined her in the car.

Only once they'd pulled out of the car park did Helen ask, "Tomorrow?"

"Adam invited us to dinner tomorrow night – not the whole group, just a few of them."

"Oh, Mia, come on. I'm not coming all the way back here tomorrow night."

"Ok, ok," Mia replied. "Let's talk about it in the morning."

"No, let's not," Helen replied. "This is not what we agreed."

"Ok, but don't spoil a lovely evening," Mia shot back. "Do you know the way home? Have you programmed the sat nav properly?"

"Yes," Helen said tersely and continued driving. She did her best to talk herself out of the annoyance she felt. She didn't want a bad atmosphere. "It's straight along this road, and then we join the camino on the right, yes?" she asked, glancing ahead of her, looking for familiar landmarks.

"Yes. You're on the right road. Look, there's that building we saw earlier, and there's the turning," Mia pointed ahead.

By the time they got back to the villa it was after 3.30 a.m. Mia had drifted off to sleep in the car instantly after the pointing out the turning, leaving Helen to negotiate the route on her own. The journey had required all her concentration as their car bounced along the dusty track in the pitch-black. Every now and again, she'd catch sight of an animal in her headlights, and then just as quickly, it was gone, leaving her wondering what kind of wildlife roamed the hills around the villa.

As they pulled up, Mia woke and denied she'd been asleep. Helen said a hurried goodnight and made her way upstairs. Exhausted, she climbed into bed and immediately wished she was back home. As she lay there, eyes adjusting to the shadowy light, she berated herself for coming in the first place. She was sick and tired of Mia getting her own way and couldn't face another day of this. This trip hadn't been about her at all. All that talk about it being a chance for her to reset. It was clearly all for Mia's benefit. She'd tell her tomorrow. Tell her she wouldn't be falling into line with her plans. She'd use the time for herself. Mia could go out on her own if that's what she wanted. Suddenly she didn't feel quite as tired and her annoyance grew further. She missed her little cottage, she missed Percy. She missed work. She wanted to be amongst her own things. She wouldn't even have been here if Phil was alive. Phil… the thought of him and the familiar pain of loss swamped her; so intense it almost winded her. She rolled on to her side and squeezed her eyes tight shut, not allowing the tears to come. She knew that would just make her feel worse.

"Goodnight, Helen. Sleep tight," Mia shouted as she made her way to her own bedroom, pulling Helen from her thoughts.

Still irritated by her sister, Helen murmured, "Good night."

When Mia replied, "I loved being out with you tonight. It really helped to take my mind off things," before closing her own bedroom door, Helen instantly felt a twinge of remorse. After what she'd told her earlier, it was obvious Mia needed someone to lean on, no matter how strong she appeared. Mia's default coping strategy was to run away from a bad situation and bury her head in the sand, whereas Helen would head for home, lick her wounds and set a plan. It had always been the same. If Mia really suspected Chris was having an affair, then she needed to talk to him. Her behaviour with Adam tonight suggested she wasn't exactly prioritising mending her marriage. She vowed she'd encourage Mia to open up tomorrow when they would discuss things properly. Yes, she wanted to be back home but she needed to help her younger sister before she ran headlong into an affair of her own.

CHAPTER 8

When she woke, the sun was shining, spilling through a crack in the curtains. Helen stretched and reached for her phone, surprised to discover it was already after nine. Grabbing her linen dressing gown, she made her way downstairs, tiptoeing so she wouldn't disturb Mia.

In the kitchen, she flicked the switch on the kettle and walked over to open the French doors onto the garden. Helen breathed in the fresh smell of the morning blossoms, picking out the distinctive floral notes of lavender. She made herself a coffee and stepped outside. The garden was stunning, its borders a riot of vibrant colour. A large oleander shrub was in full flower, its blousy pink flowers giving a heady smell, similar to apricots. Next to it, huge Agapanthus blooms towered above their foliage. She would love to recreate this look in her own garden.

She followed the winding path towards the pool, and as she approached, heard the soft sound of splashing. Assuming it was the maintenance man clearing leaves from the pool, she was surprised to see Mia, arms resting on the far side of the pool, idly kicking her legs behind her. Unseen, Helen cupped her hands around her coffee and watched her for a minute. From behind, it was hard to believe this was her gregarious little sister. She looked vulnerable, there on her own, head tilted to one side, lost in thought.

"Mia?" She turned, and almost at once, the dreamy, wistful demeanour was replaced by the Mia that Helen knew.

"So, you've finally decided to get up, have you?" she smiled at Helen, clearly delighted to have surprised her by being the first up.

"I can't believe it's this time already," Helen replied. "I never sleep in this long, but then it was rather a late night."

"It's easily done here – it's so peaceful, isn't it?" Mia assured her. "I remember the first time I came here a few years ago, it felt like a health spa – so rejuvenating."

Helen nodded and took a seat on a wooden bench beside the pool.

"It's almost hard to believe the island's party reputation," Mia continued. "You're really miles away from anything up here, aren't you?"

Again, Helen nodded as Mia climbed out, wrapped herself in a large towel and came to sit next to her. The pair watched a small bird land beside the side of the pool and hop along the tiles before Mia scared it away by stretching out her legs and raising her arms above her head.

"Oh, this sun is just glorious," she said, tilting her face towards the sky. "Hellie?" She turned to look at her sister. "You're not saying much. You're not still cross with me about last night, are you?"

Helen started, "Actually Mia—"

"Because I'm so grateful that you came, and honestly, I just thought it might be good for you to get out and just, well, have a change of scene. A little bit of fun, you know, and it was fun walking down by the marina, wasn't it?"

Helen sighed. Mia was very good at framing a situation to show her in the best possible light. They both knew the nightlife of Ibiza was hardly the first place Helen would have picked for a change of scene.

"To be honest, Mia, I'm more concerned about what you told me last night about Chris." Helen tried to read her sister's expression, which gave nothing away. "You love him… or at least you did the last time we spoke about it. You can't just turn that tap off."

Mia still looked at her impassively.

"I thought I did, but maybe I loved the excitement. I still love the holidays, the cars, the houses. But…"

"But what? You've obviously been bothered enough to employ a private investigator."

"Because knowledge is power. I need to know exactly what's going on because if it does come to a divorce, I need to be one step ahead. He has no idea I know as much as I do, and I'll leave it that way until I need to do otherwise." Mia frowned.

Helen thought about how tough she sounded. She could project the air of someone who'd had the hardest of upbringings, fighting for everything she had. She played the victim well, Helen mused.

"So, what will you do exactly?" Helen asked.

"I don't know, but one thing's for certain, if we split, he will come down hard. Exactly as he did with his first wife. He'll try and give me as little as possible, and I'm afraid I like the lifestyle too much to give it up easily. He has no more respect for me than he does anyone. The only thing he truly cares about is money and control."

Helen wondered how she'd got Chris so wrong. He'd always seemed besotted with Mia,

"Surely, being happy must be your number-one priority?" Helen studied her intently, but Mia remained silent and expressionless.

"Genuinely, you'd put up with your husband playing around because you like your lifestyle too much to give it up?"

"You make it sound worse than it is," Mia replied, meeting her sister's gaze.

"Sorry? You've said your husband is cheating and doesn't have respect for you? How could it be worse? This is me you're talking to, remember? You can be honest."

"Helen, don't. It's different for you. You're clever. You've got a career. What have I got?"

"*You* had a career, Mia."

"I had a job at Chris's company. I had no degree, no A levels."

"But you got that job on your own merit. You had the confidence to walk in and charm them into giving you an interview. You didn't even meet Chris until after you'd started there. Where has the determined, sassy Mia gone? The one who believed she could do anything?"

Mia shook her head. "I got rich, Helen."

"Oh, Mia… It's not just about the—"

"I could never do the things I do, go the places I go, buy the clothes, the bags, the shoes – all of it – without Chris's money. I could have worked in marketing forever and never made it to this stage. I know you probably find that hard to hear but it compensates for a lot."

"You need to be happy, Mia. Believe me—"

"Enough, already." Mia jumped up, pulling the towel around her. "I've already said we haven't come all this way to talk about me and Chris. We're not here for long, so let's make the most of the time we have left. Now, will you come into town tonight? *Please*?"

Helen's heart sank. She really couldn't face that trip again, and just the thought of another club was more than she could bear.

"Mia, please… I, don't wa—"

"Helen, it would mean so much to me, I can't tell you. I've already had a text this morning from Adam, and it would give me such a lift to see him. Even if it's just the shortest visit into town."

"There's no *short* way of doing it, Mia, and you know that." She paused then added, "So Adam has your number. Does he also know where we're staying?" Mia looked slightly sheepish, a rare occurrence, Helen thought.

"He asked and I told him," she said, not quite making eye contact.

"Let's talk about it later."

Mia stood up, "I'm going to get a dry bikini on and some breakfast, then I think a nice little snooze by the pool will do very nicely for us, don't you think?" She smiled at Helen. "It would mean a lot to me if you'd come, Helen. It's been a while since I've had a bit of fun. Life has been pretty miserable with Chris, but obviously, with everything you've been through, I haven't wanted to burden you with it."

With that, she turned towards the villa. Helen sat for a moment, mulling over their conversation. She was irritated by her request, but she'd do it anyway. They both knew Helen would never refuse her little sister It would be better she was there to keep an eye on things anyway.

CHAPTER 9

"I think Simon really liked you," Mia said as they lay by the pool. The pair had enjoyed a lazy day. Helen had finished the paperback she'd bought at the airport and had started another.

"Sorry?" she said, dragging her attention away.

"Simon. It was clear he really fancied you last night."

"Oh, for God's sake, he did not. We were just commiserating."

"He did. Adam noticed it too."

Helen shook her head.

"He *did*! Honestly, he did. Adam said Simon was work, work, work, and when he wasn't working, he was running or doing a triathlon or an ironman or something. When we saw you talking to each other, he said it was the most animated he'd ever seen him."

"I think you'll find he was animated because he was having to shout so loudly to be heard in that place."

"He's rather nice though, isn't he? Come on, admit it! And you've got so much in common."

"Have we?"

"He's a doctor and loves keeping fit."

"He's a cardiologist, and he takes part in extreme fitness routines. I like Pilates and a bit of swimming and running when I can manage it. Hardly the same."

"But you aren't denying he's good-looking."

"I hadn't really noticed."

Mia laughed loudly. "Now I *know* you're interested. Of course you bloody noticed. And he lives in London, which is handy. So, are you going to come into town tonight?"

Helen groaned.

"Mia, I'm honestly nowhere near ready for a new relationship, and you know how I feel about going back to a club. It's just not my thing, and we're going home tomorrow—"

"Exactly, we're going home tomorrow, and this time next week you'll be back in the surgery, dealing with someone's rash or whatever and wishing you'd taken the chance to go out and enjoy yourself and—"

"I can enjoy myself with you, *here*." It was Helen's turn to interrupt now.

But Mia continued, "How about a compromise? We just go for dinner?"

Helen sighed. She knew when she was beaten. "Ok, we'll go in just for dinner."

"Fantastic. It'll be great, promise!" Mia reached for her phone. "I'm going to text Adam. I'd say I'd get us a taxi, but Victor says it's tricky to get anyone to come out this far. That's why he leaves a car at the airport."

"Don't worry, I'm ok about driving."

"You're amazing." Mia got up and gave her a kiss on the cheek. "And don't worry, I won't forget all your lovely chauffeuring when I get my licence back."

Helen rolled her eyes. She had resigned herself to the fact that their last night wasn't going to be a gentle, relaxing evening with a glass of wine listening to crickets as the sun went down. She followed Mia into the house to get changed, settling on pale pink linen trousers and a sleeveless silk shirt. She was brushing her hair when Mia walked in. Helen caught sight of her in the mirror and turned round.

"Oh, wow, Mia, you look amazing. That is gorgeous. It's like the Marilyn Monroe dress."

It was a simple design. White with a halter neck and fitted to the waist, it accentuated her tan, and with blonde hair falling over her shoulders, she looked stunning.

Mia beamed but shook her head. "Hardly that glam, but thanks. I bought it a few weeks ago and have been waiting for an excuse to wear it."

"I feel a bit underdressed now," Helen said, turning back to the mirror, finishing off her hair and casting a critical eye over her crumpled trousers.

"You look lovely, Helen. You always do," Mia said. "And it's so warm this evening, this dress will probably be uncomfortable. It's a bit tight." She placed her hands on her waist and turned from left to right, studying herself in the mirror before adjusting her neckline to maximise her cleavage. Helen finished her makeup and made her way downstairs, where Mia was waiting. Mia drained a glass of champagne and dangled the car keys in front of Helen.

"Our carriage awaits," she beamed, pulling open the front door with a dramatic sweep of her arm. "After you."

Helen stepped outside and once again was struck by the night scent and the chatter of the insects. It was such a shame to be leaving these beautiful surroundings for the noisy chaos of Ibiza Town.

"Look..." Helen said as Mia shut the door behind them. She was lifting her face to the sky. Mia followed her gaze. The night sky was spectacular. With no light pollution, the moon and stars shone brighter than ever, lighting up the garden.

"Don't worry, there will still be a moon and stars when we get home tomorrow." Helen shook her head at her sister's lack of interest and they climbed into the car.

When they reached the town, Mia guided Helen to a small car park not far from the marina, explaining that the boys were in a nearby bar.

As they strolled along, the walkway was already buzzing with chatter and laughter. Helen was aware of the attention Mia was getting – attention she was clearly enjoying. Music played from one of the bars, and Mia broke into a dance, lifting her arms above her head in time to the beat ensuring she was noticed, just in case her dress and cleavage hadn't quite done the job. Helen wanted to tell her to calm it down, but this was typical Mia. She was on a high, excited for the evening ahead.

Nearby, a group of friends were laughing and chatting as they stood outside one of the designer boutiques. Two women from their party were inside, browsing a selection of handbags. From the little Spanish she knew, Helen heard a male voice shout "darse prisa!" telling them to hurry up, which was met with more laughter from the group.

"There it is! That's Botega's." Mia pointed to a bar up ahead. As they approached, a group turned to watch, and even though the attention was very much on Mia, Helen felt self-conscious.

"Here she is. Well. Look. At. You!" Adam's voice boomed, and Helen watched as he came out to greet them. He grabbed Mia and kissed her passionately on the lips as if they'd known each other for ages.

"Hello, Helen," he said as he pulled away, leaning over to kiss Helen on both cheeks. "Come in, come in, we've got a table at the back. It's outside."

The pair followed Adam through to the rear, where a little garden sat with several tables surrounded by fairy lights and flickering candles. It looked magical. Gentle jazz was playing just audibly above the conversation amongst the tables. Helen caught sight of Simon. He was talking to Ian and looked up as she approached, lifting a hand to wave. He was wearing a pale-blue shirt, sleeves rolled up to his elbows. It was fitted, and Helen noticed how broad his shoulders were. He was really good-looking. He beamed at her.

"Drinks? What would you like?" Adam asked before they'd even sat down. "Champagne?"

"Oo, yes, please," Mia replied immediately. "That would be perfect. Helen, are you going to join me?"

Helen hesitated a second too long and Mia answered for her. "Yes, it's just a glass, Hels, and you'll still be able to have a glass of wine with dinner." Mia turned to Adam and mouthed the word "driving".

Mia said she'd go with Adam to get the drinks, and before Helen could protest, Mia had gone, once again leaving her alone, uneasy and embarrassed as she turned to face the two men. She wished she'd already had a drink. A cold glass of champagne might go some way to help alleviate her awkwardness.

Immediately, Simon stood up and gestured for her to sit down. She guessed he could sense how she felt as he pulled a chair over from another table.

"Sorry, Ian, I'm afraid your stag party is being invaded yet again," Helen said apologetically. "Where are the others tonight?"

Ian laughed. "The others are eating back at the hotel and you're not invading – it's good to see you both. My fiancée will be delighted that Adam has made a friend out here to keep him occupied. She was always worried the trip would be solely strippers and lap dancers, but thanks to you two that won't be happening. To be honest, you're doing us a favour. Aren't they, Simon?"

Simon raised an eyebrow and smiled at Helen. Helen felt herself relaxing a little as the men laughed. He'd really caught the sun. The colour made his blue eyes especially striking. Mia and Adam returned with fizzing glasses of champagne.

"Salud!" Mia said, raising her glass to tap it against Helen's and then turned to Ian. "To you, too – here's to your wedding. To a long, happy and successful marriage."

She winked as she caught Helen's eye.

Everyone replied "salud" and Helen sipped her drink, watching as Mia turned her head to whisper something in Adam's ear before he did the same to her. Mia laughed then leant towards him, resting her hand on his arm for a second or two. There was certainly chemistry between them. Adam could hardly take his eyes off her, and Mia was loving the attention. Helen couldn't remember ever seeing her behave like that with Chris. Even in the early days of their relationship.

When Mia said she was going to the loo, Helen said she'd go with her. Although she was more comfortable than at the start of the evening, she still didn't want to be on her own with the men.

"All ok, Helen?" Mia asked without looking up as they stood washing their hands. Without giving her a moment to reply, she added, "I'm having such a great time. Adam is such easy company."

Helen nodded and smiled. "I can see. I'm glad."

She watched as Mia reapplied her lip gloss, adjusted her cleavage yet again and ran her fingers through her hair, adding volume to the sides.

It's just one more night. We'll be home this time tomorrow.

CHAPTER 10

The group had just finished dinner when Adam mentioned a party in the marina.

"It's a guy I know through work – a fund manager. He's out here for a few days and has brought some clients along. We're all welcome too. And honestly, it could be quite useful for me, work-wise."

Helen watched as the others nodded. They seemed happy enough to go along. They'd all had a few drinks and were quite relaxed. Dinner had been delicious, and despite her reservations about the evening, Helen had enjoyed chatting with Simon and Ian. She had no history here, and it was a welcome change not to be seen as The Widow. Almost as soon as the thought popped into her head, she felt guilty but Phil would have understood. She could almost imagine him standing here now, telling her to "crack on and live your life".

"We're parked down by the marina, so it'll be easy to call in on our way home," Mia said, wrenching Helen away from her thoughts.

Helen almost laughed out loud. "Oh, Mia, Adam didn't mean us! I think we can leave them to it. We've crashed their stag party enough this week." She glanced at Ian and was convinced she was right. He looked relieved. No matter what he'd said earlier about being ok with it, he was just being nice. He'd come out here for a few days with his friends and didn't need two strangers tagging along. Mia could be so incredibly unaware sometimes.

"I don't mean we are actually going to stay, I just meant we would pop in on our way home. It'll be ok, won't it, Ian?" Mia tilted her head to one side, flashing him a megawatt smile.

"Of course," Adam interjected before Ian had a chance to reply.

"I'll get the bill," Adam said grandly "and we can get going."

Helen glanced at Mia who was, yet again, studiously avoiding making eye contact with her. "Mia…" she began.

"We'll just pop in, have a quick drink and leave," said Mia firmly. "I like the idea of a yacht party, and besides, we're going home tomorrow, and it might be the last time we ever meet you." As she spoke, she looked directly at Adam, who held her gaze.

Helen didn't want to cause a scene so remained silent. As they got up to leave, Mia busied herself, making sure Helen didn't get a chance to speak to her on her own. Simon stood to the side, holding the door open.

"Oh, what joy, another night of partying in Ibiza," he said quietly, just enough for her to hear. She turned to face him, and he winked conspiratorially.

"I'm beginning to feel I've been brought here on false pretences," he continued.

"You and me both," she replied, also keeping her voice low. "I was promised a few days at a remote villa."

Simon gave a little laugh. "Do you think we are the only people ever to come to Ibiza for a relaxing break? Maybe we were both being a bit naïve. I thought it would be golf and a few drinks in the sunshine. To be honest, I'm glad you're coming along. It might just keep a lid on things."

Helen glanced sideways at Simon. He was looking straight ahead. "A lid?"

He leant towards her, and she could smell his cologne as his shoulder lightly brushed against hers. She felt the heat of his body.

"Most of us hadn't met Adam before we came here. Ian used to work with him. Apparently, he's a bit of a party animal. When we planned the trip, we all thought we'd leave the bars and clubs alone, but Adam's keen on splashing the cash and is, in fact, a bit of an idiot."

Helen was about to ask him to expand on this when she heard Adam calling for them to catch up. He'd managed to hail down a minibus and was ushering them all into it.

"This is going to take us to the marina. South entrance, please," he said to the driver.

When they arrived, Mia was the first to disembark, almost leaping out as the driver opened the door.

The marina was alive with people and parties, lights and laughter. Eighties disco music pumped out from a glass-fronted bar, and loud chatter carried on the air as guests attempted to make themselves heard above it. A juggler dressed as Pierrot was surrounded by a small crowd who gasped and cheered as he balanced a child's bicycle on his chin while riding a unicycle. The group followed Adam as he strode ahead with Mia walking briskly at his side. She would lean into him or touch his arm every now and again, laughing at something he'd said. Helen wondered if she'd even mentioned she was married.

"Wow, that's pretty impressive," Simon said.

Their group slowed, and she followed Simon's gaze to a huge yacht. Someone was waving at Adam from the top deck, glass in hand.

Two men in identical navy polo shirts and white shorts stood on either side of the gangway onto the boat. One held out a hand as Mia stepped forward. The others followed.

On board, the crew asked them to remove their shoes, politely pointing out that the owner preferred bare feet only on the polished teak. Another crew member held a trayful of champagne flutes. Adam leant forward and took two, handing one to Helen and one to Mia.

"I'm driv…" Helen started but thought better of it. She took the glass.

They were ushered up inside and up some stairs onto the open top deck where a drinks party was in full swing. She could feel the beat of the thumping jazz under her bare feet as guests shouted to each other to be heard over it. Some people were shimmying in time to the music as they drank and chatted. Helen put her untouched glass of fizz on a table and they all followed as Adam and Mia shouldered their way through the crowd towards the man who had waved earlier. Helen was behind them when suddenly she felt liquid hit the side of her face and chest and turned to see a glamorous young woman laughing loudly and gesticulating, apologising for spilling her drink.

"Oops, I am very sorry," she said in what sounded like a Russian accent. Before Helen could reply to the mystery woman had made her way through the scrum to talk to a much older man. Helen glanced down. A dark red stain was creeping across the front of her blouse.

In the press of bodies, it was increasingly difficult to move freely. Helen realised she'd been separated from the others and craned her neck to look for them. Even turning around felt impossible now. She was almost hemmed in and starting to feel claustrophobic so immediately began to retrace her steps towards the staircase, apologising as she bumped into a couple kissing passionately. They didn't seem to notice. Eventually, she was almost by the door they had come in through and managed to turn and look back at the crowd. Standing on tiptoes, she tried to scan the room.

"Are you lost?"

A deep voice beside her was almost drowned out by the music. She turned to see a man of about fifty very close to her, sipping a drink. He was wearing more jewellery than she was and was about a foot shorter.

"Er… no, thanks. I was just going to get some air."

"It's very overcrowded, yes?" He leant towards her, his face inches from hers, and Helen almost gagged from the stench of stale alcohol and cigarettes. She tried to recoil but the pressure of the crowd prevented her. Nodding, she gave a tight smile and tried to squeeze past him when she felt a hand on the back of her thigh which quickly slid up to her bottom.

For a split second, she was stunned, not quite believing what was happening as she felt the hand move between her legs.

"Get your hand off me!" she snapped, finally finding her voice and feeling her face redden.

The man lifted a hand in front of her and raised his eyebrows as if to ask a question. He was smirking.

"You're disgusting!" Helen muttered and forced her way past, moving a little quicker now, no longer worrying about knocking other guests. She reached the stairwell and made her way down to the first deck, ignoring those trying to make their way up. *They could wait. Where the hell is Mia?*

At the bottom, she looked around and saw a young woman wearing the same uniform she'd seen on the men earlier.

"Excuse me?"

Without waiting, the young woman held her arm out ahead of her pointing towards a door. "The bathroom is this way, madam."

"Actually, I was going to ask you to help me find someone. She's upstairs, and it's too busy. I can't see her, and we need to leave."

"Ok, we are just going to be starting another drinks service. I can see if I can find her then. What's she wearing?"

"She's wearing a white dress."

The waitress smiled. "There are a lot of white dresses up there. Who did you come with?"

"Adam."

Helen suddenly felt really stupid. She couldn't even remember Adam's surname. Had she ever known it? She felt like a teenager who had gate-crashed a party. To make matters worse she'd been accosted by a fat creep and had a large stain down her top. *I feel like a total idiot in front of this girl. I've had it with Mia. If the shoe was on the other foot, I bet she'd just go and leave me without a backward glance.* Helen felt like crying.

"Ok, I'll go and look for you," the girl said.

"Thank you. Her name is Mia, she's blonde, and the dress is a halter neck, if that's helps."

"Would you like a drink?" The girl smiled politely. Helen shook her head, and the waitress started to climb the stairs.

Helen made her way to the loo and pushed open the door. Inside, it was hard to believe she was on a yacht; it was so spacious, it looked more like a bathroom in a high-end hotel. Catching herself in a large mirror, she realised how bad she looked. The stain on her top had now bled into a misshapen flower. Some of the red wine, or whatever drink it was, had also dried on her face and now resembled a bruise. Her mascara had started to run in the heat, creating dark smudges underneath her eyes, and sweating had caused her hair to hang lank and shapeless.

She'd brought a small bag with her, but all it held was the car keys, a debit card and lipstick. She took a few tissues from a box by the sink and dampened some of them under the tap. There was no point trying to tackle the stain on her top, but she cleaned her face and started to apply some lipstick.

Suddenly, one of the loo doors opened behind her. Helen had thought she was the only person in there. She watched as two young women exited the same cubicle. The first, an attractive blonde, looked surprised to see her and stood, blinking as if trying to gather her thoughts. A second blonde moved a little unsteadily to the basin next to Helen as if she hadn't noticed her. She pulled a blusher brush and compact out of her bag and applied makeup furiously, almost as if she was in a race. The other girl dabbed at her nose with a tissue. She looked agitated. Helen glanced at the girl applying the makeup. Her eyes looked wild, darting from the mirror to the compact.

Helen flinched as one of them let out an ear-splitting screech, "Let's get back and *paaartaaay*!" before they left without giving her so much as a glance.

As another group came in, Helen abandoned any idea of trying to tidy herself up and left. A number of guests, chatting and laughing loudly, were swarming down the stairs from the top deck and onto the next set of stairs. Amongst them, sandwiched between two young women, was the man who had put his hands on her. Helen shrunk back against the wall to hide from him.

Waiting until the last of the group had passed, Helen made her way back upstairs. She was furious– with herself for not bringing her phone and with Mia for disappearing. She wondered if she could simply leave and ask the staff to tell Mia to meet her at the car.

"Excuse me, hello?"

Helen followed the voice. It was the crew member who had helped her earlier, who was standing at the top of the wooden stairs in front of her. "It's a lot clearer here now if you want to have a look."

Helen nodded gratefully. There was still a crowd but it was nowhere near as overwhelming as it had been. She started to make her way through, looking for Mia. The waitress had been right, there were a lot of white dresses.

Helen searched the deck and just as she was about to give up, she heard Mia's voice. She turned quickly and doubled back to where she thought it had come from.

"You are *sooo* funny." Definitely Mia's voice. Looking down, Helen caught sight of her, half sitting, half lying next to Adam on a narrow bench, which was why she hadn't been able to see them earlier.

"Mia," Helen said, and Mia looked up towards her, an inane grin on her face.

"Hi, Hels."

"Mia, I've been looking everywhere for you. I didn't know where you'd all gone."

"Well, we were here." Mia was slurring slightly.

Adam's arm crept around her shoulders and he pulled himself forward. A bottle of champagne sat in an ice bucket on the table in front of them. He pulled it out and topped up their glasses. Helen felt like screaming.

"Hi, Helen," he grinned. "Simon and the others have gone to a bar in the marina. They said it was too crowded here. We thought you'd gone with him," he sniggered and Mia elbowed him.

"What happened to your top?" Mia asked, suddenly noticing the stain.

"I want to leave," Helen replied, ignoring her.

"As soon as I finish this drink. Do you want one?"

"No!"

"How about just a soft one? I'll get it!" Adam pushed his way up out of the seat looking for a waiter, before walking towards a bar area. *Why don't they listen. I don't want a damn drink . I just want to get out of this hell hole.*

"Helen, we'll go soon, I promise," Mia said, quickly reapplying a slick of lip gloss.

"Mia, for God's sake, I want—" Helen was interrupted as Adam reappeared, holding a large balloon-shaped glass full of yellow liquid, a fruit kebab hooked over its rim.

"It's a mocktail," he announced, looking delighted with himself. "A Cinderella."

"Very appropriate. It's like me having to rush home before the clock strikes midnight," Mia said quickly, laughing at her own joke. "Leaving Prince Charming in the lurch. Unless of course Prince Charming wants to come back with Cinders?" She nudged Adam playfully in the ribs

"What's in this?" Helen asked, ignoring Mia.

"Citrus juices and ginger ale, I think," Adam replied. "He put some Angostura Bitters in it too, and maybe some Grenadine, or something that looked like that but no alcohol."

Helen nodded and sipped on the striped paper straw. She'd have preferred a glass of water to this sticky concoction, but she was thirsty, and it was cold and refreshing. She carried on drinking.

"Come and sit, Helen." Mia patted the seat beside her. "Relax."

Reluctantly, Helen slipped into the seat next to her but perched on the edge. She wasn't staying a moment longer than she needed.

"Not bad this, is it?" Adam asked. "Wouldn't it be fun to have a boat like this? Maybe not as big but something where you could bring your friends."

Helen could think of nothing worse but smiled politely and nodded. She put the drink down. She'd had as much as she wanted.

She nudged Mia and tried to speak quietly, "Ready when you are."

Mia gave an almost imperceptible nod but didn't reply. Instead, she pointed towards her own drink. "As soon as I've finished th—"

Irritated, Helen interrupted her, her tone sharp, "Mia I've had enough. First there was this disgusting creep… and then there are kids doing drugs in the loos. I'm done."

"Drugs? What drugs?" Mia asked, her eyes widening.

"What difference does it make? Come on, I'm leaving, Mia. Now."

Helen went to stand up but suddenly felt a head rush as if she'd done it too quickly. She put her hand on the table to steady herself and took a deep breath. Mia hadn't even noticed, her body turned towards Adam.

Helen tried standing up but again felt lightheaded. Oh, God, was she going to faint? She closed her eyes and took a deep breath, exaggerating the length of the exhalation, then did it again, for even longer this time. She opened her eyes and looked around her, but Mia still hadn't noticed. She was now nuzzling Adam's neck, her hand twirling her fingers lazily through his hair.

"Mia, I… Mia…" Helen called. She was leaning heavily on the table.

Mia turned around, "What is it?"

"I need some air."

CHAPTER 11

Helen woke with a splitting headache. The worst she could remember. The pain was so intense across the bridge of her nose and behind her eyes that it felt as though her skull would crack. Her mouth was dry, even the inside of her nostrils felt parched. She clearly hadn't drunk enough water last night. Hazy memories started to flood her brain and she recalled feeling dreadful on the boat. The dizziness, intense nausea and then – *oh my God, I had to stop to vomit as we got towards the car. What on earth had that been all about?* She lay there, looking up at the ceiling, trying to recall more of the previous evening. She'd been so unwell. She'd been intensely hot, the back of her neck drenched with sweat. The blind panic at not being able to take a deep breath. The anxiety at being in such a packed environment. It had all been so sudden and out of character. She remembered falling into bed, relieved to be back at the villa, but everything else was a bit patchy. *How weird.* She wondered if it might be her perimenopause. It was easy to blame the menopause for everything, but this was a distinct possibility. Headache, nausea, anxiety were all classic symptoms, and she knew that, for some women, perimenopause can come on very quickly. On the other hand, it could just have been the heat or something she'd eaten.

She hadn't enjoyed the evening. She thought back to the party and remembered that disgusting man on the boat, the way he'd touched her. The women doing drugs in the loo. She shuddered. *Thank God we are leaving today.*

She needed some water and painkillers, but just the thought of getting up was exhausting – this was going to take some effort. She swung one leg out of bed, then the other, before sitting on the edge. She took a few deep breaths before making her way unsteadily to the bathroom. She was relieved to see it was only 4.38 a.m. She still had time to try and sleep this headache off before her flight home.

Taking two Nurofen from her bag, she washed them down before climbing back into bed, pulling the sheets up under her chin. She dozed off quickly, and when she woke again it was 6.45 a.m. She felt much better this time and pulled on a short linen dress and flip flops to make her way downstairs.

It looked like Mia was already up and about. The kettle was warm, and there was a half-drunk cup of tea next to it. Helen sipped a glass of water as she made coffee and peeled a banana. She still had a headache. Not the intense pounding it had been, but there, nonetheless. She forced herself to eat, knowing it would help stabilise her blood sugar, and taking a gulp of her coffee, put on her sunglasses to shield her eyes from the glaring sun and stepped out into the garden. She walked to the pool, wondering if Mia was enjoying one last swim, but there was no sign of her. She carried on through the gardens, brushing past the oleander. Her headache made its scent more cloying than pleasant.

She went back to the house and called out Mia's name. When there was no reply, she crossed the hall and was surprised to see the front door was unlocked. Had they locked it last night? She couldn't remember.

She could hear running water somewhere outside. She followed the noise and peering round the high hedge which screened the carport, found Mia washing Victor's car, hose in one hand, cloth in the other.

"Wow, there's a sight I thought I'd never see!"

Mia spun to look at her. She looked tired, and despite her tan, her face looked pale.

"It's the least I can do."

"Absolutely. I'd have helped."

"No, it's fine," she panted.

"Are you ok?" Helen asked. "You don't look so good."

"I didn't sleep that well, I've been sick a few times and got a bit of a headache."

"Oh, not you too? I woke up with the worst headache. Dry mouth, jittery tummy. And vomiting like I did when we got off the boat. That's so not me. You'd think I'd been drinking all night."

"What's that supposed to mean?" she replied sharply.

"Sorry?"

"Sounds like you're making a dig."

"No, Mia, I'm not," Helen replied, guessing Mia's tetchiness was due to a hangover. "Anyway, I slept soundly," Helen said, hoping to soften the mood.

Mia wasn't listening. She wasn't even looking her way. She was standing back, admiring her work.

"What time did we get back last night?" Helen asked. "Was it really late?"

Mia walked to the other side of the car to inspect it then returned to where she'd just been working and began the vigorous polishing once again.

"Mia?"

"No, it wasn't too late," she said, her hand moving quickly across the gleaming paintwork

"You know we've got to go down that dusty old track on the way back to the airport, don't forget."

Mia shrugged. "I don't think there's a car wash on the way, and I had plenty of time. I got up early."

"Did you? Thank God I went back to sleep after waking at silly o'clock. I feel better for it. But wow, I felt absolutely dreadful last night. I think I must have crashed out as soon as my head hit the pillow," Helen continued.

"Same," Mia replied.

"The nausea," Helen shuddered as she recalled retching.

"Probably something we ate at that bloody restaurant" Mia said, not looking up.

"But dinner was delicious," Helen protested. "You usually know if it's been something you ate. Anyway, what could it have been? What did we have that was the same? The fish?"

"Are you all packed?" Mia snapped, ignoring the question.

"Not quite," Helen replied. "What about you?"

"I'm all ready but you'd better get a wiggle on. We have to leave soon." Mia was polishing the windscreen now. Helen thought of the car valeters Mia and Chris employed on a regular basis.

Finally, Mia stepped back and started to roll up the hosepipe. She put the cloths and cleaning products into a plastic bag, which she knotted at the top.

Within half an hour, Helen was loading her bag into the boot when Valentina drove up, smiling broadly.

"Good morning. I hope everything was good and you have enjoyed a lovely time here," she said.

"It's been wonderful, thank you. A real treat," Helen replied, and Mia nodded as she handed over the villa keys.

"I hope to see you both again—" Valentina started.

"We better get going, don't want to be late," ordered Mia, climbing into the car and urging Helen to join her. Helen offered Valentina an apologetic smile.

"What's the rush?" Helen asked, adjusting her sunglasses. The bright light was still affecting her headache.

"No rush. Just making sure we get to the airport on time."

They drove much of the way not talking. Occasionally, Helen glanced at Mia. She still didn't look great.

"How are you feeling?"

"Fine. Just a bit sick," Mia replied. "Maybe I do have whatever was affecting you yesterday."

"I hope not. I was thinking mine might be perimenopause."

Mia turned to look at her. "Honestly? Already?"

"Absolutely. It can go on for years, and some women start really early. Oh, no, what's this?" Ahead of them was a sea of red brake lights as traffic slowed.

Helen frowned. "I hope this doesn't go all the way to the airport. How are we for time?"

Mia didn't reply but looked ahead, squinting into the distance.

"Mia?"

"I don't know Helen! Just hang on!" Mia snapped. She'd opened the window and was leaning out, craning her neck.

"Can you see anything?"

"No!" Mia retorted, tersely.

"Well, maybe there is a different route we can take? In case this is going to be a major hold up?" Helen suggested as they came to a halt."

"Well, I don't know, you're the driver!"

"Ok, Mia, I was just asking. You were the one who said we had to make sure we left plenty of time." Helen replied.

"Yes and we don't even know what this is all about yet. Stop panicking."

"I'm not panicking, Mia. I'm just trying..." Helen glanced at her sister. The tension rolled over her like a bad smell.

"Are you still feeling rough?" Helen asked gently.

"Yes and all of this stop-start braking isn't helping." Helen knew better than to protest that there was nothing she could do about it and she wasn't feeling that great herself. The pair sat in silence until a few minutes later the vehicles in front of them started to move. Before long they were travelling at normal speed with no sign of what might have caused the hold up. Eventually there was a sign for the airport.

"Ah brilliant – there we go," Helen said, "It must just have been weight of traffic causing the hold up. I get that every time I use the M25." Glancing across at Mia, Helen saw she was slumped against the window, her chin resting in her hand, eyes closed. Helen smiled. She could never stay cross with her grumpy little sister for long.

"Here we are," Helen announced half an hour later as they pulled into the airport, Mia sat up and read out Victor's instructions for leaving the car. Helen started to reverse into the allotted bay.

"Just drive into it," Mia said.

"I thought I'd leave it how we found it. Parked and ready to go." Helen continued to reverse.

"Just drive it in!" Mia's tone was sharp before she added, "It'll be easier to get our bags out of the boot."

Helen did as she was asked, and after dropping the keys, they made their way to check-in.

CHAPTER 12

The tree was crashing down just a few feet in front of her, its vast canopy spanning the entire width of the car. Her screams echoed around her, drowned out by the ear-splitting crack of the huge trunk. It was too late, it was going to crush her and there was nothing she could do.

Helen sat bolt upright. Wide awake, sweating and trembling, her eyes adjusting to the darkness, she hugged her knees to her chest and rocked gently. Her mind tried to rationalise the nightmare she'd just had. Unsettled, she reached over and turned on a lamp. The tree that had crashed down just feet in front of the car hadn't been real.

There was no need for her heart to be beating so fast or for adrenaline to be coursing through her veins. She sat like this for a few minutes before getting up to go to the bathroom, where she caught sight of herself in the mirror. God, she looked dreadful, and what was that mark on her chest, just below her collarbone? She palpated the area; it was tender under her fingers. There was faint discoloration, not quite a bruise, but she couldn't recall any reason for it. She jumped as one of the curtains blew inwards, almost horizontally as the wind screamed into the room. The storm must have strengthened as she'd slept. A large oak tree outside her window was taking a battering, she could hear its boughs creaking – probably the inspiration for her dream.

She climbed back into bed, but the imprint of the nightmare was still so vivid. It had felt *so* real. No matter how much she tried to push the images from her mind, she could still see the gnarled bark of the trunk, its vast width toppling towards her. She tossed and turned for about half an hour before getting up to make some warm milk. She was used to handing out plenty of advice to patients who complained of insomnia, suggesting small changes they could make to their bedtime routine: magnesium, a ban on electronic devices before bed, a drink of warm milk. She might as well practise what she preached.

By the time she went back upstairs she felt calmer. She lay, reflecting on the trip. The beautiful villa and its gardens would stay in her memory for a long time, as would the half-day they spent with Manon, despite Mia's rudeness to him. And while she hadn't particularly enjoyed the nights out, it didn't matter now. She wondered how Mia was feeling. There'd been no talk of Adam since they'd left the villa.

How was it going to be now she was back home with Chris? Her sister's life was nothing if not complicated. She pulled the duvet tighter around her as she listened to the wind howling outside, its whistling quickly lulling her back into a dreamless sleep, waking hours later to the sound of her alarm.

By lunchtime, Helen had almost forgotten she'd ever been away. Happy to be back, she'd worked her way through an extensive surgery list without a break all morning and had another clinic that afternoon. By 5.30 p.m., she was only halfway through a number of emails when there was a knock at her door, and Stephen walked in.

"Hey, the workaholic returns. How was it?"

"Great, thanks."

"Clubbing every night?" he asked sarcastically.

"Actually, yes, well, sort of."

"Really?" He raised an eyebrow.

"Yes, really," she replied, feeling a frisson of annoyance at his surprise.

He laughed. "Good for you, when in Ibiza… although I must admit that wouldn't have been for me. I think those days are gone. I'm more dinner than disco these days. Actually, does anyone even say 'disco' anymore?"

It was Helen's turn to laugh now. "No, I don't think so. If it hadn't been for Mia, I wouldn't have gone. She was desperate to see some DJ."

"Oh, Susie said something about that, I think. Mia mentioned it at your birthday party."

"Oh, did she now?" Helen replied, frowning.

"Oh, dear, have I said something I shouldn't have?"

"I guess it's just Mia being Mia. She probably had her own itinerary ages ago. She sold it to me as a little bit of R&R."

"Was it that bad?" he asked, perching on the side of her desk.

Helen shook her head. "No, of course not. It was fun." She didn't want to appear ungrateful.

"Don't worry, Helen. I know exactly what you meant. How do you think I feel, trying to keep up with a wife so much younger than me? Susie and Mia are quite similar from what I can gather."

"It was really kind of Mia to go to the trouble, and managing to keep it all a surprise. We managed a little sightseeing and stopped at this amazing vineyard. In fact, I got you a little something." She handed him the bag with the two bottles of wine.

"Oh, Helen, you really shouldn't have!" Stephen beamed as he lifted a bottle, studying the label. "Oh, this looks exciting. Thank you very much."

"My pleasure. We really enjoyed it, and I know you like white Rioja."

"I most certainly do. It is very kind of you. I feel a bit bad about the patient participation group meeting now."

"Why?"

"You're chairing it!"

"Hang on… why am I chairing it? That's your job, isn't it?"

"Holiday, Helen. Holiday! I'm off on my own little trip that week. Four days golfing with the boys, if you can still call us that – the youngest is fifty-two." And with that, he left Helen's office with a loud "goodnight".

CHAPTER 13

"Someone looks like they've been on holiday, look how tanned you are." Teresa Stanish ushered Helen inside. She was an old neighbour who had recently been discharged from hospital, Helen had called on her way home from work to check on her. A widow herself, Teresa had helped Helen pick up the pieces in the aftermath of Phil's death, and had been a shoulder to cry on.

"I had a few days in Ibiza, we got back a couple of days ago."

"We?" the older woman asked.

"Oh, just me and Mia," Helen replied. Teresa nodded and handed Helen a cup of tea. They'd just sat down when Helen's phone started to buzz.

"Sorry, I'm just going to check this," she said apologetically.

Three missed calls, two from Mia and one from her mother, but neither of them had left a message. Not that important, she thought, and slid the phone back into her bag.

Almost as soon as she turned back to Teresa, it buzzed again. It was Mia's husband, Chris. He never called her.

"Sorry, I'd better take this. Hi, Chris?"

"Hi, Helen, sorry to bother you. Is Mia with you?"

"She's not. Is everything ok?"

"Erm… I got back from work this afternoon, and she's gone. There's no note or anything, but, well, things have been difficult lately and… oh, I don't know, she's just gone…" He sounded distracted, and his voice tailed off.

Teresa was watching her intently, which made Helen feel even more tense at the news.

"Gone? Gone where?"

"I don't know, but she's taken some of her things."

Helen frowned as Chris continued.

"Clothes, jewellery – her passport isn't here either."

"Ok, Chris, can I call you back? I'm with someone right now."

"Of course. I'm sorry. I tried your parents, Mia's not answering her phone." He was rambling.

"I'll come over and see you. I should be there in about twenty minutes. Try not to worry."

"Everything all right, dear?" Teresa asked the second Helen hung up.

"Yes, I think so… I'm not sure. It's Mia."

"I knew you were going to say that." Teresa sat up a little straighter in her chair, a knowing look on her face.

"Really?" Helen raised an eyebrow.

"I've known you long enough to know that when you frown like that, it's usually something to do with your sister."

Helen shook her head. "I'm not quite sure what's happened yet, I expect it's nothing. I'd better get off. Thanks for the tea, Teresa, and try not to do too much. Keep up with the exercises, but don't push it. I know you'll be impatient, but please be kind to yourself."

"I could say the same to you! Look at your shoulders, up by your ears."

Helen dropped them immediately, and they both laughed.

"Thanks for popping by," Teresa said. "It was lovely to see you, as always. But promise me you won't take on too much. You need to look after yourself."

Helen kissed her and once she was back in the car, dialled Mia's number. It went straight to voicemail. She called her mother.

"Have you talked to Chris?"

Meghan sighed. "Yes, we've had Chris on the phone looking for her. I don't think he believed me when I said we hadn't seen her, but I haven't heard from her since you got back. Seems odd for her to just walk out, though. Did she say anything to you?"

Helen hesitated for a second. She didn't want to mention her sister's suspicions about Chris's infidelity. "No, she didn't. I can't get hold of Mia either but she has tried calling me so she must be ok. I'm on my way there now. Don't worry, Mum."

"I'm more worried about you, to be honest, darling. I bet this is the last thing you feel like doing. Have you even been home yet today?"

"I'll just pop in. Try and find out what's going on."

"Don't take it all on, Helen," Meghan warned. "Mia is not your responsibility, and knowing her as we both do, this will be a storm in a teacup."

"I'm sure you're right. I'll call you later."

Approaching Mia's home, she dialled her sister's number one more time. Again, it went straight to voicemail. This time, she left a message. "Hey, Mia, it's me. What's going on? I'm just pulling up at yours. Can you call me, please?"

Chris was waiting for her at the front door.

"Have you heard anything?" he asked as soon as she got out of the car. Helen shook her head and went to give him a hug. His shoulders were rounded, his hair unkempt. His usual swagger and self-confidence appeared to have vanished along with his wife.

The kitchen was like something out of a magazine. It was vast, with a large table and seating for twelve at one end and squashy sofas and chairs clustered around a central fireplace at the other. In the middle of the room was an oblong-shaped island with three copper pendant lights hanging above it.

"Can I get you a drink?" Chris asked.

"A cup of tea would be nice," Helen replied, and she saw a flicker of disappointment.

"I was thinking of something a bit stronger," he said, opening the large wine fridge and pouring himself a glass.

"You go ahead, I'll make myself a cup of tea." She took a mug out of the cupboard. She was looking for the kettle when Chris reminded her that they had a boiling tap.

"Of course you do," she mumbled, moving towards it. Chris was halfway through his glass when his phone rang. His disappointment was obvious as he pressed reject.

"So, what makes you think Mia's gone missing?" Helen leant back against the worktop.

"I don't *think* she has, I *know* she has. Like I said on the phone, some of her stuff is gone, and she cancelled Mickey today. You know he's been ferrying her around since she lost her licence?" Helen nodded. "She texted him first thing this morning to say she wouldn't need him. She must have got a taxi…"

Helen studied him as he spoke. He was rubbing his temple with his thumb while cradling his forehead with the other four fingers.

"Did you have a row?"

"Not really, but Mia just hasn't been herself recently. I thought your trip to Spain might have done her a world of good – help her reset. But since she's been back, she's been a bit..." He gave up trying to find the right word.

Helen frowned. Mia hadn't been herself because she thought her husband was having an affair. Another trip away from home was hardly going to make things better. Had she discovered something else to fuel her suspicions? If Chris couldn't see why his wife might be unhappy, he was more arrogant than she'd imagined. Helen was surprised to see him looking so desperate, but this must have come as a shock. Mia walking out on this lifestyle wasn't something Helen would have expected either – especially as Mia admitted as such in Ibiza.

"When you say *reset*, is it just Mia who hasn't been herself? How have you been?"

Chris drained his glass. "I know I'm probably not the best husband out there. I'll be the first to admit I'm a workaholic. But none of this comes easy, Helen," he said, sweeping his arm in a large arc.

Helen nodded. She knew the backstory. How he'd come from nothing. How he'd built his business from scratch. He had been the king of cold-calling, taking on work that no one else wanted, working the longest hours. She watched him pour more wine.

"If I'm guilty of anything, it's spending too much time at work. But she always knew I did that. I thought Mia and I were good."

"There's no one else involved is there?" she asked, trying to maintain an air of innocence.

"I hadn't even considered that, to be honest. Unless you know something I don't." He put his glass down and looked at her intently.

"No. I didn't mean that... What I meant was..." Helen faltered. "Is there anyone else involved... for either of you?"

There, she'd said it. She'd addressed the elephant in the room, but Chris didn't skip a beat. He shook his head. "Good God, no! I love Mia, I gave up a lot for her. My first marriage hadn't been good for a long time, but I was prepared to stick it out, for the sake of the kids as much as anything else. Then I met Mia and well... you know the rest. It hasn't been easy, of course. My ex has made everything as difficult as possible. But I was prepared to put up with it all as long as I had Mia." He looked down at his feet.

"Chris, might Mia have *thought* you were having an affair?"

Again, he shook his head. "She'd have no reason to think that. I'm always in the office, on site or at home. There's no time for anything else. I haven't even had a game of golf in ages! Besides, why on earth would she think that? She knows how I feel about her."

Helen nodded, conflicted. Her gut instinct said Chris was telling the truth but why would Mia have made up such an elaborate lie about her suspicions and hiring a private investigator?

She's done this before, you know," she admitted. Chris shook his head. Helen didn't want to betray Mia's confidence, but she felt sorry for him. "It wasn't long before you two got together. She'd borrowed Mum's car, she and dad were away for the weekend, and Mia was staying at the house. Anyway, to cut a long story short, she was driving down Wenlock Road and something distracted her. She ended up crashing. The car was a write-off, but she walked away without a scratch, and no one else was involved, thankfully. When our parents came home, she wasn't there, and they didn't hear from her for a few days. My parents were frantic. They knew about the car because it had been towed to a nearby garage, and the police had informed them. Mia had simply walked away and left it. We worried she'd obtained a head injury."

Chris's frown deepened in puzzlement. "So where had she gone? Didn't she call anyone?"

"A friend's house, or at least that's what she told us. She said she'd been in shock, didn't think to call anyone and couldn't offer an explanation. The strangest part was that she'd had a bag with her, with clean clothes and toiletries."

"And she just walked back in a few days later?"

"Yes," Helen replied. "As soon as they saw she was fine, my parents were furious. They couldn't understand why she hadn't contacted them. I'd almost forgotten about it until now."

After a pause, Chris asked, "Does the name Adam mean anything to you?"

Helen felt her stomach flip. "Erm…" she started as he continued.

"About three months ago, I noticed a change in Mia. She'd become quite withdrawn – certainly from me, and I know this isn't going to sound great, but I asked Mickey to just keep an eye on things."

Helen remained silent.

"I know, I *know* it was pretty bad of me, but I just had a feeling…" He took a large gulp of wine.

"Mickey said she'd been doing her usual routine: lunches, gym, beauty salon, hairdresser, that sort of stuff. The only thing that stood out was conversations with a guy called Adam."

Helen didn't know what to say as Chris continued. "I know what you're thinking. I was spying on her. I know it sounds shit."

Helen said nothing while thoughts swirled. She was furious with Mia for putting her in this position. It couldn't have been a coincidence that she'd met *another* Adam in Ibiza. It must be the same one.

If she'd been talking to this Adam several months ago, she couldn't have met him for the first time there.

"Do you think she's leaving me, Helen? Has she said anything that would make you think she's unhappy?"

Helen couldn't meet his gaze. She felt so confused. Mia had been so negative about Chris and his feelings for her. She'd either got it very wrong or she was lying. She shook her head in an attempt to refocus on Chris.

"She means the world to me," Chris continued. "I know people think I'm the bad guy for walking out on my wife and kids, but honestly, we hadn't been happy together for years. Mia makes me so happy..."

"Chris. This will be a storm in a teacup. You know how she is, she's impulsive sometimes. Look, I've got to go back to mine, sort a few things out, and get some food in me. You should eat too. If she contacts me, I'll let you know immediately – and likewise, ok?" She turned to face him. He certainly didn't look like a man who couldn't give a damn about his wife.

"Of course. Thanks for coming over."

"Don't be silly, and please try not to worry. I'm sure it will all be fine," she said, trying to sound as convincing as she could. She gave him a hug. As she drove off, she could see him still standing there at the door, wine glass in hand.

CHAPTER 14

Helen was torn from sleep at 3.33 a.m. She was sweating, both pillows were on the floor, and the duvet was a crumpled heap on the other side of the bed. This time, the nightmare had been so graphic that it took her a few seconds to realise it wasn't real. There'd been the falling tree, again, but this time as she tried to swerve away from it, she'd turned her car into oncoming traffic. Her own screaming must have woken her. She sat up, pulled the duvet back and hugged her knees to her chest. She glanced at her phone. Mia had sent two WhatsApp messages at 2.10.

Hey! Just writing to say all ok. I needed some time. I'll be back the day after tomorrow x x

I've texted Chris too.

Coming back from where, she wondered.

She tossed and turned all night worrying about Mia. When her alarm sounded several hours later, she felt as if she hadn't slept at all. There had been no more texts from Mia.

On her way to work, Chris called. Hi Helen. Just thought I'd let you know I had a text from Mia late last night."

"Me too. I was going to call you but was worried it was a bit early." She glanced at the clock on the dashboard. It wasn't quite 8.00 a.m.

"I haven't slept much, to be honest," he replied. "I was awake when she texted, but when I tried to call her back, it went straight to voicemail."

"What did she say?"

"That everything was ok, and she'd be back the day after tomorrow."

Helen sighed. "That was pretty much word for word what she texted me. At least we know she's ok."

"Yep. Erm… thanks for coming round."

Helen sensed his discomfort. He wasn't the kind of man to show feelings openly, and he'd let his guard down last night. She forced the image of Mia snuggling up to Adam out of her mind.

"I've still no idea where she may have gone, do you?" Chris asked.

"No," she answered truthfully. "But she's got some explaining to do," she added, by way of solidarity.

"Well, I'm sure we will soon find everything out one way or another."

They said their goodbyes. Just before she pulled into the car park, she called Mia's mobile one last time. Again, she only got her voicemail.

The morning surgery was hectic. Her list was long, with her last patient of the morning finally leaving around half twelve. As she was finishing her notes Stephen came in and sat down.

"Morning, Doctor. I've got an acute case of bad time keeping and overrunning," he said without cracking a smile. "I think it's a reaction to an overdose of patients."

Helen smiled at him. "I'm sorry, Dr Walker. I'm afraid there is little we can do for that. You're just going to have to work through it until it's over and your symptoms have subsided. Just keep yourself hydrated, make sure you're chained to your desk and allow the overdose to wear off."

"Hmm," Stephen replied, leaning back in the chair and stretching his legs in front of him. "I thought *mine* was a marathon session and I wrapped up half an hour ago," he said, waiting for her to finish.

"I said I'd take four extra emergency appointments which is what really tipped my schedule over the edge," she replied, and he nodded, looking out the window.

"You're also their favourite doctor," he said. "They all ask for you first."

"No. It's because I'm a woman, and lots of my patients are women. They're more comfortable, that's all."

"We both know that's not true, but don't worry. I'm delighted, not offended. It will mean I'll be able to retire early and gallop off into the sunset on the golf course, knowing the practice will be in safe hands, and everyone will be happy."

"Don't you dare even think about that," Helen said. "You'll need to pay the school fees for years yet. You aren't going anywhere."

Stephen laughed, "Fair point."

"Now, what I really came to see you about was this," Stephen held up the latest copy of *The Lancet.*

"I was going to tell you," Helen replied, "I just wanted to wait until it was all definitely going ahead. You know these things can take ages to get off the ground," she continued as Stephen started to read aloud from the journal.

"Haemochromatosis: Helping GPs Make Earlier Diagnoses. Haemochromatosis UK and the Royal College of General Practitioners (RCGP) have launched an initiative to support GPs to improve early diagnosis rates. The partnership will assemble best-practice models and guidance for GPs and work with health commissioners on care pathways. Henry Brian of Haemochromatosis UK welcomes the appointment of the partnership's national GP clinical lead, Helen Nash, who is an experienced GP and a Professor of General Practice and Primary Care.

"'Projects such as the National Awareness and Early Diagnosis Initiative have given us a much better understanding of why some people with haemochromatosis are diagnosed late, and we need to act on these insights,' Dr Nash commented—"

"Oh, stop it!" Helen interrupted him. "I hate reading about myself!"

"Helen, it's amazing! Congratulations. I knew you were heavily involved with the society, of course, but I had no idea you were going to be the clinical lead! And you're giving a keynote speech at the conference next month. You're far too modest. You really should have told me. I'd have been singing this from the rooftops if it were me!"

"It'll be good to be involved," Helen replied. "There is a little bit of funding available, so it's not as if we are starting from the very—"

Suddenly the door swung open. It was Joanna, the practice manager, who had uncharacteristically entered without knocking to tell them there was someone at the front desk who had injured himself.

"He needs to go straight to A&E," Stephen said without asking for details, but Helen was already up and out of her chair, heading for reception.

"I thought you might say that, which is why I came to ask Helen," Helen heard Joanna say behind her.

"What have you been up to?" Helen asked as she saw seventy-year-old Peter Rainton sitting in a chair, holding a large pad already soaked in blood against his head.

"Hello, Doctor Nash," his wife replied before he had a chance to open his mouth.

"I told him we should go straight to the hospital, but he said we'd wait for hours. Look at the state of him. He needs to go to hospital, doesn't he?"

"It's not too bad. I'm sure you could do it for me." It was Peter's turn to cut in now.

"Let's have a look," Helen said. "Can you come into my room?"

"Of course," Peter nodded and stood up, dismissing his wife's offer of help.

Helen watched him walk, obediently climbing onto the couch when she asked. *He seems steady enough on his feet.* She pulled on a pair of disposable gloves.

"So, what happened?" she asked as he settled on his back on the couch.

"I was setting off for my morning cycle, and a car came up from nowhere. I think it must have just clipped my back tyre and sent me sprawling."

She gently removed the blood soaked pad. As she leant in to take a closer look a sudden wave of intense nausea took Helen's breath away. She put one hand over her mouth and reached out with the other to steady herself on the hand basin. She suddenly had an image of something coming towards her at speed. She felt out of control and began to retch, aware of Peter trying to lift his head off the couch to look at her. She forced herself to breathe deeply, head bowed over the basin, now gripping both sides. The nausea began to pass, and although her hands were trembling, she registered that her parasympathetic system was kicking in to slow her heart rate.

"Doctor?"

Helen gave Peter the thumbs up. It bought her a few more moments as she ran the cold water into the sink and cooled her wrists. Taking another deep breath, she turned to face him. "I'm so…" the nausea was there again. Not quite as strong as before but still rendering her useless. She took another breath and closed her eyes.

Peter started to sit up, but Helen spoke, "No, stay there. I'm sorry, Peter. Can you just give me a second, please?"

Helen ran out to the loo, almost bumping into Joanna on the way. She wrested open the cubicle door and dry retched into the bowl. She stayed there for a couple of minutes until the nausea passed. When she came out, she caught herself in the mirror. She was as pale as a sheet. She tried to calm her trembling hands as she turned on the taps. Behind her, the door swung open and Joanna popped her head in.

"Helen, are you ok?"

Helen nodded, washing her hands before splashing her face gently with cold water. Their eyes met in the mirror.

"Wow you look… er…" Joanna started.

"I just felt really sick – it came out of nowhere. Poor old Peter is still on the… It needs cleaning up . From what I saw I think it'll just need a couple of sutures."

"I can see if Nicki can do it."

"Thanks, that would be for the best. I'll be ok in a minute though. Can you let him know I'll be back with him shortly to check on him?"

"Of course, take your time," Joanna said. "I'll give you a minute."

As the door closed behind Joanna, Helen took slow, measured breaths. She tried to concentrate on steadying her heartbeat, but she couldn't shake off the overwhelming anxiety that was flooding through her. She pictured Peter in the room next door, covered in blood, when suddenly her brain was flooded with images that made her heart race and her mouth dry even more. It was as if she was watching a slow-motion film starring herself. She was feeling so weak as she was led to the car. Then she was driving, fast, when suddenly, the headlights caught something, she couldn't say what, a bike, a car? She was braking, her foot slamming hard on the pedal. No response! She shouted, but it was too late. She was going to hit it, and there was nothing she could do about it.

Helen gasped and leant forward, as if recovering from a hard run. Her breathing was shallow, and her chest felt tight. Adrenalin coursed through her. *What was this?* She tried to talk herself down, in the same way she'd deal with a patient presenting with symptoms like this. *Why am I having a panic attack?*

She stood still for a few seconds and stared at her reflection in the mirror. She'd feel a great deal better once she got home, after a meal, and a warm, soothing bath. The self-talk started to calm her.

At home, Percy came rushing to greet her. She bent to stroke him as she gathered up the post. He weaved in and out of her legs as she walked to the kitchen, and she fed him before she turned to prepare her own supper. She was unwrapping the tuna when the phone rang. She ignored it, suspecting it was a scamming call.

As she sat down to eat, Percy jumped onto the chair next to her and started to wash himself, not even glancing in her direction. The phone rang again.

"Oh, for God's sake!" she said and gave it two more rings before pushing herself up from her chair and going to the phone.

"Caller withheld" read the display, confirming her suspicions. She pressed the reject button, returned to her meal and flicked through the post.

She felt much better after eating and relaxed back in her chair. She checked her phone. Three missed calls. One from Mia, two from a number she didn't recognise and a voice message. After listening to the message, she realised the unknown number was also Mia. She dialled the number back. There was a slight delay before the unmistakable sound of an international dialling tone.

Mia picked up almost immediately, blurting out, "Helen, I've been calling you. Where are you?"

"At home. Is everything ok? Where have you been? Are you abroad? I thought you were coming back."

She thought better about adding that Chris has been worried sick. She knew Mia wouldn't appreciate it.

"There was something I needed to sort out," Mia said.

"Needed to sort what out?"

"Don't worry about it, it's been taken care of. Has anyone been in touch?"

"With me? About what?"

Mia hesitated, or maybe it was the phone connection, Helen wasn't sure. "You're sounding very cloak and dagger, Mia."

"I just wondered if anyone has contacted you about me?"

It was Helen's turn to hesitate now. She wondered whether this was a trick question. "Chris called me, if that's who you mean."

"Chris? Why?"

"I think he was probably wondering *where you were*, Mia," she replied, her tone heavy with sarcasm.

"Did you speak to him?"

"Yes, of course. He was worried about you. We both were."

"He'll have let you think he was."

Helen remained silent. She wasn't going to get into this right now.

How their marriage worked was up to them, but the Chris that Mia had described to her certainly wasn't the same man she had spoken to yesterday.

"Helen, I'll come round and see you tomorrow evening when you've finished work."

"Ok. You didn't answer my question – where are you?"

"I'll explain everything tomorrow."

CHAPTER 15

Helen left the surgery promptly at six the next day. She was keen to see Mia and find out what was going on. Mia could stay for an early supper, and they could talk as she cooked.

Mia jumped out of her Range Rover as soon as Helen arrived home.

"Wow. Someone's eager to see me!" Helen said, giving her a forceful a hug. She noticed immediately that Mia seemed anxious. Her body felt so rigid and she was glancing around her.

"Is everything ok?" Helen asked.

"Let's go inside."

As she opened the front door, Percy greeted them, curling round Helen's feet.

"Can we talk as I prepare supper?" she said as she retrieved Percy's food. "There's more than enough for both of us if you—"

"Not for me, thanks," Mia leant up against the kitchen countertop.

"Can I get you a coffee then?" Helen asked putting a pan on the hob and pouring in some oil.

"No, thanks." Her voice was tense. "I've been back to Ibiza."

Helen looked at her, not comprehending. There was silence before both women started to speak at the same time.

"What for?"

"I went to see Adam."

Helen let out a long breath and proceeded to chop an onion.

"I wanted to see him again. As soon as I got back to the UK, I wanted to go back. He changed his flight so he could stay on for another few days. He made me feel excited about life, young again, I don't know… it's just right between us."

Helen put the knife down as Mia continued. She was talking quickly.

"I wanted to spend some proper time with Adam, get to know him better."

"Haven't you already spent time with him?" Helen asked.

"Sorry?"

"I think you met Adam before Ibiza."

Mia blinked repeatedly. *I'm right. I can tell by her face.* Helen knew her sister well enough to recognise the signs. Blinking was her giveaway.

"Mia. Please don't lie about it. Your private life is your own, but I don't want to be part of any deceit. And using me so you could meet up with your boyfriend on holiday is just—"

"Helen, I—"

"Please, I really don't need to know. You can just be so cavalier about hurting people—"

"You don't know *anything*!" Mia shouted.

"About what?" Helen replied, not hiding her impatience now. *This was Mia at her most attention-seeking, trying to turn the situation to her own advantage.*

"About me, my life. You don't care."

"Mia, stop it. I admit, I have been a bit preoccupied since Phil's death but come on, you know you've always been a priority."

Mia stared at her, with a petulant look that Helen was so familiar with.

"I'm not cavalier about hurting people." She lowered her eyes, pouting but Helen wasn't going to fall for it, not this time.

"Did you really think Chris was having an affair? Was that the truth about hiring a private detective? I don't know what to believe any more, Mia. I'm not sure I can trust you."

Mia's expression changed. Her eyes flashed. She looked furious, unused to Helen challenging her.

"You really don't remember, do you?"

Helen sighed, visibly frustrated. "What is all of this about, exactly, Mia? Don't remember what?"

"The night we went to the boat party."

"Of course I remember the boat party."

The silence returned, hanging in the air between them, filling the room. Mia looked down at her feet.

"Helen, we had an accident."

Adrenaline flooded through her as the vision she had seen the day before came hurtling back into focus. Her heart was pounding, drumming inside her chest so loud it was almost drowning out Mia's voice.

"You hit someone. He was suddenly right there in front of us. There wasn't anything you could have done to avoid it."

The room was spinning now. Helen reached out to steady herself on the work surface, but she missed, and her legs buckled. In a flash, Mia was at her side, catching her and pulling out a chair for her to sit down. Instinctively, Helen leant forward and tried to calm her breathing as another wave of nausea overwhelmed her. Her chest felt as if it was in a vice.

"Oh, my God! That was the image. The moped, I couldn't stop."

She felt Mia's arms around her shoulders and she forced herself to look up at her. It was Mia's turn to look confused now.

"I've had these strange erm... episodes. The other day at work and..." she rushed towards the sink, lightheaded. She watched her hands trembling against the white porcelain. "Why the hell haven't you said something before now, Mia?"

"I didn't think we'd hit him. He was just there, in front of the car, and then...Oh, God, Helen, it just happened so quickly. Surely, you remember?"

Helen blinked and squeezed the bridge of her nose between her thumb and forefinger, trying to think.

She remembered leaving the party, she remembered walking with Mia to the car, the nausea, the throbbing head. She tried to concentrate. What else? She had a vague image of a small reflector light and trying to brake, but was that a false memory? Was she just trying to visualise what Mia was claiming? She could remember trying to brake, but the car not slowing quickly enough. Then the seatbelt; it had been stuck. She suddenly had an image of Mia standing in front of the car.

"You said it was ok," Helen said. "I can remember that."

"I thought it was."

"So what happened?" Helen's tone was sharp. She was alarmed that her memory was so patchy. Mia wasn't helping.

"Tell me what happened. Help me out here, Mia. I can't bloody remember!" Mia looked scared. It was a look Helen couldn't remember ever seeing on her sister's face.

"When you rounded the corner on the big bend, you hit a young guy on his moped, and he went over the top of the crash barrier."

Helen's hands flew to her mouth. "Oh, my God! Is he dead?"

"He's in a coma in hospital. They don't think he's going to make it."

"Oh, God." Helen's voice was barely a whisper now.

"Have the police contacted you?"

"No," Mia replied. Her tone was soft.

"So, how did you…"

"Victor told me."

Helen frowned.

"Adam was meeting me at the airport. Victor said I could use the villa again, but we'd have to take a different route as the road was closed. He said there had been an accident on the main road by the camino. When he described it all, I put two and two together."

Helen felt her heart racing as she tried to take it in.

"We need to go back, speak to the authorities," Helen said, a sickening feeling in the pit of her stomach as she realised the enormity of what Mia had told her. She searched the darkest recesses of her mind. Maybe it all made sense now; the dreams, the images had all been trying to tell her something.

Mia shook her head. "No, Helen." Her voice was quiet, calm but steely.

Helen frowned again. *"Of course* we do. That poor young man, his family. The police will want to—"

"No, Helen." Mia's voice was firmer.

Helen started to reply but jumped as she saw black smoke rising from the forgotten pan. She took it off the heat and opened a window. "We have to face up to this."

"Helen, let me make one thing very clear. You staggered off that boat. You looked totally pissed. We walked from the boat to the car and passed plenty of people on the way who will have assumed that you were. Do you honestly think the police are going to believe you weren't feeling very well when you can't remember much about the evening. And the fact you had a bad headache the next day doesn't look good either. At the very least, you'll get done for drink driving, leaving the scene of an accident, failure to report an accident and then, God forbid, if the worst happens, manslaughter."

Her words hung in the air along with the acrid smoke from the pan. Helen put her hands to her face.

"We can't just ignore it. We have to—"

"Helen, I wouldn't even have told you—"

"You wouldn't even have told me?" Helen's voice was high-pitched

"No. The only reason I've told you is because of Simon."

"What? What's Simon got to do with it?"

"He's been trying to get in touch with you. He asked Adam to see if he could get your details, but you can't contact him. We don't want anything else connecting us to the area that evening."

Helen didn't reply. It was all too much to take in. She had seriously injured someone, couldn't remember much about it, and Mia had kept it from her. He might die. His family would suffer the same pain she had suffered over Phil. Her head was spinning.

"There is nothing to link us with the accident, Helen. No one need ever know we were anywhere near the scene that night. We need to stand firm. Don't get in touch with Simon. Or anyone else who could link us. We need to put as much distance between us and Ibiza as—"

"I'm a doctor, for God's sake, Mia. I'm supposed to *help* people..." She paused, unable to find the words.

Mia watched her, uncharacteristically cowed. "Helen, this isn't just about you! What about me? If Chris finds out about me and Adam, what's going to happen? If you end up in jail, what would that do to mum and dad? What good would it do anyone? It was a horrible accident. No one else is going to get blamed for it. I swear, if you keep quiet about this, I won't mention Adam again. I'll make it work with Chris."

Helen shivered as Mia spoke again, "Look, I'm going to pour you a drink. Have you got some brandy?"

Without waiting for a response, Mia opened a cupboard and poured two glasses of Courvoisier from a bottle covered in dust. Helen peered down at the brown liquor, her stomach in knots. Whether it was the thought of the world carrying on as normal while she'd received a life-changing shock, or the terrifying idea of returning to Ibiza and handing herself into the police, she didn't know, but Helen started to sob uncontrollably.

Mia put her arm around her shoulders and pulled her towards her. "Ssshhh, it's going to be ok. Everything will work out, no one will ever know," she cooed.

"You've always been there for me, and now, you've got to let me help you, trust me."

Mia was rubbing Helen's back now, and Helen carried on crying until it felt as if she had no tears left to shed. Mia went outside and told Mickey to come back later – she'd text him when she was ready – and then made them supper. Helen couldn't eat anything, and she wasn't much up for talking either. Mia sat there until she was satisfied that Helen would go to bed, assured that Helen wouldn't tell anyone about the accident.

CHAPTER 16

Helen laid in the darkness, mulling over the events of the previous evening. It all made sense now. The panic attacks, the nightmares. Her subconscious had been trying to tell her something. She'd agreed with Mia to keep the truth of the accident to herself just to buy some time. She'd been exhausted and, when Mia finally left, had fallen asleep quickly. But now she wide awake even though it wasn't yet 4.00 a.m. She let her mind wander back to the night of the accident. The meal in town, the party on the boat. She recalled feeling unwell, desperate to leave, pushing her way through the crowds to get off the boat and walking back to the car with Mia. Why couldn't she remember hitting the motorcyclist?

Her heart racing once more, she rolled onto her side, pulling the duvet around her and buried her head. How would she get through today? Or tomorrow? Nothing would ever be the same again. Eventually, she gave up on sleep and went downstairs to open her laptop. Entering "car crash Ibiza" into Google threw up thousands of results. The first page concentrated on a British teenager knocked over as he crossed a road two years ago. She scrolled through various pages, her stomach churning with fear at each click that she'd find her case, but couldn't find anything relating to their accident.

Pale early morning light crept into her kitchen. She had been sitting there for over an hour, the conversation with Mia replaying in her head. As she sat back from the screen and closed her eyes, her mind drifted back to her early days as a registrar. The lack of sleep, endless callouts and self-important consultants more concerned with bringing down their golf handicap than with weekend admissions. It had been such a long slog to get to where she wanted to be. She thought about her patients and how they'd feel about her when they discovered what she'd done. She thought about how proud her parents were of her career and Mia's promise to patch things up with Chris. Tears slid down her cheeks.

She made coffee and cupped her hands around the mug as she looked out onto the garden. Phil had loved this time of morning. What would he have said? God, she missed him.

Percy meowed beside her, and she bent down to scoop him up, burying her face into his fur. What would happen to Percy if she went to jail?

Maybe Mia was right. Maybe she didn't have a choice.

The first three months were the worst. Helen would spend hours trawling the internet for news before manically erasing her history. She even found out how to wipe her hard drive and did that periodically too.

At the end of every day, she would crawl into bed, exhausted, only to wake at three or four in the morning. She still couldn't recall the crash in its entirety but would have occasional flashbacks when she was least expecting them. She also had vivid nightmares where she'd be braking so hard that she'd wake with cramp in her calf.

She surprised herself at how she managed to hold it together at work. The surgery and patients became her escape. The practice was as overstretched as ever, and she was happy to stay late or take on extra home visits, anything that kept her mind from revisiting Ibiza.

Initially, Mia had been supportive and encouraged Helen to stay strong. In the days immediately after her return, she would remind Helen of what she stood to lose, but as time passed, insisted they spoke about it less.

"There's no point spending the rest of your life thinking 'what if', Helen. You've got to move on."

And that's what she tried to do. As three months turned into four, then five, six and more, Helen found herself able to breathe a little easier. She wasn't searching the internet quite as often, and although she still woke in the early hours, it wasn't with quite the same frequency.

Occasionally, she would catch her mother eyeing her. It was the same look she remembered following Phil's death. "Is everything ok, darling?" Meghan would ask, and Helen would be consumed with guilt as she reassured her that everything was absolutely fine.

Mia's fling with Adam – or whatever it was – seemed to have been forgotten as she seamlessly returned to being Mrs Chris Carlyle, with the lavish holidays, expensive clothes and jewellery. The day she got her driving licence back, Chris presented her with a shiny new convertible for sunny days.

Helen dared to hope it may all be ok, that the accident hadn't been as bad as they'd feared. That maybe, just maybe, the moped rider had got away with bumps and bruises and was blissfully unaware that in another country, a local GP had been going out of her mind with worry. She even started to think about the future, even planning a trip to Cornwall.

Almost ten months after Mia had broken the news, Helen was getting ready to leave the surgery when her intercom buzzed. Her pulse quickened when the receptionist told her who was on the line.

"Dr Nash speaking."

"Hello, Doctor Nash, this is Detective Chief Inspector Pete Benson at Homicide Command, Metropolitan Police."

His voice was clipped, formal. She noticed her left hand starting to shake and pressed her palm onto the desktop to steady it.

"Is this a convenient time?" he said.

"Er… yes, of course. How can I help?"

"We're investigating the death of a seventeen-year-old male motorcyclist. He was killed overseas, involved in a road traffic accident…"

Her stomach lurched. Now both hands were shaking uncontrollably.

"Hello? Are you still there? Hello?"

Helen flinched. She could hear a loud ringing inside her head.

"Yes, I'm here," her voice flat, as if it was coming from somewhere else. "I, er… I just—"

"I know you'll be busy. I'll get to the point. It was a man called Paulo Notarianni. I believe you knew his family? He was in Italy, near Pontechianale. They were due to fly back the day of the accident. Hit by a speeding car as he crossed the road. Had his headphones in apparently. They thought he might make it, but he wasn't the strongest from a health point of view, I understand, which is the reason for my call."

Helen gulped as if she'd surfaced from a minute under deep water, her lungs burning. She realised she'd been holding her breath. "Sorry to hear that," Helen managed to push the words out.

"Yes, I know, it's a sad state of affairs," the inspector replied. "But because of his pre-existing medical condition, I wondered if you'd be able to testify at the inquest?"

"Yes. Of course, I'm just... just... Yes, of course I'll be a witness. I know the family well. Paulo had focal seizures, but they were under control."

"Yes, that's what his parents said. But even though he hadn't had a seizure for years, it's still something that needs to be taken into consideration. I just didn't want you to get the summons and not know why. It should be with you in a week or so," Benson said.

Helen's goodbye was barely audible. She buried her face in her hands and closed her eyes. She could still feel a tremor in her left hand. She didn't know how long she had been there when there was a knock at the door. Before she had a chance to respond, Stephen walked in.

"Hey, I wondered why there was still a light on. I thought I was the last one to leave tonight... oh, what's the matter...?"

Helen shook her head. She wanted to tell him that she was fine but couldn't form the words.

"Are you ok? You're white as a ghost. Are you crying?"

"No... I mean yes, I'm ok. No, I haven't been crying. I just rubbed my eyes, I think."

"Something's the matter. Come on, you can tell me," Stephen said. She shook her head again. "Look, I've dumped on you often enough. To be honest, I was delighted to see your light on as I needed to offload again."

"So, offload," Helen said. Sitting upright, she turned towards him, grateful for the opportunity to shift the attention away from her.

"No. Your turn! Tell me what's the matter."

"It's nothing, well no... not nothing, just a shock, you know."

"No, I don't know, Helen. Oddly enough, mind-reading is not one of the skills I've brought to my practice quite yet. I'm working on it, of course."

He pulled up a chair and sat very close to her, looking uncharacteristically interested.

"I've just had a call from the police about a patient. He was only seventeen, killed in a traffic accident."

"Tragic."

"He died abroad and had underlying health issues," she continued, her hand still shaking. "There's going to be an inquest. I know the family."

"Oh, how sad. I'm sorry. All the more reason to come for a quick drink."

"No," she answered, a little too quickly, immediately feeling guilty. "I'm sorry, I can't. I've got plans."

"Ok. No worries. I should get back myself, really. I'm just looking for an excuse."

Helen frowned. "Because?"

"No, let's not go there tonight. You've had enough bad news for one day by the looks of things."

"Stephen it's fine; really, I am."

"No, it's nothing," Stephen said, smiling. "Come on, let's call it a day. You sure you don't want that drink?"

She shook her head and picked up where she had left off before the police call, packing up for the day. It was only as she drove out of the car park that she dared to relax.

CHAPTER 17

Helen had been looking forward to spending time with Caroline. Close friends since medical school, she had been Helen's bridesmaid, and every year since the wedding they continued the tradition of a girls' date – usually a day's shopping in London, followed by dinner. It was one of Helen's highlights of the year, but the unsettling call from Detective Benson had dulled her enthusiasm.

They met at Liverpool Street station. As always, Caroline looked stunning, drawing appreciative glances from both men and women as she walked across the concourse. Tall, blonde and glamorous, she looked more like a model than a clinical psychiatrist. She enjoyed her looks but made no secret of the fact that her career was more important to her than anything. She had been doggedly determined to rise to the top of her profession as quickly as she could. Most of her time was taken up with a successful practice in Harley Street where she had a long waiting list of high-profile patients, all desperate for an appointment with the psychiatrist they'd heard so much about.

The two women embraced warmly.

"I've been looking forward to this so much. It's so good to see you. You look amazing, Caroline. What a gorgeous coat!"

"Thank you! And you look as pretty as ever. Oh, it's so good to see you, I've missed you!" Caroline hugged her again, tighter this time. "And congratulations on the haemochromatosis initiative. My brilliant friend!"

They hadn't seen each other for months, but they fell quickly into the easy conversation of close friends. Chatting as they walked to their favourite coffee shop, Helen couldn't help but laugh as Caroline brought her up to speed with the latest details of her love life.

"I had another disastrous date last week."

"I thought you said you were done with blind dates?" Helen raised an eyebrow.

"I was, but well, you know … he looked very attractive in the photo." Helen grinned as Caroline continued. "He was into shooting. I should have said no on the strength of that alone but bloody hell, I can't tell you how boring he was. He actually started reeling off stats from his flipping Strava app. Who does that?"

They were still giggling as they sat down. Helen was happy to let Caroline lead the conversation. It was good to see her old friend and allowed her a brief respite from the torturous thoughts of Ibiza.

"So… come on, tell me what's up." Caroline leant in towards Helen as soon as the waitress left.

Helen frowned and shook her head. "What do you mean?"

"Oh, come on, Hels, you haven't been right since we met at the station. There's a black cloud hanging over you, and you've hardly said a word."

"I have!" Helen protested. "Honestly, Caroline, you're too much of a psychiatrist sometimes. Not everyone needs their heads examined."

"Harsh," Caroline replied, feigning hurt. "But all the same, I'm right, aren't I? Something's going on."

Helen struggled to meet her gaze. She wasn't surprised Caroline was suspicious, but no matter how bad she felt about keeping it from her, she couldn't possibly open up.

"I think I've just been missing Phil a lot lately," She felt so guilty saying it.

"Here we are, two cappuccinos," the waitress announced. "Who's having the soya?"

"Mmm, delicious," said Caroline as she sipped her coffee. Helen followed suit, grateful for the interruption.

"So, what's been making you miss Phil now more than ever?" Caroline probed as Helen shifted uncomfortably in her chair.

"Oh, I don't know, just life without him. Anyway, let's enjoy today. Where are we going next?"

"Don't try and fob me off."

"I'm not. Caroline, please, it's nothing, it's just… I don't want to talk about it." Helen looked down at her coffee, the smoothness of the froth destroyed where she'd taken a sip. She picked up her teaspoon and began to stir gently, trying to repair the symmetry.

Helen could feel Caroline studying her. She'd known her long enough to understand when she was hiding something – it didn't take her degree in psychology to know the signs.

"Ok, but I'm here when you do."

Helen continued stirring her coffee, not looking up.

"Right then," Caroline announced decisively, "I'd like to go over to Marylebone High Street." She smiled broadly as Helen raised her eyes and returned her smile.

Later the pair headed to The Courtauld Gallery to see a Seurat exhibition. A love of art was something they had shared since the early days of their friendship. They wandered through the rooms, marvelling at the works.

A group of teenagers made their way towards them, shepherded by one of the curators.

"You can see the little dots of colour and how they've been applied in patterns to make up the image." The guide stepped aside allowing the students to take a closer look.

Helen noticed a young man towards the back of the group. He was craning his head, peering left and right of the person in front of him, trying for a better view. The guide must also have seen him as she said, "Can those at the front move out a little so everyone can see properly, please? Can everyone see now?"

A chorus of mumbled yesses followed. Satisfied, the curator began her speech about Seurat. "His work *A Sunday Afternoon on the Island of La Grande Jatte* altered the direction of modern art. It's pretty big, isn't it? Three metres wide."

Caroline nudged her, whispering, "Shall we go?"

Helen nodded. As they headed towards the exit, she looked up and noticed the young man watching her. He was wearing a bright yellow T-shirt with a pink palm tree and the word Ibiza emblazoned across his chest. From nowhere panic swept over her. Her heart was racing, palms sweaty, a flush of heat at the back of her neck. As much as she tried to calm herself, there was no escaping this overwhelming anxiety. She'd seriously injured someone. Someone probably not much older than this boy. She may even have killed him, and yet here she was, enjoying a day out. Her legs buckled.

"Helen," Caroline grabbed her, pulling her back to the present. "Darling, what on earth's the matter?"

Helen shook her head.

"Why don't you sit down, let's get you a glass of water—"

"No, please, I just need some fresh air." She was aware of people looking at them and tried to compose herself.

"Ok, ok." Caroline steered her outside.

Helen stood, her back against the wall of the gallery and closed her eyes, breathing deeply, trying to shut out an image that had jumped into her mind. One of her walking away from the boat party, leaning into Mia …

"Helen?" Caroline sounded worried.

"I'm sorry, I don't know what came over me…" she started, opening her eyes.

"Don't worry," Caroline replied, studying her face. "Let's get you out of here." Before Helen could protest, they were climbing into a cab.

Helen sank back into the seat.

Caroline rested her hand on her shoulder. "All ok?" she asked.

"Yes – honestly, I'm fine. I think it was just a bit hot in there," Helen replied, the colour returning to her face. "The exhibition was good," she said.

"Yes," Caroline replied, respecting her friend's swift change of subject. "Almost as good as the large Seurat in New York. Do you remember?"

"Of course," Helen nodded.

"We did the Guggenheim and the MoMA then," Caroline continued.

"Fabergé," Helen said with a weak smile, remembering the stunning jewellery exhibition.

"That's better."

"What?" Helen asked.

"You, *smiling*. I haven't seen enough of that today."

Helen was grateful for the taxi driver's interruption, announcing their arrival at the Savoy. A uniformed doorman stepped forward to help them, and they climbed the stairs to the American Bar. Despite the early hour, it was already busy. Laughter and chatter filled the air, and glasses clinked above a tinkling piano. They were led to their table, and Caroline ordered for them both.

"Two Kir Royales, please," she said, "and two glasses of water."

"I love this feeling," Caroline said as she glanced down at the collection of bags by her side. "Knowing that I will unpack all my little goodies when I get home. Honestly, I think I enjoy it as much as Christmas!"

A waiter appeared carrying their water and two glasses fizzing with beautiful pink bubbles. Caroline raised her glass towards Helen. Here's to friends and shopping trips – long may this tradition continue." They touched glasses and both took a sip.

"Totally delectable," Caroline declared in a silly voice. Caroline could always amuse Helen when she mimicked one of their professors from med school. Caroline took another large sip and sank back into the padded banquette, stretching out her arms to rest them on the plush teal upholstery and looked around. Two men in suits on the table next to them were speaking in low voices, and on their other side, a group of four women chatted excitedly, periodically erupting into peals of laughter. A pianist began playing an up-tempo version of *Fly Me to The Moon*, and there was the clink of ice and glasses from behind the bar.

"God, I love this place. If you had to conjure up a scene of the perfect cocktail bar it's this, isn't it? Ambience, clientele, music. They just get it so right."

"It is lovely," Helen agreed, feeling better, though was sitting perched at the front of her chair, her body tense.

"So… how's work?" Caroline asked.

"Busy as always. How about you?"

"Manic. I've had to get very stern with myself and say no a bit more. I've seen far too many people with burnout and know how easy it is to get to that stage. I'd like to go to South America this year and have a proper break. I've spoiled too many holidays in the past answering emergency calls and having to fly home early."

"You've always worked too hard. I'm glad you're trying to get a bit of balance now." Helen replied.

"Yes. And you? Are you managing to get balance? I always thought you were good at that. Even with everything you've been through with Phil. You've always had it sorted."

Helen took another gulp and finally managed to sit back into her chair, turning her body slightly to cross her legs. Helen felt a flush in her cheeks as the alcohol started to take effect. "I don't think so."

"Oh don't give me that! You have always had life sorted, Helen, don't deny it."

Helen dropped her gaze.

"But you're not yourself today, that's for sure been out of sorts all—"

"Please, just leave it," Helen said sharply. She was blinking furiously.

"Of course. I'm sorry. Let's just…"

"I'm sorry too. I just can't, erm… I just…"

Caroline must have known she'd said enough and changed the subject.

On their way to Après restaurant, Caroline said, careful to keep the conversation light, "How are your parents? I haven't seen them for ages."

Caroline was in safe territory as Helen brought her up to date with news about Meghan and Roger. They had always been fond of Caroline. She smiled broadly as Helen outlined their plans for a trip to celebrate their golden wedding anniversary.

"And Mia? What's she been up to? Still living her best life, happily married to the *millionaire*?"

Helen knew that Caroline knew Mia didn't like her. The feeling was mutual, but they were careful not to show it too much. Mia was manipulative and Caroline knew there was far more to it than her being simply the "strong personality" Helen claimed her to be.

"Actually, she's..." Helen began but again the conversation was broken by the taxi driver announcing their arrival.

Après was intimate, with low lighting and a hum of chatter from other guests. They were greeted at the door by a friendly maître d'. As he led them to their table, they passed a small family group. In the centre of their table was a beautiful, two-tiered cake. A chef in whites stood by, beaming as they praised his creation.

As soon as they sat down, Caroline ordered a bottle of wine.

"We don't have to drink it all!" she said as Helen protested. "And what were you going to say about Mia in the cab?"

"Oh, God. You know Mia. I'm not entirely sure how it's all going for her, to be honest. We had a few days away ..." Helen faltered as she began recounting their trip. Caroline was watching her intently. "Erm... we had a few days away, and she told me things weren't great with Chris and her. Then everything seemed to be ok. I don't know."

"You never really do know with Mia, do you?" Caroline knew she could have gone on, but Mia was Helen's sister after all and she was careful to keep it gentle.

"No. But she's been trying to help – in her own way – since Phil died."

"*Really?*" Caroline tried not to sound too surprised, though failed. In the first few months after Phil's death, it had been Caroline who Helen had gone to stay with and Caroline who Helen called first thing in the morning. Mia hadn't been much help at all. She had carried on with a long-planned trip to Australia, departing two days after the funeral.

"Where did you go?" Caroline continued.

"Sorry?"

"You said you had a few days away, with Mia. Did you go somewhere nice?"

The wine arrived, and Helen took an extra-large gulp. Caroline pretended not to notice.

"Ibiza."

Caroline burst out laughing. Oh, my God, did you really? When?"

"Not long after my birthday. She gave me the tickets as a surprise."

"Hilarious. I love it! Did you go clubbing?"

"Erm, sort of…"

"*Sort of?*" Caroline was clearly intrigued judging by her tone. "Helen, this is so funny. Why didn't you tell me before? Why Ibiza?"

Helen forced a smile. "I know. Crazy, isn't it? She, erm, she borrowed a villa from a friend. It was her idea of getting me away from things. Change of scene and all that."

"Ok, and did it work? You're not sounding all that enamoured about it."

"It was nice. The villa was truly lovely." Helen felt a knot of anxiety start again.

"Helen?" Caroline's voice was sharp, pulling her back into the present, concern etched on her face.

"Helen, darling, please, what on earth's the matter?" She reached over and put her hand over Helen's. Helen couldn't help but shake.

As Helen welled up, Caroline leant closer towards her.

"Don't. No. I…" Helen swallowed hard. "Please… it's nothing."

"It's not 'nothing', Helen," Caroline said quietly. "But I get it if you don't want to talk about it here. Although you clearly do need to talk about it, and if anyone can help, I can."

Caroline slipped her arm around Helen's shoulders, gently pulling her towards her. As a waiter approached, Helen felt Caroline shake her head to send him away.

"Do you want to leave?" she asked quietly.

"No." Helen's voice was barely audible.

"Ok, let's eat. I don't know about you, but I'm feeling tipsy! I could do with something to soak up this alcohol." Caroline slid back round to her seat.

"Look at this menu. Oh, my God, I want everything!"

Helen nodded gratefully, doing her best to ignore the overwhelming urge to sob hysterically. As Caroline talked about her choices, Helen stared down at the table, unable to look up and meet her friend's eyes. She knew if she did, she'd tell her everything.

"Do you need some help deciding?" Caroline offered.

Helen shook her head. Caroline's solicitous tone made her feel even worse and unable to stand it any longer, Helen pushed the menu away.

"Caroline, I'm sorry. This was a bad idea. I've got to go." She stood up and grabbed her bag before Caroline, her face a picture of astonishment, even had a chance to reply. "I'm really sorry."

She hurried to the door and was gone in seconds.

CHAPTER 18

Are you free tonight? I need to talk.

Helen texted Mia as she wrapped up work for the day.

She'd thought she'd never get through her patients today. Starting work with a hangover hadn't helped, but the previous night's emotions made her realise that she couldn't go on living a lie. She'd texted Caroline and told her she would explain everything but there was something she needed to do first. The weight of it had become unbearable – she had to speak to Mia.

As she was leaving the practice Stephen's wife, Susie, arrived, immaculately groomed and glamorous as usual.

"Hi, Helen," she beamed, planting a kiss on each cheek. The unmistakable scent of Molecule Number 1 enveloped her. Helen returned her smile as convincingly as she could, desperate to get to the car.

"I'm collecting Stephen. We're meeting friends for dinner."

"Very nice. Where are you off to?"

"Rollo's."

Helen raised an eyebrow. "Very fancy, lucky you. Is it a special occasion?"

"No, not really. I just wanted to try it and persuaded Stephen to take me. I booked it two months ago – couldn't get a table any earlier."

She leant closer to Helen and whispered almost conspiratorially, "To be honest, now it's here, I could do without it. I've been out with girlfriends in London today. Mia was with us too, and we ended up having a late lunch after shopping. I haven't even been home. Mia dropped me off. Her driver collected us from the station."

"Secret's safe with me!" Helen winked at Susie, hoping to disguise her surprise at hearing her sister's name. "Well, have a wonderful evening," she said over her shoulder, not wanting to delay her departure a minute longer. She started the car and drove off as quickly as she could.

Mia texted back just as Helen arrived home:

Can it wait until tomorrow? Just coming back from London.

Helen didn't like that Mia was lying. Scooping up Percy who was waiting by the door, she scanned her mail and checked her answer phone –a routine she had started after Mia had persuaded her to take their secret to the grave. The light remained a steady green. No new messages. She wasn't even sure what she was expecting.

Mia I really need to speak to you.

This one was sent via WhatsApp. It was read almost immediately. Half an hour later, Mia called.

"All ok, Hellie?" She sounded weary, as if the call was an effort.

"Mia, I can't do this anymore." There was silence. "It's making me ill. I'm not sleeping, I'm having nightmares, palpitations, anxiety attacks. It's affecting my work too. It's just so, so… wrong. You're not going to change my mind." She kept talking, but Mia wasn't trying to interrupt. She wasn't saying anything. Helen could hear her breathing and then the sound of her heels across the floor followed by a door closing.

"What's happened, Helen?" Mia asked, not trying to hide her exasperation.

"Nothing has happened. Nothing specific, I just can't go on like this. I'm going to speak to Mum and Dad before I tell the authorities."

"Oh, stop!" Mia practically spat into the phone. "Don't be ridiculous. You know you can't do that. You'll destroy everything."

"I already have destroyed everything as far as I'm concerned. Lying is only making it worse."

"I'm coming over. Just don't do anything before I get there."

"Mia, I have said everything I need to say. Nothing you can do will make me change my mind. I need to do this. I'm going to tell Mum and Dad before I go to the police – they need to—"

"What about me? I lied for *you*." Mia was struggling to keep her voice low.

"I know, Mia."

"I've protected you – nothing's changed. We can continue to—"

"No, Mia," Helen said defiantly. "No more. I'm going to keep you out of it altogether. Don't worry. I will say that it was me who asked you not to come forward. I'll say it was my reputation we were trying to protect."

"I'll be with you soon. Don't do anything until then." Mia hung up.

Helen suddenly had an image of Phil. He had his back to her, looking out to the garden. She concentrated on the slope of his shoulders, the breadth of his back, not allowing his image to turn from the window and look at her, judging her, wondering why she'd left it this long before facing up to what she'd done.

She was going to break her parents' hearts. How would she tell them? What words would she use? She looked down at Percy, who was oblivious to the chaos that was likely about to unfold. He curled a little paw over the front of one eye as he groomed himself.

She was halfway up the stairs when there was a loud knock at the door. Surely, that couldn't be Mia already, could it? How long had she been standing there in the kitchen after their phone conversation? Had she lost all track of time?

The knock came again, even louder now, more insistent. She made her way back down and opened the door. Caroline was huddled under the shallow porch, trying to keep dry from the rain.

"Caroline!"

"Yes, thank you, I'd love to come in." She almost pushed past Helen into the hallway.

"The heavens opened just as I pulled up. I'm hardly dressed for this."

Helen looked at her, open-mouthed, trying to make sense of her being there. Caroline rarely visited. She lived two hours' drive away. It's why they always met up in London.

"Caroline… I'm sorry. I was just… I… this is a surprise but—"

"I can't get you out of my mind. I know you well enough to know this is something you need help with. You wouldn't have run out on me like that if it wasn't serious. So, you might as well put the kettle on and make us both a nice cup of something hot and tell me what on earth is going on."

Whether it was her loyal friend's determination to find the truth or the fact that she hugged her so tightly, Helen couldn't be certain, but her composure shattered. The mask she'd been wearing all day, along with the cloak of responsibility, was cast off as she buried her face into Caroline's already damp jacket and sobbed. She allowed herself to be led into the kitchen and guided into a chair. Caroline sat down next to her with an arm around her shoulders. Once Helen had managed to compose herself, Caroline passed her a tissue and lifted the kettle onto the Aga. She opened cupboard doors and drawers, looking for everything she needed to make tea. Helen didn't offer any guidance but sat like a child, dabbing her eyes with the tissue.

"Well, I'm glad I came. Even the traffic jam on the M11 was worth it," said Caroline, placing a steaming mug of sweetened tea in front of her friend.

Contrition swept across Helen's face. "God, of course, you must have had a hell of a journey. You've come so far and I—"

"You know that doesn't matter. Come on, tell me—"

Helen jumped as another knock at the door brought their conversation to an abrupt halt. She steeled her nerves and got up to answer the door.

It had been several years since Caroline had last seen Mia, and at first, when Helen entered the kitchen with her sister, she didn't seem to recognise her. During that time Mia's hair had grown much longer and several shades lighter too, with soft blonde waves framing her face. But there was nothing soft about her expression. Mia's eyes flashed with fury as she barely acknowledged Caroline and stepped into the kitchen.

"What on earth have you done, Helen?" Mia's tone was sharp. "I might have known *she'd* be involved." She nodded towards Caroline.

Caroline stood. "Mia, look—"

"Stay out of this. It's none of your business," Mia snapped. "Helen, come on, we've been through this."

"Mia, *stop*!" Helen's tone was firm. "Nothing has changed as far as you're concerned, but it's not about you, is it? It's me who is living the lie, living with the guilt, and I can't go on anymore."

Mia stepped closer to Helen, their faces nearly touching. "What has she said to you?" she asked, tilting her head towards Caroline.

"Nothing. And I'm so sorry you've been dragged into this, Caroline. You're right, we have known each other a long time, and I'm so sorry I wasn't truthful yesterday. I haven't been truthful for a long time. I've—"

"Caroline, trust me, you need to go. I will look after Helen." Mia's tone was more placatory as she placed her hand on Helen's arm. "It'll all be fine."

Caroline looked at Helen, speaking softly, "Helen?"

Before she had a chance to reply, Mia answered, "It's all going to be ok. Nothing to worry about. I'm here now—"

"I hit someone, Caroline." Helen said firmly, ignoring Mia's loud gasp. She spoke directly to Caroline. "I may even have killed him. In Ibiza," she said, taking a seat. "Mia has just been trying to protect me. I was driving and hadn't been feeling well, I may even have blacked out, I don't know. I can't remember all of it, but we hit someone."

"Ok, ok," Caroline said, trying to sound calm, as if what Helen had just told her was an everyday occurrence.

"You had an accident. You haven't murdered anyone." Caroline had a passive look to her face, as if trying to process the information from a therapist's objective viewpoint. She looked from Mia to Helen and back again.

"Exactly!" Mia interrupted again. "And she didn't know she'd done it, of course."

"See? Caroline agrees. It was an accident. What's the point—"

"Do you want to tell me exactly what happened?" Caroline interjected, holding up a hand to silence Mia. "Mia, just let her talk."

"Yes… I'm sorry, Mia. I know you're just trying to protect me."

"Yes, I bloody well am!" Mia shouted, and the sharpness of her tone made Helen jump.

Caroline glared at Mia. Undaunted, Mia returned the look before turning back to Helen. "You are about to cross a line, Helen, and if you do, there is no going back. Before you make any decisions, I need to tell you something – in private."

Not giving her a chance to protest, Mia grabbed Helen's shoulders and propelled her out of the room, slamming the door behind them. In the dim hallway she brought her face close to Helen's. Helen was sandwiched between the cold wall behind her and the warmth of her sister's body. Mia's eyes were wide as she whispered into Helen's ear. "He died! The motorcyclist you hit, he's dead! Nothing you say now will change that! You know what you stand to lose, who will suffer. It won't just be you. Think about our parents," she hissed.

Helen felt the room spinning as she took in the news. She pressed herself harder against the wall for support.

"He died? Oh, my God! He died? How do you know? Why haven't you said anything?" Helen's voice was barely a murmur.

The door swung open and Caroline stood looking at them.

"For this very reason," Mia snapped, ignoring Caroline. "Because you are going to destroy everything. Your life, my life, everything. And for what? You're not going to make anything better – you'll just make it far worse."

Helen felt broken, her head bowed and for a second, she thought she was going to do what she'd done so many times in front of her domineering younger sister and capitulate. But when she looked up, she saw Caroline staring at her, a fierce determination and belief in her friend's eyes. It was the same expression she'd seen many years ago when they were both exhausted junior doctors, surviving on adrenaline. It always gave her strength then and did so now.

"Mia, when did you learn this?" Helen asked.

"It doesn't matter, does it?"

"Of course it matters. It all matters." Her voice was quiet but resolute.

"Helen, we need to talk. Caroline should go. I will look after things from—"

"No, Mia," Helen insisted. "Caroline, I want you to stay. I'm going to tell you everything."

Mia started to speak, but it was Helen's turn to shout, "No, Mia. Just go. *Now!*"

"Mia, do as she says," Caroline said.

Mia turned towards Caroline, her eyes narrow, blazing with anger. She looked as if she was about to speak, but something prevented her, and she turned on her heel and left, slamming the front door behind her. Helen sank into a chair.

"Let's start at the beginning," Caroline said, taking a seat next to her.

Helen took a deep breath.

CHAPTER 19

Caroline insisted on staying the night, and they sat up talking until way past two. Helen recounted the story from beginning to end, how Mia had been asleep as they drove, waking as they hit the young man. She told her about the about the anxiety attacks, how keeping quiet had been her idea, but she had always regretted it and so now she was putting it right. Caroline listened attentively before quizzing her.

"Are you sure it was your idea not to report the accident?" she asked.

"Yes," Helen said, burying her face in her hands. "The whole thing is such a terrible mess. Of course I should have reported it but, oh, I don't know, Caroline. I just got myself into such a state. I kept thinking what it would do to my parents. They're getting older, it would destroy them if I went to jail."

Caroline nodded. "Of course, I can see why you'd worry but it just seems so out of character for you to …compound the issue."

"There was Mia too," Helen added.

At the mention of Mia, Caroline frowned. "With all due respect, I can't believe you're still putting her before yourself, even in this situation."

"It was more than that," Helen replied and let out a deep sigh. "She'd been having a few problems in her marriage. She and Chris have worked through them. They're fine now but when we were in Ibiza she hooked up with this guy. She finished it but has never told Chris. She said if he ever found out it would be the end of their marriage."

"Mia has put you in a very compromised position, Hels," Caroline said.

"No! – it's not her fault," Helen replied sharply. "I was the one behind the wheel and I should have spoken out ages ago. It's too easy to blame someone else."

"But …" Caroline began then saw that Helen was weeping again. "Ok, that's enough. I've got the picture. There's no point going over and over it. Let's call it a night."

When they finally got to bed, Helen struggled to sleep, her brain churning as she considered her predicament. Unable to tolerate the torturous mind loop, as soon as it was light, she made her way quietly downstairs.

She had just made a coffee and sat down at the table when Caroline opened the kitchen door.

"Oh, Helen, you're up already! I was creeping around trying not to wake you. Did you manage to sleep at all?"

"Not really." Helen shook her head. "What about you? It's still very early."

"I've got to get home and change before work."

"Caroline, I know it might sound as if I'm lying, but I honestly can't remember any detail of the accident or what happened…"

It doesn't sound as if you're lying, Helen – not to me. I see this sort of thing all the time in clinic," her friend explained. "Your brain has registered an overwhelming trauma and has blocked the memory to protect itself. If I had to take a guess, I'd say that your lack of recall about the accident is dissociation."

Helen nodded. "I'm so glad you know, Caroline. I've hated keeping it from you.

"Can I make some coffee?" Caroline offered.

"I can't believe I've lied about it for so long," Helen murmured. "What must you think of me?"

"Helen, we've been through this. There's no judgement. You've been totally overwhelmed by this, and in fact, there is an argument that you haven't lied about it because you didn't know it had happened. But that's the next step. That's what lawyers are for."

"I *have* lied, though. I've lied since I learnt about it." Tears streamed down her face. "I'm going to get struck off aren't I and I'll end up in jail. Oh God..."

"Are you sure you don't want me to come with you to your parents? I can always come back this afternoon when clinic is finished, and we can go together."

"No, I need to get this done. I'm going to call work and tell them I'm not coming in. And then I'll sort out a lawyer."

Caroline made them coffee, and they sat in silence as they drank, both contemplating the enormity of the situation. Caroline gave her a tight hug before she picked up her bag. Helen walked her to the door and whispered, "Goodbye, and thank you."

Helen leant against the door frame until Caroline's car was out of sight.

PART TWO

CHAPTER 20

"What time's your flight?" Caroline asked down the phone.

"Eleven thirty. Mia's dropping me at the airport. I've got to call in at the solicitors on the way."

"Well take care, and call me when you can."

"Of course."

Helen was exhausted. It had been months since she'd been charged. The Guardia Civil had pushed for reckless homicide, but her legal team had managed to reduce it to negligent manslaughter and fleeing the scene of an accident.

Despite her guilty plea, it would be several months before the case concluded. In the meantime, to comply with the Spanish judicial system, she'd had to make repeated trips to Ibiza.

When Helen first told Stephen about the accident, she'd expected him to ask her to leave the practice, but he'd been adamant she was to stay on until they knew the outcome.

"I can't work as normal," Helen said. "Not when everyone knows what I've done. My credibility is shot."

Stephen reminded her that until it became public knowledge, no one would know.

"We can deal with all of that when it happens. But in the meantime, you're still the best GP I know. You've managed perfectly well all this time. Work gives you something to focus on. Surely, it would be worse without it?"

Helen protested, claiming she didn't deserve such support, but Stephen insisted. "You're staying! We need you. Take it one day at a time, Helen. Look at the big picture. You're a good doctor, a good person. It was a tragic accident."

And for a while, she managed. Having a Spanish lawyer as well as an English solicitor was eating up her funds, but she had no choice. She told Mia and her parents that she was fine for money, but the truth was she'd probably have to sell her beloved cottage.

She lost weight. Her hair, previously long and lustrous, became dull and brittle. If she'd been a patient, she'd have diagnosed extreme stress and instructed them to be kind to themselves, take time out, do things they love. Options not available to her.

She was on her way back to Ibiza. She'd stay for just a night, as she usually did, at the small, central hotel, and be back in at the surgery the day after next. No one at work, other than Stephen, would be any the wiser as to where she had been. But she knew she was on borrowed time. No matter how tight a lid they kept on it, the truth was bound to get out. When this was all over, she'd be suspended, at the very least, and probably struck off the GMC register. The career she had forged with such care and determination, the career she was so proud of and which had kept her sane when Phil died, the career she loved, in ruins.

Mia dropped her at Stansted just after nine. She'd offered to accompany her, but Helen preferred to go alone. "You've already done so much. This is just routine. I'm fine on my own."

Surrounded by excited holidaymakers and carrying just a small overnight bag, Helen was soon through the security checks and waited patiently for the gate number. As soon as they landed, she was the first through arrivals. As her taxi pulled away, a uniformed police officer caught her eye, turning her anxiety to paranoia.

She had come to hate the twenty-minute journey from the airport to the hotel.

"Welcome to Ibiza, how long are you staying?" the taxi driver asked, in perfect English, smiling at her in his rear mirror.

"Just tonight. It's a short visit."

"A business trip?"

"Yes," she turned to look out of the window.

"What business do you do?" he persevered.

"Oh, I'm sorry…" She pulled out her phone, pretending to be absorbed in emails until they drew up outside the hotel.

After checking in and a quick freshen-up, Helen made her way to the same café she always went to on these visits. She sat at a table outside and ordered a bocadillo and a cappuccino before turning her face to the sun. She closed her eyes, listening to the hubbub around her. She shivered, despite the warmth. She dreaded these trips to Ibiza. It was time to visit her lawyer's office, so she finished her drink and set off.

Elisa Ramirez was an experienced, no-nonsense lawyer. Petite and stylish, she had an air of authority that Helen found intimidating yet comforting. Today, she wore a classic navy shift with white lace collar and high-heeled shoes. Her glossy dark hair was arranged in a neat chignon. Greeting Helen with a firm handshake, she introduced her colleague, Alvaro, and invited her to sit next to him. She didn't waste time with pleasantries.

"So, Helen," she said in fluent, American-inflected English, "we are still waiting for the full register of detention, which tells you exactly what charges you're facing." Elisa had spent a decade working in the states before settling in the Balearics. "Up until now, it was pretty much what we thought. Your version of events was accepted. The police had almost finished their investigation."

"But now, some new CCTV footage has come to light."

Helen's heart skipped a beat. The atmosphere changed, and the walls seemed to press in on her.

"What CCTV? I didn't think there were cameras on that stretch of road?"

"That's correct. It's not from the accident site."

Helen frowned again, confused. "Where then? The police said that even if there had been CCTV in operation that any evidence would have been wiped by the time their investigation started."

"Yes, that is true," Elisa continued. "But this is from one of the boats. A super yacht at anchor just outside the marina. It hadn't berthed because it was too large, so there were no records, and of course, the yacht had left long before the guardia were aware of your...involvement." Elisa chose her words carefully.

"It belongs to a Russian oligarch. It's a ridiculous-looking thing. Almost like a naval vessel. It has state-of-the-art security."

Helen nodded. She recalled some of the boats they'd seen as she had strolled along the marina. They were like floating hotels. The one that had hosted the party had been enormous. Helen stayed silent as Elisa continued.

"These days, many wealthy owners have installed super security on their mega-yachts to protect them. Piracy and paparazzi are just the tip of the iceberg. Yacht security consultants have never been busier.

"Unfortunately for us, the prosecutor put out an appeal to all yacht owners within the vicinity that evening. The boat was a considerable distance offshore, but the camera still picked up clear footage of you and Mia walking towards the marina exit."

Elisa paused, as if waiting for a reply. Helen nodded, encouraging her to continue.

"You appear very drunk, Helen."

"But I've told you, I wasn't drinking. I had just one glass because I was driving."

"I'll show you." Elisa aimed a remote control at a TV monitor. The screen flickered into life. At first, all that was visible was a side view of a large motor yacht. Then the camera began to pan around. Helen watched in horror as she saw herself staggering into frame. She was leaning heavily on Mia, her legs buckling every now and again when they would pause and restart. One arm was draped around Mia's neck, the other dangled by her side. Mia held Helen tightly around her waist. The footage was short. The pair were out of sight in just a few seconds, but it was enough. There was no doubt about it. She looked completely inebriated.

CHAPTER 21

By the time she left Elisa's office it was almost 8.00 p.m. Helen was struck by how hot it still was. She'd lost all track of time, and after several hours in the air-conditioned office, it was disorientating to be amongst crowds dressed for a balmy evening. As she walked to the hotel, she passed couples and groups of friends enjoying the last few rays of sunshine, sipping drinks and watching the world go by. Two young children ran along the pavement, knocking into passers-by and laughing as their parents called out to them. She jumped as a crowd of young men rounded a corner in front of her, one of them stumbling and bumping into her. He mumbled an apology in English. To the rest of the world, life carried on as normal, but she felt as if hers was on a runaway train, gathering speed as it careered downhill. There was no going back, no applying the brakes. She had to stay onboard until the end, until it finally jumped the tracks and came to a shuddering and violent standstill.

Helen knew from her first meeting with the investigating magistrate that a custodial sentence was a definite possibility. Elisa had assured her that the fact she had taken full responsibility, albeit later, would stand her in good stead. There was even a chance of just a suspended sentence and a fine. Mia was the only witness, and her statement supported Helen's account that it was a terrible accident. However, her lawyers had warned that she too may also face charges for her involvement.

The more details Helen learnt, the more traumatised she became. The man she'd killed, José Catrimano, was one of four children. He still lived with his parents at their family home. He had been on his way back there after visiting his girlfriend.

Helen had wanted to visit his family, or at least write to them, but her lawyers had stressed that under no circumstances was she to make contact. Mia had also piled on the pressure.

"He's not a patient, Helen. You can't make this better. The last thing his family will want is to see you. What do you hope to achieve?"

Everywhere Helen went, she would see young men and wonder how old they were, how full of life they were, wonder at what life held in store for them and wish it had been her who had died.

Her parents had been more supportive than she felt she deserved, and Helen couldn't bear the pity in their eyes. Being confronted with their anger or disappointment would have been easier, and she told them as much, but Meghan was quick to reassure her, "It was a terrible accident. I'm just so sorry it happened."

Helen stuck to the story she had told the police. They hadn't realised they'd hit someone at first, but when they did learn the truth, it had been her idea to conceal it and that Mia had wanted them to come forward.

Now, with this new CCTV evidence, the prosecution would likely accuse her of lying and claim she'd been well over the drink driving limit. After seeing the footage, Helen wondered if her own lawyer believed her version of events.

"The fact that the prosecution didn't have a chance to undertake blood or breath tests can actually work against you," Elisa said.

So far, news of her arrest hadn't made the British press. Elisa had said they should remain that way until the case went to trial. The accident had occurred at a notorious black spot which had a higher-than-average record of fatalities. Although it had made the local paper at the time, coverage had been limited, with just four paragraphs given to the story.

To her surprise, Helen slept for six hours when she got back to the hotel. She'd ordered a light meal from room service and had curled up in bed, exhausted but expecting to lie there for hours, her mind whirring. She woke only when she heard movement in the corridor outside, and for the first few seconds, struggled to remember where she was. Her head was pounding, and her jaw ached. She'd probably been grinding her teeth. She remembered the headache she'd woken with the morning after the accident. Had that been a consequence of her subconscious working to suppress her memory? She hadn't suffered from headaches before Ibiza. Tension was a regular part of her life now, a price she had to pay. A small price compared with losing a son, a brother, a boyfriend.

CHAPTER 22

Helen had just completed her morning surgery when Stephen walked in with two steaming mugs of coffee.

She smiled gratefully. It was extraordinary how the two people she would never have expected to be able to count on were Stephen and Mia. She'd always judged both to be a little selfish, putting their own needs before others.

"How's it all going?" He perched on the end of her desk, handing her the coffee. "How was the latest trip?"

"Rough." She shook her head.

Stephen didn't reply. They'd talked this through so many times already, exploring how whatever the outcome, the burden of guilt Helen was carrying was exacting a heavy toll on her.

"Any nearer to a conclusion?"

"I had thought so, but now, there's some new evidence. It's CCTV of Mia and I just before the accident. I look totally pissed."

"But you're never totally pissed."

Helen shook her head and said, "It doesn't matter, does it? I certainly look it.'

"But Mia's corroborated your story, that you were unwell."

"My sister is hardly going to be seen as an impartial witness. I just want it to be over and done with. The sooner this is resolved one way or the other, the better for everyone."

"What sort of afternoon have you got ahead, then?" Stephen said, changing the subject.

"Busy as usual. Thank God for that too! I'm grateful for work. And to you for allowing me to—"

"Please, you know we couldn't manage without you. In fact, I was going to ask you if you'd sit in on the chronic disease management meeting this afternoon. It was meant to be me, but I can't make it now."

Helen glanced at her diary. "Of course. Usual time?"

"Three thirty, for an hour, yes."

Helen said she was going to take an early lunch break. The fresh air would be good. It was a glorious day, and she'd take a walk down by the river.

"Can I come?" Stephen said. "I've got half an hour, and I could do with stretching my legs."

"Of course."

"I'll meet you outside in a few minutes. Let me just tell the front desk we're both going out."

Helen left the surgery by the back entrance, a heavy fire exit door which closed softly behind her. Loud birdsong competed with the gentle hum of the local traffic. She really wouldn't need her cardigan, she mused and started to unbutton it.

"Dr Nash?"

Helen turned to see a young woman. She didn't recognise her, although the woman smiled broadly. Helen guessed she was early thirties. She wore a pale pink dress with a white sweater knotted around her shoulders, long blonde hair in a ponytail.

"Yes," Helen said returning her smile. Had they had already met?

"Carrie Aulden. I'm with the *Cambridge Herald*."

Helen blinked; her smile froze.

"I wonder if I could have a word?" Before she had a chance to reply, the woman leant in towards Helen and added, conspiratorially, "About Ibiza."

Helen felt her stomach lurch, and at that moment, the door opened. Stephen took one look at his colleague and switched his gaze to the young woman.

"I don't think I—" Helen started to say.

"We can do this inside if you prefer?" There was an edge to the woman's voice.

"Is everything ok?" Stephen asked. Helen looked at him and then back at the young woman.

"I've been advised not to speak to—"

"It's better you give me your side of the story, Dr Nash. My editor wants me to write it anyway, so it would be in your best interests to take this opportunity to get the facts straight."

Helen noticed a man carrying a camera approaching them. Stephen saw him at the same time and stepped in front of Helen.

"Dr Nash doesn't want to talk to you. I'd like you both to leave, please."

The cameraman was now next to the journalist. "Who are you?" she asked, looking at Stephen. Without waiting for him to reply she spoke directly to Helen, "Are you sure you don't want to speak to me?"

"No," Stephen said, his voice so loud it made Helen flinch. The man aimed his lens towards her, and she lowered her eyes. With his arm around her shoulders, Stephen ushered her back towards the door. He tried to prise it open but it had locked behind him. He thumped on it with his fist and when no one opened it, turned towards the front entrance, half-pulling Helen with him. Helen could hear the click of the camera shutter as they walked. She kept her head down.

As they reached the double doors, Joanna was standing inside talking to Nicki. An elderly patient was at the dispensary window collecting his prescription. They all looked up as Helen and Stephen crashed through the doors with the cameraman and journalist following close behind.

"Do not let them in," Stephen growled over his shoulder as he propelled Helen into his office.

CHAPTER 23

Helen was trembling as she sat down in Stephen's office. She sipped a glass of water, using both hands to steady it.

"You need to go home, take the rest of the day off. We can sort emergency cov—"

"No, I'll be fine," she insisted. "This was always going to happen. I just thought I might get away with it for a bit longer. I know a couple of patients have been waiting for ages for their appointments; I can't let them down." Helen sighed. "I probably won't be able to continue working for much longer, so I've got to try and tie up as much as I can."

"Ok, enough of that talk," said Stephen. "Look, I know Mike Davis, the editor of the *Cambridge Herald*. We play golf together. Why don't I give him a call and see what he knows about that journalist?"

Helen doubted he could persuade an editor against running the story. It would be a big deal for a local paper. She could only imagine what the headline would look like.

"GP Flees Party Island After Hit-And-Run", or "Cambridgeshire Doctor Leaves Motorcyclist to Die".

She took a deep breath, "If you think it might help, but honestly, Stephen, my lawyers told me to expect press attention and not to engage. Now, in the meantime, I've got to get on with work. I've got the chronic disease meeting this afternoon."

"Are you sure you're up to it? I could cancel my plans. It was meant to be me after all."

Helen assured him again that she was fine. She freshened up before making her way to the meeting room.

She smiled at her colleagues as she took her seat. Helen tried her utmost to concentrate on everything the chairwoman was saying. Every now and again, she would interject with a question. Outwardly, she was fully engaged in the meeting. As soon as it was over, she started the afternoon surgery and worked through it without a break. She had just one patient left to see when the front desk called her.

"I've got your mother on the line, Dr Nash."

Helen glanced at her watch. She was running twenty minutes behind schedule. She thought about the last patient in the waiting room, watching the clock as the second sticked by.

"I've just got one more patient to see."

"She sounds worried," the receptionist added. "Says she left a couple of messages on your mobile."

"Ok, put her through."

Helen drew in a deep breath as the call was passed over.

"Mum, is everything ok?"

"Helen, I'm so sorry to call. I know you're busy." Meghan sounded stressed. "But we've had someone here. I didn't realise she was a reporter at first, and I'd already confirmed where you work, and oh, I'm just so sorry..." Meghan spoke rapidly, hardly drawing breath.

"Mum, please don't worry, it's fine. The legal team said this might happen, remember?"

"Oh, yes, of course, but I just thought it might not make the papers. At least not yet."

"No, me neither. But I don't suppose there's much we can do about that."

"Everyone reads the *Cambridge Herald*, Helen – all of our friends do."

Helen's heart sank. "Mum, I'm so sorry."

"No, I didn't mean it like that. I just meant—"

"I know. Look, I've got to go. I'll call in on the way home, ok?"

As she hung up, Helen heard her father's voice, and she was overwhelmed with guilt. Her parents didn't deserve this. They'd suffered enough when she told them about the accident. Now their lives were about to be turned upside down. She prayed Mia wouldn't face charges too. It would just be too much for their parents to bear.

After her last patient, she checked her phone. Missed calls from a number she didn't recognise as well as a few texts. She'd deal with them later. On her walk to her car she was aware of the looks from some of the staff but smiled warmly at them, managing to avoid conversation. God knows what they must be thinking having seen the commotion at lunchtime. They'd know soon enough what it was all about.

As she drove along the leafy lanes on her way home, she wondered how much longer she would have the freedom to live like this. She'd been trying her hardest not to Google "Spanish prison life".

The road stretched ahead of her. She noticed a group of magpies on the grass verge –four for a boy.

Once more, she trawled her memory, desperate to recall the accident. She saw snatches of scenes but nothing definitive. She could picture herself at the party on the boat, the encounter with the creepy older man and her urgent need to leave. She remembered Mia helping her off the boat and then being violently sick. She couldn't remember the drive, apart from the sensation of braking hard. After that, she could recall nothing else until she was getting into bed at the villa. The images were like fleeting stills from a film she had seen a long time ago.

She'd recounted these same memories so many times to her legal team, and the Spanish investigating officers, but wondered if any of them really believed her. Thank God for Mia. She'd flown to Ibiza several times with her. Her sister had made a statement, corroborating her story, insistent that Helen hadn't been drunk. They hadn't even been driving fast. Helen was a very careful driver. They thought they had hit an old bike. Her sister would never lie. She was a doctor first and foremost. She would never knowingly leave someone to die.

She was almost at her parents' home when Stephen called.

"Hi… are you on your way home?"

"I'm going to my parents. That journalist has been in touch with them."

"That's what I'm calling about. I've just spoken to her editor. He said she's been working on the story for almost a fortnight. She got a tip-off from a contact in Spain. He wasn't going to tell me whom. She found out that a Cambridge GP had been involved in a fatal accident, but it took her a while to identify you as the driver."

"Oh, God." Helen pictured Carrie Aulden digging for details about her.

"It's amazing how these things get out," Stephen went on. "She's a good reporter, he said, with a nose for a story. I wondered if her contact had been someone who works at your solicitor's office."

"No! They wouldn't do that, would they?"

"Well, of course they're not supposed to, but who knows, the journalist might be friends with one of the secretaries. You just don't know."

"It was always going to get out. I don't deserve anything less, Stephen."

"They're still investigating, aren't they? You were involved in an accident. It was tragic, but it was an accident, nonetheless."

"I left him to die, and I hid the truth."

Stephen ignored her. "They're going to hold off for another few weeks. They won't print anything unless anyone else gets hold of it. Then he said they will have no choice as it is their, er..." Stephen hesitated, "he said it was their scoop."

Helen pulled up at the side of the road. She was just a few hundred yards from her parents' house. They didn't need to hear this conversation.

"Ok. Thanks for talking to him. Although, it doesn't really matter whether it comes out tomorrow or in a few weeks."

"I just thought it would give you some breathing space, and you never know, you may have a sentencing date by then."

"Thank you," she said again, "for trying to help. I appreciate it."

The truth was she no longer cared. She knew he was trying to help, but her reputation was already damaged. She'd never feel good about herself again. But what was a reputation compared to a life? She felt like more and more of a fraud with every patient consultation. She, who was meant to help people, to improve their lives, she'd gone against every instinct and oath she's taken as a doctor.

Her heart broke a little more when she saw her parents' worried faces as they opened the door.

CHAPTER 24

Helen turned down her parents' offer to stay for dinner. She told them she needed to get back to do some work and check on Percy. The truth was she couldn't bear the weight of their sadness any longer. She could see her own fear reflected in their eyes.

"On the plus side, Mia has proved more of a support than any of us would have dared to hope," her mother said as she sipped ginger and lemon tea.

Her father sat by her side. He'd aged in the last few months, Helen thought. She'd done that.

She forced a smile. "Yes, she has. She's been so kind. She even offered to help financially. I won't need it, but—"

"She needs to take some responsibility," her father said. "You wouldn't have been in that car or at that party if it hadn't been for her."

"Dad!"

"Well, it's true. Don't tell me you haven't thought that yourself. I know you had your arm twisted."

"It doesn't matter, Dad, none of it matters anymore. It was my fault, and what's done is done."

She bowed her head and squeezed her eyes tightly shut. She wouldn't cry in front of them.

"Helen, darling, "Meghan said as she leapt up and put an arm around her, but her father continued, "*Her* holiday, *her* friend's car, *her* party, she also left the scene that night, but still, you insist on protecting her."

"Dad, we've been through this."

"She's always been your blind spot," he said quietly.

Helen sighed. She got up from the table to say goodbye and to plead with her parents not to worry. "Looking to apportion blame doesn't help anyone. And I know it's coming from the best possible place, Dad," she added, kissing him on the cheek. "But it'll be ok. I'll be ok."

As she pulled away from their house, she answered a call. There was a click on the line and a slight delay before the voice came through, "Hello, Helen? It's Elisa. I'm sorry it's a little late. Is it ok for you to talk?"

"Yes, of course."

"Oh. Are you driving?"

"Yes, I'm on my way home."

"Ah, ok, I'll call when you are back."

"No, this is fine. The journey will take me another half an hour or so."

"I think it might be better if we talk when you're not driving."

Helen paused. "Is it bad news, Elisa?"

"Just call me when you get back. Call me on this number."

Helen tried her utmost to concentrate on the road. As soon as she got in, she poured cat food into a bowl for Percy and called

Elisa. She paced the room, glancing at a photo of her and Phil on the beach at Southwold, looking at each other and laughing. Another lifetime.

"Thanks for returning my call, Helen. Ok, I've got an update for you. It's a bit complicated, I'm afraid."

Helen felt her pulse quicken.

"Is this because of the CCTV?"

"It's changed things, yes. The police are now challenging your version of events and are pushing for charges relating to you being under the influence of alcohol."

"Oh, Elisa," Helen sat down next to the fireplace.

"They are saying that was the reason you didn't come forward immediately. I'll be frank with you, Helen. The prosecutor, Oscar Albon, is young, ambitious and making a name for himself. He's already talking about pushing for the maximum sentence."

"But I really wasn't, I wouldn't."

"I believe you weren't drinking," Elisa continued. "I know that was backed up by Mia too. It's just unfortunate there are no other witnesses. And frankly, drunk or not, you were clearly not fit to drive.

"On the plus side, it doesn't look as if Mia will be implicated at all and, as I've already told you, the fact that this is your first ever offence will help."

"Ok," Helen murmured.

"I am afraid to say you are going to have to come back to Ibiza for formal charging. We don't have a date yet, but it is imminent. I can't be confident that you will be granted bail either. I'd get your affairs in order, just in case."

Helen told her she understood and would wait to hear more

before arranging flights. Elisa said she'd liaise with Helen's lawyer in the UK.

When the call ended, she sat alone in her thoughts, the only noises an occasional bark from a distant dog and Percy purring next to her on the sofa. The shrill tone of the landline yanked her back to the real world. The room was in total darkness.

"Hello?"

"Oh, you are there, then?" Mia sounded annoyed.

"Er, yes. Is everything ok?"

"I've been calling your mobile. I've left voicemails. I've texted you."

Helen glanced over at her phone. Its screen was dark. How long had she been sitting here? She'd lost all track of time.

"Helen? For God's sake, you sound out of it," she snapped. "What's happened about Ibiza? I've heard from my solicitor. There's been a development apparently – something major that's going to affect the case?"

"Yes."

"*Yes*? What do you mean? What is it? Why didn't you call me?"

"I've only just heard myself, Mia. Calm down."

"Calm down? You're telling *me* to calm down? Seriously?"

"Mia, as far as you're concerned, nothing's changed. Your involvement in the accident is not in question, nor your knowledge of it. The development is only going to affect me."

"Oh, ok." Mia's barrage ceased.

"It's going to be drink driving. Causing death by reckless driving or whatever the official charge is in the Balearics."

Helen could hear Mia breathing. It was fast, too fast. Anxious, noisy breathing. In normal circumstances, she'd have told her sister to calm down, but she wasn't going to attempt that again.

Then a loud sigh erupted before Mia spoke again, "But, Helen, you weren't. I thought they'd accepted that? Why would they think otherwise? What's happened?"

"There's CCTV."

"What? We've already been through all of that, there were no cameras, the accident was way out of town."

"They got CCTV images from a boat."

"A boat?"

"Not the boat where the party was, another one, anchored offshore. Some super yacht."

"I don't understand."

"I've seen them, Mia. They're very clear. It's us, leaving the party. And I look drunk. Very drunk. It's our word against theirs."

"When you say us, just you and I?" Mia asked

"Yes. There are a few other passers-by but it's us they're interested in, obviously. The images are clear. I'm leaning into you and look pissed.

"But they've spoken to some of the party guests. No one said you were drunk."

"No one said I hadn't been drinking either. At the end of the night it was just you and Adam. The rest of the group wasn't there. Mia, come on, you remember how packed it was. No one knew how many people were on there. Nobody was counting. Even the guy who held the party admitted he didn't meet us."

"But if you hadn't been breathalysed or had a blood test, how can they decide you were drunk?"

"I can be charged with driving while unfit, and it's up to the prosecution to persuade the jury that, in all probability, I was."

"But—" Mia started again.

"Mia, please. I'm tired. I've had enough for today."

"But what about me…?"

"Mia, whatever happens, this was nothing to do with you. It's my problem. Nothing's changed. Look, I've got to go – goodnight." She ended the call.

CHAPTER 25

Helen woke with a start. This time, she could remember the dream vividly. She had been walking along a beach, the tide creeping in under her toes, her feet leaving imprints in the soft sand. Someone was walking next to her. But they left no footprints. She had been trying to see who her companion was when she came to. She had a feeling it was Phil and was desperate to see his face.

Blinking, she looked around her bedroom. Light was already spilling through the curtains. It was 6.02 a.m. Memories of yesterday's calls with Elisa and Mia flooded back, and with it, the now-familiar anxiety. She felt Percy stirring by her feet.

She turned on the radio, trying in vain to concentrate on the soothing voice of the presenter. After a few minutes, she got up. Percy leapt off the bed at the same time and scampered ahead of her down the stairs. "You'll trip me up one of these days," she said, reaching for the banister.

She was on the bottom step when she noticed the white envelope in the middle of the hall. Someone must have pushed it though the letterbox with a lot of force. It was handwritten with her name on it, but there was no address. Probably from Neighbourhood Watch, she imagined, as she slid a finger under the seal, or maybe something about the new housing development nearby. She'd been actively involved with that before her life had been turned upside down.

Dear Dr Nash,

We met recently when I came to the surgery along with our photographer. I wonder if you could please give me a call? I'd like to talk to you about your version of events, as we discussed. I understand you are facing new charges, and the Cambridge Herald was promised an exclusive interview with you. I would like to think I could be a support to you at this time, and when we are in a position to print the story, I can assure you that I will give a thorough and wholly accurate account.

If it helps, please Google my name and see some examples of the kind of feature work I do. I am not in the business of scandalising.

My contact details are at the top of this letter. This story will soon be in the public domain, so I'd be grateful if you could get back to me asap. You can call me any time.

Kind regards,

Carrie Aulden

Helen read it again. Percy stood impatiently next to his empty bowl. Robotically, she fed him and made herself a coffee before rereading the letter for the third time.

An "exclusive interview" about her role in a young man's death. She needed to be at work in less than two hours; she had a full patient list. How much longer could she continue with this charade?

The thought of sitting in front of a journalist, trying to persuade her that she was a decent person, that she hadn't meant to kill anyone, or lie about it and cover it up for months afterwards, was the last thing she could do. She almost wished they would simply write what they wanted. Her reputation couldn't be made any worse.

She knew she would have to tell Stephen about the new charges, and that she would likely need to travel to Ibiza within the next few days. She'd try to wrap everything up at work today and make tomorrow her last day. She'd tell the rest of the staff herself. It was unfair to leave Stephen with that. He'd already taken a risk by sticking by her, allowing her to continue working. God knows what the General Medical Council would have to say about that when it all came to light.

She'd need to let her solicitor know about the letter from Carrie Aulden too. "*This story will soon be in the public domain*" and "*I'm not in the business of scandalising*" buzzed round and round in her head. She imagined photos of herself plastered over the papers. She thought about her patients, poring over every detail. Some of them had been with her for many years, right from the first day she started. They trusted her, relied on her.

Her phone pinged. A text from Mia. *Very early for her.*

Are you ok? Can I help with legal fees, etc? You said you'd ask, and you haven't mentioned anything. You must have paid for stuff by now?

Helen quickly replied:

All fine, thanks. I would ask if I needed it but thank you x

Helen pushed send. Mia was trying her best. If only the solution was as easy as throwing money at the problem.

A few hours later, she was talking to her last patient of the morning surgery.

"So, let's start off with this and see how you get on?" she said to the man in front of her. "If you find your symptoms haven't improved within a week, then come back. But don't leave it any longer."

He nodded and smiled. "I will, thank you very much. I feel better already. My wife said to come and see you."

Helen smiled as she passed him a prescription. *He's going to need his meds adjusting in a couple of months and I bet won't be here.*

"You shouldn't have left it this long but you'll have to come back so we can see if the pills are doing the trick. If you can't get in to see me, don't wait. Make an appointment with one of my colleagues. All your notes are on the system."

Helen completed her notes diligently as the morning surgery ended. As she went into the kitchen, she noticed Stephen's door was firmly shut.

Nicki was sitting at the little table eating her lunch.

"Looks very healthy," Helen nodded towards her colourful salad.

"It's awful, but I've got a wedding in six weeks and I need to lose half a stone," Nicki complained.

"You do not need to lose half a stone."

"My ex is going to be there. I'm not going to give him the satisfaction of seeing me looking awful!"

"You could never look awful." Helen meant it. Nicki was a pretty, petite blonde with a big heart and personality to match. She was always the life and soul of any party. "You'll look fabulous, and he'll see how much he's missed out on."

"Oh, you're good! You know exactly how to make people feel better. No wonder you're such a great doctor."

Helen smiled and filled the kettle.

"Tell me to mind my own business, but is everything ok, Helen?"

Helen kept her back to Nicki.

"You just don't seem like yourself."

They had worked together for years. *Would Nicki ever trust her again when she learnt the truth?* Helen turned to face her. "Nicki, I—" she started.

"Ooh, yes please, I'd love one, just a splash of milk, no sugar!" Stephen strode in, interrupting them.

"I was hoping to catch you. Can I have a word?" Helen asked him, grateful for the distraction.

"Certainly, as long as you find me a biscuit with that tea. My office in five minutes? I've just got to drop these off." He raised the thick pile of papers he was carrying.

Helen held a mug up towards Nicki, "Did you want one?"

"No, thanks. But I'm free after work if you are?"

Helen lowered her eyes as she spoke, "Thank you. I'll see."

"Just look after yourself."

Helen took a deep breath and carried the two steaming mugs into Stephen's room. She could hear his voice travelling along the corridor from reception, pausing while someone laughed at something he'd said. She sat down next to his desk, sipping her tea. She'd have to say goodbye to all of this. She wondered if she'd ever practise medicine again.

Stephen shut the door behind him, sat down and picked up his tea. "So… Dr Nash, how can I help you today?"

His broad smile was replaced with a frown as she started to explain.

CHAPTER 26

As she thought he might, Stephen did his utmost to persuade Helen to continue working until the very last minute possible.

"Helen, it's never over until it's over. I just think it will be better for everyone if you stay. You, your patients and obviously me, me, me! I can't imagine this place without you, and how will I manage the workload? There's never going to be any sneaking off early for a round of golf now."

Helen was adamant. She couldn't bring herself to smile, although she appreciated his attempt to lighten the mood. She would speak to the staff at the end of tomorrow; it wasn't right to walk out without saying goodbye and leave Stephen to face them on his own.

"It'll be difficult enough for you to get cover at such short notice. Hopefully, that lovely locum will be happy to come back in the short-term until you find someone more…" She couldn't bring herself to say "permanent".

She asked Joanna to call a staff meeting for the next day and ate lunch at her desk, using the time to clear the few personal belongings that had accumulated over the years. It took longer than it should have done as she lingered over a photo of Phil and carefully packed a small vase she'd been given from a patient. She'd received it in her first month here, and it had sat on the shelf next to several textbooks ever since. She'd taken great pleasure remembering the patient's gratitude at what Helen had considered was just doing her job.

The internal phone buzzed, and the receptionist told her Carrie Aulden was on the line.

Helen hesitated. She didn't want to speak to her. She hadn't had a chance to catch up with her lawyer yet.

"Can you take a number and tell her I'll get back to her, please?" She would hide behind the officious receptionist while she still could.

A minute later, the phone rang again. "Sorry to bother you again, Dr Nash, but Carrie Aulden has asked me to pass on a message. She says she needs to speak to you very urgently. I've got her number."

Helen said she'd deal with it. For a few moments, she tried to quell the disquiet that coursed through her body. She was sitting with her hands clasped in her lap, shoulders rounded, head bowed when a sharp rap at the door jolted her upright.

"Come in," she said instinctively. Joanna's face peered round the door. Her eyes were wide.

"Dr Nash, there are two journalists in reception asking to speak to you; one said he's from the *Daily Mail* and another I didn't quite catch. Also, a van's just turned up with what looks like filming equipment."

Helen's breath caught in her throat, and she felt her face flush. On her desk, her phone flickered into action. A number she didn't recognise flashed up.

"Is Stephen around?" she asked.

"Erm, I think he said he was going to stretch his legs. Shall I see if I can get hold of him?"

"Yes, please, and Joanna, is there any chance you could bring that meeting forward to now? I need to speak to you all sooner rather than later. It won't take long."

"As in *now*?"

"Yes. As in the next half hour if possible, please. Do you think you might be able to put those journalists off?"

"I'm sure we can, and as we are theoretically on lunch, I should be able to get most of us together." Joanna's eyes had gone from wide to full-blown saucers.

"Thank you. I've just got to make a call. I won't be long."

Joanna closed the door behind her. Helen picked up her phone, ignoring the missed calls and messages and scrolled through her contacts for her UK solicitor's mobile number.

Louisa Neville picked up almost immediately.

"Louisa, I've got journalists here at the practice. A woman from the Cambridge paper has been in touch, and I promised I'd speak to her first, but now others must have found out and they've come to see me at work and—"

"Woah – slow down a minute. What do you mean they're at the practice? Have you spoken to them?"

"Not yet. I've asked the practice manager to keep them at bay. But I think there are more outside."

"Ok. First off, do not speak to any of them. When you said you've promised to speak to someone, you haven't yet?"

"No."

"Good, and don't. To any of them. No matter what they promise. They'll say they want to allow you the chance to give your side of the story and that they won't sensationalise it, but you have no control over what appears, so don't give them anything at all."

There was a discreet knock at her door, and Stephen appeared. He had the same wide-eyed look as Joanna. Helen motioned for him to come in as Louisa continued.

"I was going to call you about the new charges anyway. It looks like you're going to have to be in Ibiza this week. I'll fly over with you."

Helen heard someone in the background, and Louisa said she needed to go. "I'll be on my mobile if you need me, but when you get home, shut the door and close the curtains. Unplug your landline, if you have one, and use your mobile only. Do not answer any unknown numbers. Just don't engage." Helen was still frozen, holding the phone for a while after Louisa had hung up.

Stephen broke the silence, "Bloody hell. It's all kicking off out there."

"I'm going to explain to everyone what's going on, and then I'm going home."

"Don't worry about being noble now, Helen. I can speak to the others."

"I owe them an explanation, Stephen. I can't just walk out."

"Ok, if you're sure. Joanna has got everyone together in the dispensary. She's locked the front door too."

Helen stood up. "Right then!"

She felt strangely calm, as if she was observing herself. She made her way to the dispensary, averting her gaze away from reception. She didn't need the distraction of whatever lay outside the surgery doors.

As she pushed the door open, the room fell silent. Joanna and Nicki stood next to two of the receptionists. The two pharmacists were resting against a large filing cabinet. Stephen came in behind Helen.

"I wanted to explain to you all what's going on," Helen announced without any preamble. "This is very hard for me to say, but I'd rather you hear it from me. I should have told you all before now, and I'm sorry. I'm deeply sorry." Her voice faltered as she took a deep breath and collected herself.

"I was involved in a car accident. When I was on holiday in Ibiza."

The faces stared back at her. No one moved. The tension in the room was palpable.

"I hit a young man, and he died."

Helen heard a sharp intake of breath. She didn't look up but took a second before she continued. "The thing is, I, er... I didn't know I'd hit anyone. I can't remember anything." She caught the look of horror on Joanna's face.

"When I came home, I started having nightmares and flashbacks, and I couldn't understand why. But then some evidence came to light, and it all began to make sense. And now, well... now, I'm facing charges."

No one spoke for a few moments until Nicki said, "So that's why all the journalists are here?" She exchanged a look with Joanna and continued, "It must have been terrible for you. But it was an accident. This press attention seems a bit over the top. There's a camera crew out there now too."

"It is. But that's just—" Stephen interjected.

"The police think I was drunk," Helen said. "I wasn't, but it's my word against theirs, and they've got some pretty incriminating CCTV footage."

No one spoke, and the weight of silence hung heavy in the room. Joanna shifted from one foot to the other. Stephen looked at the floor.

The phones, which had been ringing in reception throughout their meeting seemed to get louder.

"So, I can't carry on working, I'm afraid. Not now, with all of this going on. It's not going to be easy for any of you, and I'm so sorry for bringing this negative attention to the practice, I truly am. I'll be leaving today."

Silence descended again until Nicki stepped forward, walked up to Helen with her arms outstretched and enveloped her in a tight hug. At that, Helen's composure shattered, and she couldn't hold it together any longer. Tears slid down her face as she allowed Nicki to pull her in, supporting her weight. Stephen ushered the others out of the room. She could hear him telling them to keep a dignified silence and say nothing when it came to the press.

"Don't be rude, it won't help, but don't speak to anyone. We will tell the patients that Dr Nash has taken leave for the time being, until we know the next steps."

Without saying a word, Nicki pulled out a packet of tissues and passed one to Helen. She watched as she dabbed at her eyes.

"I'm so sorry I didn't tell you before."

Nicki shook her head and shushed her.

CHAPTER 27

Helen zipped up her jacket, pulling the collar tight to her ears, as if she could somehow disappear into the folds of its fabric. There were at least ten reporters outside now and easily as many photographers.

"Ready?" Stephen asked. He had insisted on walking her to the car. "Keep close."

As soon as they stepped out of the back door, there was a scramble as lenses swung in her direction. The noise of the shutters ricocheted around the car park like gunfire. She put her head down as Stephen strode forward, holding his arm straight out in front of him to clear their short path to the car. He walked carefully but as fast as he could. Helen followed, her eyes trained firmly on his heels, not looking left or right. A woman tried to step between her and Stephen.

"Dr Nash, have you got a comment for the *Argos*? I hear you've written to the Catrimano family. Have you met his parents?"

Stephen turned to look behind him, but Helen sidestepped and carried on walking, her gaze firmly to the ground. Holding the keys inside her pocket, she squeezed the fob and unlocked the car. Stephen stood to one side, using his body to block the group who now encircled them, and she slipped into the driver's seat.

"Move out of the way, please," he said politely, staying behind her car as she reversed, waving her out.

"Who are you, sir? Are you a doctor here?" a booming male voice asked.

"Do you work with Doctor Nash?" someone else shouted.

Helen's car swung out and pulled forward. She saw Stephen in her wing mirror turn to put his head down and hurry back inside.

As she left, Helen expected the media pack to jump into their cars and follow her. She joined the line of traffic snaking its way along Trumpington Road and dared to look in her rear-view mirror. She couldn't be certain, but it didn't look as if any of them were behind her. There were roadworks in the distance; she could see the temporary traffic lights changing from red to green. The traffic barely moved.

"Come on, come on," she muttered under her breath, urging the car in front to magically leapfrog its way to the front of the queue and clear a path for her.

Her hands gripped the steering wheel so tightly that her knuckles were white. A tremor travelled up her arms, into her shoulders, which were now up around her ears. Adrenalin coursed through her.

Her phone rang, and she flinched. It was an unknown number so she ignored it. Her car was inching forward, and the lights turned red just as she approached them. The phone rang again. The screen was packed with notifications of unread text messages and missed calls. She turned it off. Something caught her eye at the side of the car; a motorcyclist was right next to her, and although his face was obscured by a visor he was looking into the window. Helen jumped. She looked away, willing the lights to change when he tapped on the window. She tensed, then realised he was pointing at her wing mirror, her indicator light was flashing. She adjusted the stalk. She must have left it on since she left. He gave her a thumbs up as the lights changed and pulled off. She let out a long sigh, realising she'd been holding her breath.

As she drove, Helen replayed the scene at the surgery. The look of horror on Joanna's face when she had told them she'd killed someone. The exchanged glances between the pharmacists. Nicki had jumped in with support and sympathy for which Helen had been enormously thankful, but that was Nicki's default setting. The others had looked shocked and horrified. Of course they had. But they knew her. They knew her patients loved her, knew she was a conscientious professional and a kind person. They'd been with her at office Christmas parties, they knew she remembered their birthdays. But a jury of strangers wouldn't know this. She didn't stand a chance.

As she approached Saffron Cottage, she saw them. A large white van parked at an angle, cars she didn't recognise, the woman by her gate talking to the camera. Several photographers. A reporter was talking to her elderly neighbour, Teresa, and taking notes.

She froze. She didn't know whether to reverse, leave before they saw her, or face the mlée and make a dash for the front door. As if they could hear her thoughts, two reporters looked in her direction. One of them mouthed her name. It was their turn to freeze now as they waited to see what she would do next.

Others followed their lead, turning to look in her direction, and she saw the confusion on Teresa's face. For the second time that day, camera lenses were aimed straight at her. The journalists stood still, forcing her to slow to an unbearable speed. She edged forward tentatively until they reached an impasse, no one moving. They were calling her name, and she wondered whether to blast the horn. *Would it make me seem aggressive and paint me as a road raging menace?* She decided not to press down on the wheel. There were photographers on both sides of her. Teresa strode towards her and told them to move.

"Clear the way! Immediately. She's trying to get to her house."

Helen could have kissed her. Teresa continued to shoo them, buying her a few precious seconds. As she stepped out of the car, she was met with a barrage of noise. She heard her name being called, voices clamouring for her attention. She kept her head down as she forced her way through the frenzy to the front door. She fumbled for the right key, dropping the bunch as she raised it to the lock.

"Dr Nash?"

"Do you have a comment for us, Dr Nash?"

"Do your patients know you might be facing criminal charges, Dr Nash?"

"Have you always holidayed on the party island, Dr Nash?"

They surrounded her. Even the way they called her "doctor" felt aggressive, hostile. She was struggling to get enough air into her lungs, and then finally, the key turned, she was inside. She slammed the door behind her.

CHAPTER 28

Her back against the door, chest heaving as if she'd run hard for miles, Helen slid down its smooth wooden surface. As she touched the floor, she folded forward, her head sinking between her knees. She could hear snatches of conversations outside.

Percy ran towards her. He stood on his hind legs, tentatively placing his front paws on top of her knees, nuzzling her head with his own. When she didn't respond, the nuzzling grew more insistent until she reached out to stroke him. He purred and pushed his way onto her lap, squeezing into the gap between her thighs and chest.

They stayed there until a loud knock caused them both to jump. Helen started to stand up as an envelope was pushed through the letterbox, landing with a thud. She left it and made her way to the kitchen where she pulled down the blinds and unplugged the landline.

Her hands were shaking so much she could barely turn on her phone. There were thirty-eight missed calls. She tried Caroline first, and when it went straight to voicemail, dialled Mia's number.

Her sister answered after several rings. Helen could hear music and chatter in the background.

"Hi, Helen."

"Mia, I'm at home. There are journalists outside. They came to the surgery. They're calling me, putting notes through the door. I don't know what to do."

Silence.

"Mia?"

"Yes, I'm here, hang on, let me just go somewhere quiet." Helen heard footsteps and a door closing before Mia said softly, "I'm a bit, erm, busy at the moment. Have you spoken to your lawyer?"

"Yes, before I left work. She said not to engage with anyone."

"So that's exactly what you've got to do. You've just got to sit tight and see this through. If you don't leave the house and don't speak to them, there's nothing they can do."

Before she had a chance to reply, Caroline's number flashed up on the screen.

"Got to take this. I'll call you back," Helen said and hung up. As soon as she explained the situation, Caroline said she would come over and collect her.

"You can't stay there! Sort Percy, pack a bag. Bring your passport and anything else you might need so you can fly back to Ibiza without going back home. I'll be with you by seven at the latest. I've got one thing I need to do this afternoon, but I'll see if I can bring it forward."

Helen didn't think about protesting. She was just so grateful that Caroline was offering a solution. Upstairs, she set about filling a wheelie case with anything she might need. She called her mother, trying to sound as calm as she could.

"I think it would be better if I went and stayed with Caroline for a few days. Just until the furore calms down a bit. Mum… please don't worry, I'll be fine."

When Meghan didn't reply, Helen knew she was crying.

CHAPTER 29

Helen's front garden and driveway were swarming with people. Amongst the scrum, several villagers had come out to see what was going on. Caroline parked a little way back, as near as she dared to Helen's house without alerting the crowd. She texted to say she'd arrived, to which Helen texted back:

Don't get out of the car. I'll be right out

With the engine still running, Caroline watched in her rear-view mirror. The media pack surged towards the cottage as soon as Helen opened the door. Within seconds, she was engulfed. Cameras flashed, and microphones were thrust in her face. Helen was barely visible amidst them, though she could make out her head covered with a jacket.

Her progress to the car was painfully slow, and Caroline resisted the temptation to rush out and help. Surrounded, Helen held an arm in front of her as she inched her way forward. Caroline pressed the button and lowered the passenger window when Helen was close, but a woman stood in front of it blocking her path.

"Please," said Helen, trying to reach for the car.

"Why did you leave the scene of the accident, Dr Nash?"

"Didn't you try to save the moped rider, Dr Nash?"

"Let her pass!" Caroline yelled in the loudest, most authoritative voice she could muster.

Undeterred, the woman blocking Helen from the car remained with her back to the car. At the same time, Caroline heard the whirr of a camera lens as she too was photographed. She did the only thing she could think of and leant on the car horn, allowing its blare to echo through the crowd. Startled, the obtrusive woman turned, and Helen used the opportunity to push past her. Once she was inside, Caroline locked the doors and pulled away as carefully as she could. Helen kept hidden under the jacket. Several photographers carried on snapping but no one tried to follow them. By the time they turned out of the village, Caroline felt herself relax a little as the adrenaline started to leave her body. She took a proper look at Helen and was shocked. Her face was drawn and pale, and she'd lost a noticeable amount of weight since she saw her last.

"Thank you," Helen said, her voice barely a whisper.

"Don't mention it," Caroline replied, pulling onto the motorway. "But, what the fucking hell!" she said.

Helen nodded. "I know."

They barely spoke, both lost in their own thoughts. Caroline drove on autopilot, seeing again the images of her friend trying to fight her way through the press pack. She looked across and saw that Helen's eyes were closed. She switched on the radio and let the calming melodies of Classic FM fill the car.

When they reached Caroline's house, Helen looked even worse.

"Why don't you go and soak in a hot bath. The spare room is all ready for you. Help yourself to anything you need, and when you're ready, we'll have something soothing. I think we've earned it."

In the kitchen, Caroline stretched and let out a long sigh as she heard Helen moving around upstairs. She felt exhausted. God knows how Helen must feel. Caroline caught up on her emails until she heard Helen emerge from the bathroom, and then warmed a pan of milk to make two large mugs of frothy hot chocolate. She set them on a tray with a small plate of biscuits and carried them into the living room where Helen was waiting, perched on the end of the sofa and wrapped in a dressing gown that swamped her now tiny frame.

Caroline handed her a mug.

"Thanks. I'd better check my phone," Helen said.

"Do you really need to?" Caroline asked. "Can't you just leave it for one evening?"

Helen blew gently on the steaming liquid and said, "It's my parents and Mia, they need to know where—"

"I called your mum earlier. I explained what was happening and said we'd let her know if anything changed."

"How was she? Did she mention Dad?"

Caroline hesitated. Meghan had broken down and sobbed. She'd added that Roger hadn't been coping well at all.

"She was fine. They both are. They're relieved that you'll be staying with me."

"Oh Caroline, I'll never be able to thank—"

"Don't be silly. You know you'd do exactly the same for me."

"You'd never be in this situation, let's face it."

"Nonsense! An accident can happen to anyone."

"It was what happened afterwards that has made everything so much worse. I've been such an idiot."

Caroline leant forward, making sure to keep looking her friend in the eye. She kept her body relaxed, one hand open in her lap while she nursed the mug with the other. Non-verbal communication was something she used in a professional capacity every day. Without Helen realising it, Caroline was asking her to open up.

"The weird thing is I still can't remember it– the crash," Helen said. "I can't remember hitting him. I can definitely remember trying to avoid it. I can remember feeling as if my foot would go through the floor on the brake pedal. There are chunks of that evening that I just can't recall. I can remember the party, and I can remember arriving back at the villa. There are just bloody gaps. Oh, God, it's so, so…" She took a sip of the hot chocolate.

"The mind is very good at protecting us from trauma. It may all come back to you at some point."

"I just wish I'd come clean earlier. I might be able to look at myself in the mirror by now."

Caroline hesitated for a few seconds, "But you have told the truth, haven't you?"

"Yes, erm… no, I mean when Mia told me," Helen took another sip.

Caroline took a biscuit. "Mia told you?"

"Oh, God, Caroline it's so complicated. So bloody stupid…"

Caroline studied her friend closely as Helen continued, "I can trust you, I know that. But this has to stay between you and me."

Caroline nodded.

"Mia had been having an affair with this guy, Adam. She let me think that she'd met him for first time when we were in Ibiza, but I discovered afterwards that she'd known him well before then. She orchestrated the timing of our trip to coincide with his."

I bet she did, thought Caroline.

"She said that if it came to light that I had been driving when we had the accident, no one would believe I hadn't been well over the limit. I hadn't, I swear I hadn't but I'd left the party barely walking properly. So many people would be affected by the fallout if I came clean, and of course, it wouldn't change what had happened. I knew it was wrong, of course it was, but I just went along with it. I don't know what I was thinking. I could see some sort of logic in what she said. I couldn't face having her and Chris breaking up on my conscience as well."

Caroline placed her hand on Helen's knee, "You did the right thing in the end. That's all that matters."

"Yes, but at what cost? My poor parents. Mia is walking on eggshells, terrified the truth about her and Adam will come out. I'm likely to face a horrendous trial now, unless I plead guilty to all the charges, and even then, I'll probably go to prison."

"You've got to stop worrying about everyone else, Helen. Your parents, Mia, they will all be ok as long as you are. And you will be. Look, why don't you try and get your head down. It's been a hell of a day, and I think we could both do with some sleep."

Helen nodded and stood up, picking up their mugs.

"Leave them. I'll sort it all. Just go to bed!" Caroline smiled and gave her friend a hug.

When she heard Helen close her bedroom door, Caroline opened her laptop and keyed "Cambridge doctor accident Ibiza" into her search engine. She stifled a gasp as she was directed to a Twitter link.

> A woman from Cambridgeshire has been arrested on suspicion of causing death by dangerous driving and being unfit to drive due to drink and drugs on the island of Ibiza. The woman, believed to be a GP, has not had her passport confiscated and has been allowed to return home to the UK before facing charges.

Scrolling, she found other links:

> Balearics prosecutors have located a car believed to have been used in a fatal hit-and-run accident involving a British tourist.

> Cambridge GP helping Ibiza police with enquiries following fatal accident.

None of them mentioned Helen by name. Not yet.

CHAPTER 30

By the time Caroline came down the next morning, Helen had been awake for hours. The hot chocolate had helped her get to sleep, but she'd woken early, turned on her phone and been catapulted into hell.

Missed calls, voicemails and texts littered her screen but it was the WhatsApp from Mia that made her feel sick.

Why aren't you answering? You're all over social media. Call me.

She'd sent it at midnight and included links to several web pages. Sitting up in bed and trembling, Helen had begun to open them.

Holiday Island Horror Crash

British GP Helping Ibiza Police With Enquiries

Moped Rider Killed In Hit-And-Run

Balearics Police Investigating Fatal Road Accident. British GP Helping With Enquiries.

Headlines from other Spanish sites flashed up too. She clicked on one with a photograph of a stretch of road. Tired bunches of flowers lay on the ground, some tied to the guard rail.

The first photograph she saw of herself was alongside a piece in the *Daily Mail*. It had been taken as she left the surgery yesterday. Although she had her head down, she was clearly identifiable. There were more. Some of her in the car park, some with Stephen, another leaving her front door. The more she scrolled, the worse it got, although all the stories seemed to stick to the same limited information. The British press were clearly reporting as much as they could while they had the chance. As her lawyer had pointed out, legal restrictions would kick in once she was officially charged. When she could stand reading no longer, she'd got up and gone downstairs. She was still sitting at the kitchen table when Caroline came down.

Helen's head was bowed, her chest barely moving. Caroline took a step closer.

"Hey," Caroline said gently. "For a second I wondered if you were asleep, you were so still, Helen?"

Helen opened her eyes. Her face was ashen. She felt shaken. "I'm everywhere, Caroline. Photos of me, the surgery, my house. It's out there now."

Caroline paused. Helen could tell she was evaluating the best words to say.

"It was just a matter of time, Helen."

"Yes, but… I don't know, I just didn't think it would be so… mainstream." She ran weary fingers through her unkempt hair. "It's on all the news sites here. And in Spain and on social media and God knows what else. One Twitter thread even had a comment about the caring profession not being so caring. God almighty."

She dropped her head into her hands. Caroline gently patted her friend's back.

"Look, at least you're not having to keep the secret anymore."

Caroline set two places for breakfast and placed a cappuccino in front of Helen, saying, "Don't let that go cold."

Helen picked up her coffee and took a sip. "Thank you," she murmured, cradling the mug. "Thank you."

"Just get something inside you," Caroline pushed a bowl of granola towards her as a shrill phone alarm sounded. Helen jumped and let out a scream. Her coffee spilt on the table.

"Sorry, sorry, that's mine. I forgot to turn it off." Caroline acted quickly to silence the sound.

Helen's eyes were wide, like a rabbit caught in the headlights.

"I understand how hard this must be," Caroline said, "but you've just got to go through the process. I guess you'll speak to your lawyers today, let them know what the situation is and see what the next steps are? And it goes without saying, you're welcome to stay here as long as you like."

By the time Caroline left for work, Helen had convinced her that she was a little calmer. She'd promised not to check any more social media or answer unknown numbers.

"I'll be back after lunch. I can work from home this afternoon."

"Please don't do that for me, Caroline. Honestly, I'll be fine."

"I know you will, but I'd like to. If you feel like some fresh air, you've got the park over there. The press won't know where you are just yet."

Helen attempted a smile. She wasn't going anywhere. The thought of being recognised left her in a cold sweat.

When Caroline had gone, Helen texted Mia, aware that although she had been awake for hours, it was still early, probably too early to call. She sent a short message, and within seconds, Mia called.

"I'm going to face fucking charges," Mia snapped before Helen had even had a chance to say hello. "I knew this would happen. I just knew it, and I begged you not to say anything, and now, look, we are both in an unholy mess, and it's getting worse. You're worried about losing your precious career, but what about *me*? I'll lose my marriage, my home, everything!"

Stunned at her sister's outburst, Helen couldn't think straight. "What's happened?"

"So, when you were having a lovely time with your friend last night, ignoring my calls, my lawyer called and said that because of the new evidence, I might not be off the hook after all."

"I wasn't having a *lovely* time. I turned off my phone because of the journalists, they were all over my home, and it was late. I thought that—"

"Well, whatever you thought, you were wrong. Because of the CCTV, the prosecution will push to charge me for helping to cover up that you were pissed."

Helen closed her eyes. "Mia, you know that's not true. Why are you saying that?"

"I dunno, maybe you did drink more than you said. But if you'd just fucking listened to me, we wouldn't be in this mess. All I was doing was trying to protect you, but of course, *you* know better than me, don't you? Look at the mess we're all in! How could coming forward have helped anyone, ever? But hey, as long as you feel you've done the right thing for YOU that's fine isn't it?"

Helen was holding the phone to her ear long after Mia had hung up.

CHAPTER 31

As Stephen swung into the practice car park, he held his breath, wondering if any reporters were lurking. They hadn't been around as much recently, but still he made a dash from his car to the door. His editor friend had warned him that the press would be working hard in the background, gathering as much information as possible to colour forthcoming features and keep the story running for as long as there was public demand for it.

"The gloves will be off after the trial," Mike had cautioned. Stephen had asked him what the gloves had been doing up until then. Had they ever been on?

He'd remained fully supportive of Helen, but the consequence had been far greater and more sustained than he'd ever imagined, particularly at work.

He answered queries from Helen's patients, reassuring them that their care would continue uninterrupted. At home, Susie questioned his unwavering belief in his colleague.

"I just can't believe how she could have lied about it for so long and then drag poor Mia into it too. Honestly, Stephen, I don't see how you think it's ok to defend her."

"It wasn't as if I was actually defending her," he claimed. "I was trying to maintain a strong front. It was all about the practice and reassuring the patients."

"What gets me the most is the fact that she went back to work and carried on as normal. I mean, how could she? It seems so calculating," Susie continued. "I always thought there was something up with Mia after Ibiza. I couldn't quite put my finger on it, but she wasn't the same."

Stephen listened, nodding agreement every now and again, praying that Susie would never discover that Helen had confided in him as soon as she had. He had begun to question whether or not his decision to encourage her to carry on working had been the right thing to do. With hindsight, maybe he ought to have "referred up" to his superiors, or at least the governing body. Maybe he'd be called to account too.

The next morning, he cast an eye around the surgery, able to relax only when he saw it was just a normal day. The front desk staff were sitting at their screens and fielding calls and answering queries as per usual. Recognising a particularly challenging patient in the reception area, he avoided eye contact, praying she wasn't on his list that morning. Helen had always handled her brilliantly.

He would have to deal with the now-routine questions about what was happening with Dr Nash. Most patients didn't ask, but those that did could quickly put him on the back foot. Some were braver than others and would ask outright if he'd ever believed she could have been so cold-hearted. Others skirted around the issue, fishing for nuggets of information on top of what they were being fed by the papers.

"You're very busy, I had to wait ages to get an appointment."

"Will you be getting another permanent doctor?"

"Dr Nash won't be coming back, will she?"

"Did Dr Nash tell you she'd been involved in an accident?"

"I bet you feel a bit let down, don't you?"

He fielded their questions as best he could, hiding behind the claim that he wasn't allowed to talk about it, but he stressed what a good doctor she was and always had been. He'd move the conversation on as quickly as possible.

He'd just taken off his coat when there was a knock at his door, and Joanna appeared with a coffee. "Good morning!" she beamed as she set the steaming mug down. Helen had always teased him about Joanna, claiming she had a soft spot for him.

"Thank you very much. Lovely morning, isn't it?" He slid into his chair.

"What's this?" He leant forward, peeling the sticky note off his screen. "Who's Simon March?"

Joanna shrugged. "He called early this morning. Very early – the phone was ringing as I opened up. He said he was from St Faith's hospital."

"Did he say what it was about?"

"Nope. I assumed you would know."

"I've never heard of him. I haven't had any connection with St Faith's recently either. You sure he didn't give *any* clue as to what it was about?"

Joanna looked blank. "Yes, I am sure."

"But he asked for me specifically?"

She hesitated. "Erm… I think so, or maybe the head of the practice. I'm sorry, I really thought it was someone you knew or maybe a referral."

"Don't worry. I'm sure it's nothing. With everything that's been going on, I'm probably being overly cautious. You never know what ruses these journalists will use to get through."

"Oh, yes! I hadn't thought of that," Joanna frowned.

Stephen shrugged and glanced at his watch. "Don't worry, just ignore it. If it's legit, he'll get back to us.

"Has there been any more news? Any development?" Joanna asked.

Stephen shook his head. He wouldn't tell her even if there was. Joanna thrived on gossip.

"Do me a favour and send the first patient in on your way through will you, please?" he asked, peering at his screen to read the first name on his list. "Oh, God, not Mrs Hill," he groaned, realising it was the woman he'd avoided in reception.

Joanna smiled as she closed the door.

CHAPTER 32

Helen flew back to Ibiza once the Guardia Civil announced they were ready to charge her. They had finished their investigation, and her legal team had been in touch with the Foreign Office to discuss whether she might receive a custodial sentence.

She risked booking a return flight, praying that Elisa's guess was correct, and Spanish police wouldn't demand she relinquish her passport. With a sinking feeling, she used her credit card to make a reservation at the usual hotel. She'd already spent thousands. It had wiped out her entire savings, and as there seemed to be no end in sight, Helen had decided to get her house valued. She would start the selling process before the court case. In the event she went to jail, her parents had agreed to take Percy. They'd even offered to move into Saffron Cottage when the papers printed a photo of her visiting her lawyer in Ibiza for fear that it might be a target for burglars.

Mia's mood waxed and waned. Sometimes, she would be positive and upbeat, adamant there would be no way anyone could prove Helen had been drinking. Other days, she was highly agitated, convinced it would end badly for both of them. Helen dreaded her being in this mood as Mia would become angry, blaming her for going to the police. Caroline would constantly reassure Helen that she had done the right thing, that Mia had been wrong to try and hide the accident. But still, Helen worried more about Mia than herself. No matter how dark her thoughts became about her own future, it was nothing compared to the guilt she felt about implicating her sister.

She suffered from crippling survivor's guilt too. In spite of Elisa telling her that her letter had been well received, she still hadn't been allowed to speak to José Catrimano's family. The thought of seeing them for the first time in the courtroom was too awful to contemplate, but Elisa had been firm. The letter was enough.

On the day she was to be charged, Elisa collected Helen from the hotel and drove her to the police station. Helen had pictured this scene so many times, torturing herself with images of intimidating police officers as she stood amongst criminals waiting to be arraigned.

In fact, it was nothing like she had imagined. The station was noisy, packed with people but clean, and the uniformed charging officer addressed her courteously, waiting patiently as Elisa translated.

It was several hours before the formalities were completed, but the process was relatively straightforward. Helen learnt she was facing charges of manslaughter, driving under the influence and leaving the scene of an accident. The court date was likely to be within four months. She was allowed bail and could return to the UK.

Helen wondered what the Spanish police were thinking as they read out her rights. Did they see a heartless British tourist who had visited their country, blatantly disregarding the law before returning home, leaving heartbreak and devastation in her wake? Her father had spent years as a local magistrate. How would he have judged someone like her? She knew the facts of the case looked cold and hard.

There had been no mention of Mia's involvement. Helen's hopes that this was a good sign were quashed when Elisa said that any action against Mia depended on the outcome of Helen's trial.

"If you are convicted of driving while under the influence, then they will go after your sister for her involvement in covering up the crime and leaving the scene. Helping you, effectively. But let's not think about that… unless we have to," Elisa added quickly.

They returned to Elisa's office where they completed more paperwork and talked through the bail conditions. Someone ordered food, and Helen made a half-hearted attempt to eat. By the time they finished, it was getting dark, and she took a taxi back to her hotel. Exhausted, she fell into bed.

CHAPTER 33

It was almost 7.30 p.m. by the time Stephen said goodbye to his final patient.

"It's a shame you left it so long. I'm not that scary, am I?" Stephen winked as the patient left, then sat back and stretched. His back hurt. He stood and moved his hips from side to side, trying to loosen up. He was signed up for a golf competition on Saturday. He should have squeezed in a bit more practice, or at least gone to the driving range. He just never had time these days.

Out of the corner of his eye, he noticed the pink Post-it note again.

Keying "Simon March" into Google offered a choice of news, images, maps, videos and more amongst more than 649,000,000 results.

He tried "Dr Simon March St Faith's" and the results reduced significantly. Clicking on the first one took him to the Institute of Psychiatry. There was a profile of Simon March, a handsome, athletic-looking man in a suit and tie. Mid-forties, he guessed.

> Dr March is a highly qualified and eminent Consultant Psychiatrist who practises at St Faith's Hospital in London. He has wide experience in all fields of adult mental health and emotional disorders, and in 2005, won the Intellect and Medical Future award.

The biography went on to list his training, qualifications and accreditations.

Looks like the real deal, Stephen thought and checked his watch. It was late, but he had left a mobile number. He'd give it a try.

When he dialled the number, it went straight to voicemail. He left a brief message as he put on his coat. He was hungry and hoped Susie had cooked one of his favourites. There had been a lot of salad and fish recently.

He was dreaming about a juicy steak when his desk phone flashed. There was no one on reception to answer it now. He thought about picking up but couldn't face it. He'd had enough for one day. The light went out, and he dipped into his pocket for his car keys. The light flashed again.

"Sod it," he said out loud, pressing the intercom.

"Dr Walker speaking." He employed his most officious tone. He wasn't going to be delayed a moment longer.

"Hi, it's Simon March. Sorry I missed your call. Thanks for ringing back."

"Ah, no problem. How can I help?"

"Erm, I just want to check something. A Dr Helen Nash who works with you. Is she the same doctor who's been in the papers about the RTA in Ibiza?"

Stephen sighed, this was a journalist after all using the cover of a doctor. "How can I help?" he repeated curtly. If this guy didn't have a plausible answer within the next few seconds, he'd hang up.

"I met her in Ibiza, we had dinner together. In fact, I tried to contact her several times when I got back to the UK."

Stephen remained silent. This call had taken an unexpected turn. Had Helen mentioned meeting anyone in Ibiza? He racked his brain. No way. She wasn't over Phil. He didn't believe him, "Look if you are trying to get information for some grubby little story, you're wasting your time. I have nothing to say, this nuisance call is being recorded and I will be passing your number to the police."

The call wasn't being recorded, but he was pleased with himself for suggesting it.

"What? No, no. I met Helen in Ibiza when I was there for a few days. A few of us were there for golf – a sort of stag party. Her sister was seeing one of the guys in our group. That's how we met up."

Stephen frowned. Now he knew he was lying. Mia was married. This was getting more ridiculous by the minute.

"I would have called the police, but I wanted to speak to Helen first. Hopefully, I can help."

"In what way do you think *you* might be able to help?" Stephen asked, not bothering to hide the sarcasm in his voice.

"By setting the facts straight!" It was Simon's turn to sound terse now, as a silence hung between them. "Because I think I was with Helen the night of the accident."

"You *think* you were?"

"Look, I know how this might sound, but having read about it in the papers, it all seems to fit. I met Helen for the second time on the night before she was flying home. A few of us went out for dinner.

We were invited to a party on one of the boats in the marina. We went to the party and then got separated."

Stephen was annoyed with himself for picking up the phone. This guy was either a journalist or a crank.

"Ok, well, I suggest you tell your story to the police. I can't help I'm af—"

"She should have been prepping for her GP appraisal, but her sister had secretly persuaded her senior partner to rearrange her appraisal date."

Simon had his attention now and Stephen sat back down. "Ok," he said, "but I'm struggling to see how you might be able to help."

"It's what I've read about the accident," Simon said. "It's just not true."

CHAPTER 34

Helen decided to get up. It was only 5.30 a.m. but she'd been lying awake for God knows how long. There was no point trying to get back to sleep. She had to be at the airport soon for her flight home. She dressed and made her way downstairs. The boutique hotel felt eerie with no one else around apart from a lone receptionist at the front desk.

Outside, in the dim early morning light, Ibiza Town seemed a totally different place without the crowds and noise. She made her way down the narrow street, dwarfed by tall, whitewashed buildings which crowded in on her. Between them, vines coiled their way across, stretching high above her from balcony to balcony. Bougainvillea clung to the walls, giving the street the appearance of a garden tunnel peppered with shuttered windows.

She walked for about twenty minutes, making a mental note of a particular building or landmark to help her find her way back. She turned onto the Plaza Del Parque as the sun started to rise and was soon down by the port. There was more activity here. Men were fishing, and there were signs of life aboard several of the boats. A deeply tanned man with a thick black moustache and small canvas hat was putting out a sign advertising his fishing charters and boat rentals.

A little further ahead, she could see the marina. Improbably large boats loomed high above the landscape, some with spinning marine radars which caught the sunlight. As she walked closer to the marina, there were yet more people bustling around the boats. She saw crew members, some dressed in white shorts and polo shirts, their yachts' names embroidered on their chests. They swarmed over the decks like ants, polishing chrome, laying up tables, cleaning windows.

Some of the restaurants at the water's edge were showing signs of opening. Waiters prepared for breakfasting yachties coming onshore as tables were laid and chairs wiped down.

The sights and smells were so reminiscent of holidays she'd had in the past. She remembered one in particular – a flotilla holiday in Greece with her parents when she was about six or seven. Mia hadn't arrived yet. It was just the three of them. She recalled a little motorboat pulling alongside in the early morning light, selling all manner of delicious-looking breads and pastries. Her parents laughing as she called to the baker from the deck. She smiled at the memory, which was quickly replaced by one of Phil. They were jogging together in the cool streets of early morning Puglia before heading back to their hotel for breakfast. She remembered it had been a wonderful day, and the recollection caught her off guard for a moment. Dismissing it with a sigh, she carried on walking. She'd always enjoyed these early hours, stealing time before the world woke up. Her mind wandered back to Cambridgeshire. She could just imagine her cottage right now – the sun rising over the old apple tree, the sound of a cockerel in the distance. Her bucolic idyll, her sanctuary. It wouldn't be hers for much longer.

Her thoughts were interrupted as a group of young people disembarked from a large yacht a few yards in front of her, chattering and laughing. They were English, most in their early twenties, tanned and with lots of blonde, tousled hair. They all wore the same uniform – navy shorts and pale pink polo shirts. "Habibi" was embroidered in navy across the left breast. She glanced up at their boat. "Habibi Cairo Yacht Club" was painted in navy blue lettering across its stern. She wondered if they'd sailed all the way from Egypt. A member of the group stopped in front of Helen trying to light a cigarette, forcing two of his colleagues to wait. One of the waiting girls moved closer to him and cupped her hands around his to help.

For a moment, Helen felt like a voyeur. It was a tender moment that would have normally made her smile, but right now, it just made her feel sad and more alone than ever.

She made her way to the old town, taking in the ancient stone walls that surrounded it and noticing all the museums. She lingered, remembering her reluctance to come to Ibiza. If only she hadn't, if only she'd stuck to her guns, if only Mia hadn't been so insistent. If only...

She tried to push the thoughts away, but the overwhelming feeling that a prison on this island may actually become her home filled her with fear once again, and her pulse quickened. She forced herself to carry on walking. By the time she arrived back at her hotel, it was as if someone had waved a wand, and the town had woken up. In her room, she stepped into a steaming shower, turning her face upwards as the water gushed over her.

CHAPTER 35

Although shocked by what Simon had told him, Stephen was still reluctant to give out Helen's number.

"With all due respect, she's had all sorts of people trying to con her into interviews. Let me speak to her first. I'll give her your number, and she can get in touch with you if she wants to."

Simon agreed, and as soon as he said goodbye, Stephen tried Helen's phone. It went straight to voicemail. He then called Susie, explaining he was running late. On his way home, he tried Helen repeatedly.

He didn't know why she'd refused to change her number or get a second handset when the press attention first started. She'd now taken to sometimes turning her phone off altogether.

He wasn't going to mention Simon March to Susie. She would be on the phone to Mia and her other friends at the first opportunity, delighted to be the first with new information. By the time he got home, Susie had already eaten, leaving him to reheat supper in the microwave. She sat beside him as he ate.

"Any update on Helen?" she asked before he'd managed to take a mouthful.

He shook his head. "This is delicious," he lied, working his way through an overcooked piece of salmon and a large green salad.

She smiled. "What kept you so long?"

"Oh, don't! A very long surgery and extra emergency appointments. Then I had some calls to make."

She nodded. "This is only going to get worse, isn't it? Are you going to get another GP?"

"We're trying. Joanna is on top of it, but these things don't happen overnight."

"No. Helen left you in a right mess, hasn't she?"

Not this again, Stephen thought. The truth was that he was growing tired of constantly having to justify Helen's actions as well as his own. He was no longer even certain of how he felt. Had he been a fool to believe her? *How much could you really know someone?* he mused. And could he really believe Simon March? Had he been an idiot? Had he backed Helen when plenty of others had questioned her version of events? It wasn't only his wife and Joanna who'd lapped up the papers' accounts, reaching their own conclusions.

Once Susie had gone upstairs, Stephen went into his study and tried Helen. Again, it went straight to voicemail. On the off-chance, he called her landline, but it rang and rang. She must have turned the answer phone off too. He'd have to wait and see if he could reach her in the morning.

He went over his conversation with Simon March as he drifted off to sleep. If what he was saying was true, Helen had lied, and she and Mia had cooked up a story between them. He was glad he hadn't given Helen's number to Simon. He wanted to hear what she had to say for himself.

CHAPTER 36

The airport was busy. The queue through security snaked further than she'd ever seen it. The metal detector arch was working overtime, bleeping and flashing red lights with annoying regularity meaning that the security officers had to keep forcing passengers to step to one side and succumb to a thorough pat-down while the line behind them grew. Helen had this part of the journey down to a fine art. She didn't wear a belt or jewellery, not even an under-wired bra, making sure she made it through security without drawing unnecessary attention to herself.

She put her phone and watch alongside her bag in a tray.

"No liquids in here?"

"No," Helen shook her head at the uniformed official.

"Shoes off, please," he added, sliding another tray towards her. Helen wondered if this is what it would be like in prison. She imagined herself waiting to be issued with anonymising blue or grey sweatpants and shirt, having her photograph taken, and oh, God, would there be strip searches? She shuddered, squeezing her eyes shut to try and clear the image. When she opened them, the man was looking at her quizzically. She attempted a smile and stepped forward to take her place in the queue.

On the other side of the arch, people protested as their hand luggage was picked out from the X-ray belt. One woman, a few steps ahead of her, looked puzzled as a member of staff unzipped her bag, pulling out a large bottle of perfume and an even larger container of body lotion.

By the time she got through, her gate had already been announced. She was grateful for that. She'd learnt over the past few weeks just how ingenious some journalists and photographers were at tracking her down. The last journey home had been delayed for almost four hours, and she'd spent it watching all the waiting passengers feeling vulnerable and unprepared, suspicious of everyone, waiting for them to question her or take her photo. The days when she might have spent time browsing the shops oblivious to those around her seemed a lifetime ago.

The monitor said her flight was boarding, but airline staff were still working their way through priority passengers. It would be a little while before she was called. After years of travelling with Phil, when they always booked extra-legroom front seats, Helen now sat several rows back, tucked in by a window.

The return journey was uneventful, and to her delight, no one was booked into the seats next to her. She held her breath as she walked through arrivals, head down, praying no photographers were waiting to pounce. The way was clear. Maybe she was getting paranoid.

By the time she finally arrived home, she was aware of the tension she'd been carrying because her neck and shoulders now ached. Her post was stacked neatly on the hall table, and her mother had put fresh milk and home-made soup in the fridge. Helen made herself a cup of coffee and turned on her phone. The screen flickered into life.

Twenty-four missed calls and ten text messages. She frowned as she clicked on the list of numbers. Stephen had called her eight times. There was a call from her solicitor too and one from Caroline. She didn't recognise any of the others.

The first text was from Stephen.

Call me as soon as you get this, please.

She dialled into her voicemail.

"*Hi Helen, it's Stephen. Not sure where you are but can you give me a buzz? Call me as late as you like.*"

Stephen had left another message which was followed by a call from Caroline.

"*Hey how's things? If you change your mind about being home alone just come back and stay with me. You know you're always welcome. Hope it all went well. Call when you can. Lots of love.*"

Glancing at the time, Helen called Stephen's number. She had a horrible feeling it would be a problem with one of her patients. He'd sounded worried. She knew he'd be in surgery now and got ready to leave a message. He answered on the first ring.

"Hi, thanks for ringing back. Erm… hang on a sec, can you?" She heard him saying goodbye to a patient.

"Sorry about that. Where are you?" he asked.

"Back home. I've just got in. What's the matter?"

"Can I come round? I'll try and finish on time and come straight over."

"Yes, of course. Is everything ok?"

"See you then." He hung up.

Less than two hours later, Helen jumped when she heard Stephen knock. She ushered him in and locked the door behind him.

"Please tell me it's not Catherine Wilmot's baby," she asked.

"What? Oh. No. Nothing like that. You were spot on about that. She's absolutely fine. Back at home, all well."

Helen sighed, "Thank goodness." She ushered him into the kitchen.

"Coffee? Tea?"

He shook his head.

"Helen, look, I'll get straight to it. I've been in touch with Simon March."

Helen looked at him nonplussed. He seemed to be waiting for her to react in some way, though she didn't know how.

"He says you met in Ibiza."

Her look of puzzlement continued for a few seconds then her expression softened. "Oh, Simon, yes, sorry, I'm not sure I ever knew his surname. Nice guy. Where did you meet him?"

"He called me."

She frowned, unsure where this was going.

"He told me you'd been invited to the party on the boat," Stephen said, "but neither of you wanted to go."

Helen nodded, thinking through the series of events she remembered from the trip and where he was in it all.

Stephen had paused, as if waiting for her to give him a clue about who he was and why he had called him. She still wasn't sure of the truth, so her face remained passive, giving nothing away.

"The thing is, Helen," Stephen said, finally interrupting her thoughts, "he said a few things that don't make sense."

She still didn't reply. She couldn't articulate her thoughts at this moment.

"None of my business, of course, but apparently, your sister was having a relationship with a guy who was out there at the same time."

Helen shifted uncomfortably, she could feel her face flush .Stephen stared at her.

She swallowed hard. "Yes," she replied ,it was barely audible.

"What happened when you left the party, Helen?"

She looked directly at him. "You know what happened."

"I know what you *told* me. And what you told the police."

"Hang on. What is this? Are you accusing me of ly—"

"Simon said he met you after you'd left the party," Stephen cut in. "He bumped into you and Mia on your way home. You were in a bad way."

Helen's chest tightened, her stomach churned. She was back there again, leaving the boat, carefully, one step at a time. Moving away from the noise. Feeling sick, so sick, trying to breathe. Leaning on Mia, then a voice, a man's voice. Someone else by her side, helping her walk. *Had that been Simon?* Her legs felt weak and she leant heavily against the kitchen island.

"He met us after we left? Was he there? Oh, my God, Stephen, I can't remember."

She felt as if she might faint and wobbled slightly. Stephen pulled out a chair, urging her to sit down. He poured her a glass of water.

"Are you ok?"

"Yes, I am. Please, carry on. What did he say?"

"He saw the piece about you in the *Daily Mail*." Helen shuddered. "He'd been trying to get in touch since you left Ibiza, but apparently you'd put the blocks on that."

Helen shook her head. *Had I? I know Mia said he had asked Adam for my number but it was too much of a risk in case he tied us to that night.*

"When he saw you and Mia after the party, you could barely stand. You were throwing up. Mia said she was taking you home and would keep an eye on you."

"God, Stephen. I think I remember hearing his voice now. When I was being sick. Where was he?" She put her head in her hands, resting her elbows on her knees as she leant forward. "I wish I could remember."

"Have you ever considered you might have had your drink spiked?"

Helen shook her head, though said, "It crossed my mind, but Mia wasn't well the next day either. It was probably something we both ate."

"But you've seen the after-effects of GHB, haven't you?" Stephen continued.

"Yes, of course. In A&E, we had a whole raft of kids in one after another. It was endemic in that area of London."

"So, don't you think, from what you've told me, that it could have been that?"

"Has Simon suggested that? I don't understand. What about Mia's symptoms? They were enough to wake her in the night, and she had the nausea too. If you mean the memory loss, Caroline says it's my brain trying to shield itself from the accident."

She was looking directly at him, but it was if she wasn't seeing him. She was replaying the events of the night that she could recall.

"I've got Simon March's number. I think you need to call him."

She nodded, "Yes, I will. I'll tell Elisa too."

Stephen shifted in his seat. "Erm… actually, Helen, there's something else." He kept his eyes locked on hers as he cleared his throat. "He said you *weren't* driving. You couldn't– you were incapable. He was really concerned and suggested you go to hospital, but Mia was adamant she'd take care of you. He helped you into the passenger seat. You were barely conscious."

CHAPTER 37

Stephen answered the door and ushered Caroline in. She kissed him on both cheeks. "How lovely to see you again. It's been ages!"

"Yes, it has," he replied, leaning towards her and lowering his voice, "I hope you didn't mind me calling. I just thought you'd be the best person."

"God, no! Of course. Where is she?" Caroline asked. Stephen nodded his head towards the sitting room and whispered, "She's not great."

Helen was sitting in a chair by the window, a blanket around her shoulders. The room was warm, but she looked freezing, her skin a pale-blue hue – it looked like shock. Caroline walked over and hugged her friend tightly.

"I'm so sorry. I can't believe you've come all the way here, again!" Helen said.

Caroline smiled, and said softly, "I was nearby, I had a conference in Cambridge, remember?" Helen shook her head. "I'm sure it wouldn't have registered. Not with everything else going on. Darling, it was serendipity." She turned towards Stephen. "When Stephen called, I was delighted to come. I was just saying it's been so long since we were all together."

"Can I get you a drink, a cup of tea or something?" he offered.

"No, Stephen," Helen cut in. "You've done enough. Please, go home, and thank you. I really appreciate it. I'll bring Caroline up to speed and call Elisa first thing in the morning."

"Ok, if you're sure." Stephen picked up his jacket, and Caroline followed him into the hall.

"Blimey, she looks terrible," she whispered. "What on earth's happened now?"

"I'm going to let her tell you," he replied quietly. "It's a bloody mess."

Caroline closed the door behind him and turned back to Helen. "Before anything else, you've got to eat and drink something. I need to, even if you don't." Helen nodded and started to stand up, but Caroline pushed her back down, "No, I'll order something."

"No one delivers out here," Helen replied.

Caroline shook her head, laughing, "Of course they don't. I forgot you live in the back of beyond. Ok, what have you got?" She found a quiche in the freezer and put it into the oven then pulled up a chair next to Helen.

"Right. Tell me the latest then."

Helen recounted the tale. As soon as Caroline heard Simon's name, she almost choked. "No way! I know him really well. We worked at the Maudsley together. He's a brilliant psychiatrist. A great guy too. Why have you never mentioned him?"

Helen shook her head. "He was, er… is a lovely guy, I agree, but I sort of forgot all about him after, after…" Caroline nodded sympathetically. "I spoke to him this evening, just before Stephen called you," she went on quietly. Her hands were clasped in her lap, but she couldn't stop them shaking. Caroline waited patiently for her to continue. "He saw me with Mia after we left the party. Said he helped me into the car. I was barely conscious." She pulled her gaze from her wine glass to look directly at Caroline. Tears were running freely down her face. "He…" she faltered, "he…said Adam helped get me into the passenger seat and watched Mia drive us away."

Caroline gasped loudly. "Sorry," she whispered and took another large sip of wine, forcing herself to sit back in the chair. She'd been perching on the edge, her body tense, willing Helen to talk. They sat in silence as the enormity of Simon's claim dawned on them.

"Mia was driving," Caroline said finally.

"So he says," Helen replied.

"But you don't doubt him? I mean, why would he say that?"

Helen shook her head. "I'm not saying I doubt him. There's other stuff too, things that make me think…oh, I just don't want to…" Caroline could see she was torn. Something was holding her back. She guessed Mia would be at the heart of it.

"You don't want to believe your sister could do this to you." Caroline finished the sentence for her. "What other stuff?"

"He said Adam was in the car too."

Caroline blinked, taking it in. "What?"

"He said Mia persuaded Adam to come back to the villa with her."

"Oh my God, you've got witnesses!" Caroline perched at the front of her seat again. "Why don't the police already know this?"

"They didn't speak to Simon. He'd left the party well before we did."

Caroline paused for a few seconds trying to make sense of it all. Helen closed her eyes and massaged her temples.

"What about Adam?" Caroline asked.

"He never mentioned it in his statement. Mia will be behind that. She wouldn't have wanted him to be linked to her. The CCTV evidence is definitely just of Mia and I."

"So what are you saying? Simon's wrong?"

"Simon said he saw us near the car." Helen squeezed her eyes tight shut and pinched the bridge of her nose.

"Are you ok?" Caroline asked. The colour had drained from Helen's face. "Yes, fine. Just, you know …"

Caroline nodded.

"I'm confused, Hels." Caroline looked puzzled "What has that got to do wi—"

"The CCTV only covers the marina." Helen said "The car was outside."

There was silence for a few moments as Caroline processed the information. "Fucking hell," she said finally.

Helen gave a deep sigh. "Caroline, can you make yourself believe something that you know, deep down, isn't true?"

The expectant look on Helen's face told her friend this wasn't a rhetorical question.

"Most definitely. The brain creates false memories all the time. We have all experienced that to some extent or another. But suppressing your reactions is not the best way of coping. Sometimes, we suppress a natural reaction or thought to protect ourselves. In some cases, we suppress to protect someone else," she added, watching Helen carefully.

Helen's body language changed. She was frowning and sat up straighter.

"If Mia was driving, it's as bad as it gets. She definitely *had* been drinking. She's said so in her statement too."

"Wasn't she banned from driving at the time too?"

Helen nodded.

"You said there were other things?" Caroline asked

"What?"

"You said 'things', plural. What did you mean?" Caroline pushed her again, and when her friend hesitated, Caroline placed a gentle hand on her knee. "It's ok," she urged.

Helen took a deep breath.

"Simon was in Ibiza with friends for a stag party. We met when Mia and I went into the old town at the beginning of our break. We had a couple of evenings with them. I got on well with Simon but hadn't exchanged contact details or anything. We probably would have done, but then, well…"

Caroline nodded.

"When I spoke to him tonight, he told me he'd tried to get in touch when he got back to London." She bowed her head, adding quietly, "He wanted to find out if I was ok after that last night."

Caroline nodded again. That sounded like Simon.

"He said he hadn't even known my surname, so got hold of Mia's details through Adam. When Mia met Adam on that first night, they hit it off. Or at least that's what I thought then …" She paused.

Caroline knew to say nothing, not wanting to break the spell. Helen was coming to terms with what she'd learnt. Her subconscious was being unlocked, whether she liked it or not.

"Simon confirmed that Adam and Mia had known each other way before Ibiza. I had suspected that was the case but it's even more involved than I'd thought. In fact, they'd been having a relationship for several months. Adam is married too."

"Wow!" Caroline drained her glass.

"When Simon finally got in touch with Mia, she assured him I'd been fine after the drive home; it was simply a bug. She also said I didn't want to see him again and that I had told her not to give him my number. That I was still grieving for Phil."

"What a bitch," spluttered Caroline. "Sorry," she said immediately but Helen just shook her head.

"He wasn't put off that easily. He wanted to hear it from me. He said he thought we had a connection."

"Mia must have been panicking like hell. Did she ever tell you that Simon had been in touch?"

"Sort of. She said he'd been trying to find me but that we needed to put as much distance between us and Ibiza as possible."

"I bet she bloody did," Caroline couldn't stop herself.

"The thing is, Caroline, when I think back to that night, the night of the accident, it doesn't fit. There's still gaps but I can definitely remember myself braking. I was braking so hard but nothing happening. That's what I told the police."

"Yes but think about it!" Caroline sounded agitated, "you've probably done that many times as a passenger too, Hellie, it's instinctive! God I was in the car with my seventeen-year-old nephew the week after he'd passed his test. It was absolutely terrifying. I spent most of the journey pushing my feet into the footwell. I think we do it automatically whether we're driving or not."

Caroline saw Helen grow even paler. Her chest was rising and falling quickly.

"After the accident I noticed a graze on my chest. It was just here," Helen laid her fingers below her right collarbone.

"It was on a diagonal and not quite a bruise. The skin wasn't broken, but it was red and sore."

Caroline nodded, not sure where this was leading.

"It looked exactly like the mark a seat belt would leave, you know, if we'd braked suddenly."

"But that doesn't make sense," Caroline interrupted. "If that was the case, the belt would have been on the other side."

"No, it wouldn't. It would have been here." Helen tapped the right side of her chest again. Caroline frowned. "But . . "

"Left-hand drive, remember?" Helen interrupted.

The friends stared at each other.

"Oh God, of course, You'll have been in the right-side seat – the driver's side in the UK – which would account for your false recall that you were the driver." Caroline clapped her hand over her mouth.

"I just can't believe that even Mia would go this far. I know this is horrendous, Helen, but you've got to face facts. Mia was driving, and she's letting you take the rap for it." Caroline had never felt so sorry for her friend. She looked broken, but there was too much at stake now.

"You can't protect her this time."

CHAPTER 38

Helen insisted on waiting until morning before calling her lawyers. Caroline had tried to persuade her to do it straight away, before Mia had a chance to get involved but Helen was adamant.

They talked for hours. Caroline was more open and honest than she'd had ever dared to be before about Mia. She told Helen that her sister's personality traits, mood swings and lack of respect for those who cared for her all pointed towards something much more than just bad behaviour.

"I'd say she has antisocial personality disorder. In fact there are enough red flags to suggest she meets the criteria for psychopathy," Caroline said. She didn't need to spell it out. Helen had always known Mia had shown psychopathic tendencies. She told Caroline she had always chosen to ignore it, hoping she'd change. As soon as she admitted it, she felt a wave of relief at finally sharing it.

"It's not your fault. Even the greatest doctors can't cure everything," Caroline said as she hugged Helen.

While they talked, they had totally forgotten about the quiche which had burnt to a cinder in the Aga. Lightheaded from the wine and fuelled with adrenaline, they both managed a smile as Caroline rustled up beans on toast.

Caroline was dressed and ready to leave by first light. She crept downstairs, carrying her shoes, stepping lightly onto each stair. She opened the door to the kitchen as quietly as she could and was surprised to see Helen already there, sitting in the chair by the window.

"Oh! I assumed you'd still be asleep."

"Good morning," Helen gave a weak smile. "Did you sleep ok?"

"Very well. I'd forgotten how quiet it is here.

"You stayed a lot after Phil died," Helen replied. Caroline nodded. "You're a great friend, Caroline, really the best. I don't know what I'd do without you."

"Don't be silly. We'll always be there for each other. Now, are you sure I can't stay today? I can come to your lawyers with you, drive you to see Meghan and Roger?"

"No, I'm certain. You need to get back to work."

"How is today going to play out?" Caroline asked. "Will you ring your Spanish lawyer first? They're an hour ahead, aren't they?"

"I'll call her after I've spoken to my parents. I think they deserve to be the first to know."

"Ok, but please, promise me, don't contact Mia?"

Helen's shoulders slumped. "How am I going to explain this to my parents Caroline? How can I tell them that Mia has lied throughout and was clearly prepared to stay quiet as I face a jail sentence. Has Mia really been able to do this to me?

"I know this is tough, but you are strong," Caroline cut in. "You're going to have to stay resolute. Mia will just try and manipulate the situation as she has throughout this whole sorry affair."

Caroline put her hand on Helen's shoulder. "It isn't easy for you, but Mia won't be able to help herself. I'm not being melodramatic when I say this is your life at stake here. It's not simply a case of you standing up for Mia. You need to stop protecting her and start protecting yourself and everything you hold dear instead. It will be even harder for you in the long run if you don't hand this problem over to the authorities. I'm going to get going, but Stephen's going to call in. Please don't be alone. It isn't good. But promise me you won't contact—"

"I won't," Helen assured her. "Now, go. The M11 will be a nightmare if you leave it any later. You've been amazing. I'll be fine. Just go!" Helen walked her towards the front door.

"Thanks again." The pair hugged, and Caroline noticed how thin she was under her sweater.

As soon as she was in the car, Caroline texted Simon March.

Hey, long time no speak. Hope all well and you're enjoying the new post. When you get a minute, could you give me a call about our mutual friend, Helen Nash. X

Her sat nav told her she'd be at the office in seventy minutes. If that was correct, she'd arrive in plenty of time for her first patient. She might even have time to stop for a coffee. She tuned into Radio Four. The health secretary was being subjected to a grilling.

"*Referral rates are increasing, staff teams are stretched to breaking point and yet, this government's attitude to mental health services doesn't seem to have changed, despite your promises. What do you have in place to deal with it?*"

Her phone rang, cutting through the radio.

"Good morning, Caroline." Simon's voice was exactly as she remembered.

"Hey, Simon, thanks for calling back. How lovely to hear you again."

"I couldn't believe it when I got your message. How are you?"

"All good, thanks. I hear you've been promoted."

"Keeps me busy. So… you know Helen Nash?"

"Very well, actually. My closest friend. We were at med school together and shared a house for a large chunk of it."

"Ok. So, I guess you've been pretty involved in this whole situation. An absolute mess by the sounds of things. How's it got to this stage? Her believing she was driving? Do you know the whole story?"

"I don't think so," Caroline admitted.

"So, you don't think she's telling the truth?"

"I didn't say that. Helen wouldn't dream of lying. It's just who she might be covering for."

"Her sister," Simon said.

"Yes. They're like chalk and cheese, but Helen has always been extremely protective of Mia. The family have given her everything, and in return, all she's given them is grief. She's a master puppeteer, pushing everyone's buttons and pulling strings to get what she wants. Showering her with love and kindness just hasn't been enough. There's always been some drama or another with Mia, right from an early age – bullying, drugs, shoplifting and the rest." Caroline didn't hold back.

"So, what's her situation now? She's a bit old to be a wild child."

"Oh, on the surface of it, she's turned over a new leaf. Married to a wealthy guy, playing lady of the manor, but she's still bloody manipulative and controlling. From what I've witnessed over the years, she never takes responsibility for her actions either."

"I think I'm getting the picture," Simon interjected. "Lack of empathy and narcissism by any chance?"

"Hell yes! Of course, the narcissism is under the radar. She might play charming, but she's convinced of her own superiority and believes she can play everyone."

"So, you're suggesting ASPD?"

"Without a doubt. Until last night I'd never actually voiced that out loud. Helen's no fool, Simon. She just hasn't wanted to face the truth about Mia. After hearing what you said, there's no way she can defend her sister any longer, but she is reluctant to let her take the blame. I know her. I've tried to explain that Mia has a problem."

"So what have you told Helen?"

"That her sister was ticking far too many boxes on the psychopath list.

"And she accepted that?"

"She said she did; I'm still worried she'll ignore it. I think it will take a lot for her to tell the truth."

"What? She'll take the rap for driving?"

"Possibly. Listen, Helen's got a blind spot when it comes to Mia. Helen's husband used to say the same. Mia never liked Phil and she can't stand me."

"Mia even used Phil's death to her advantage," Caroline continued. "On the surface of it, she played the supportive sister, but it was really all about her being in control. I'd even say she was gaslighting. When Phil died, I went to stay with Helen. Mia hated that. She wanted to be seen as the number-one carer. It was always about her."

Simon paused, as if digesting the information. "Has Helen ever mentioned having her drink spiked?" he asked.

"Not to me. Why?"

"Because it had been. If you'd seen her that night, there'd have been no doubt in your mind either. Looking back on it, it seems so obvious but I don't know Helen and just accepted Mia's explanation that her sister wasn't well. But what I didn't tell Helen when we spoke yesterday was what I'd heard from Adam."

Caroline frowned as she passed the sign for a large drive-through Starbucks. She'd love a cappuccino right now, but there was no way she was interrupting this conversation, "Go on."

"Adam is a right jerk, if I'm honest. He was a friend of the groom, someone he used to work with. He and Mia were an item before Ibiza, although they pretended they were meeting for the first time."

"Yes, Helen told me that. It sounds like something Mia would have cooked up. Dragged her sister out on the pretence of a holiday for her. She's a piece of work."

"On our last night, Adam got pissed again and told us a bit about it but with the caveat of what goes on tour, stays on tour, etcetera, etcetera. Just a total knob. We'd all had enough of him."

She nodded silently as Stephen continued.

"He clearly enjoyed a bit of coke. He offered us all some most nights, and he and Mia made no secret of the fact they'd been enjoying it before the party. We'd only been on the boat for a short while, but you could see how it was all going down. Ian felt uncomfortable for being involved in such a sleazy party just a few weeks before his wedding. I said I'd be delighted to leave with him."

Caroline listened intently.

"The party was getting busier and busier. Far too many people packed in like sardines, you could hardly breathe. It was dreadful. Ian suggested we go back to the marina. It was only Adam who wanted to stay. He said that he and Mia were having a great time, and he'd meet us at the marina a little later."

There was a long pause. Caroline wondered if they'd lost connection, but then he spoke again.

"And this is what I didn't feel I could say last night. Apparently, Mia thought it would be a good idea to get Helen to relax a bit, allow them to enjoy the party a while longer."

Caroline could hardly bear to hear it.

"She put GHB in Helen's drink."

"No…No way!"

"Yes! He said she'd done it for a laugh, not a full dose, just a 'tickle' as Adam put it."

"For fuck's sake."

"I know, pretty shocking, isn't it? With the seventy-two-hour window for toxicology screening, there's no way of proving it, but it certainly fit with what I saw. More to the point, it would offer an alternative as to why she looked out of it on the CCTV. After a small glass of champagne earlier in the evening she refused everything. She always made it clear she was driving and stuck to soft drinks.

"Is Mia still seeing Adam?"

"I have no idea. I last saw him at the wedding where he was with his wife and kids. He kept out of my way, probably terrified I'd drop him in it. I hardly spoke to him, but I had no idea about the accident at that stage. I only found out about it when I read the papers."

"Helen needs to know all of this, Simon. You'll have to tell the police."

"I know. There was always a part of me that thought that idiot Adam might just be making it up, bragging maybe. But it does all fit.

To be honest, Caroline, I really liked her when we met. I wanted to see her again, but when I heard that she wasn't keen on me and not ready for another relationship, I had to respect that."

"And it was Mia who told you that?" Caroline asked.

"Yep, she was as clear as crystal. Helen absolutely didn't want me to contact her."

CHAPTER 39

After Caroline left, Helen replayed her conversation with Simon over and over in her head.

Torn between despair at Mia's betrayal and rage as she thought about the heartache this had caused her parents, Helen decided she needed to speak to her sister.

Despite her promise to Caroline and matter how things looked, she needed to hear it from Mia herself. She wasn't going to go behind her back without at least giving her a chance to answer Simon's claims. Part of her still clung to the hope that there might be a reasonable explanation.

Mia was quiet at first. It was only when she relayed his comment about Mia driving that she reacted.

"Hels, Hels, listen to me," Mia cut in. "I didn't want it to come to this. I just wanted to protect you. I…" she sounded uncharacteristically tense. "The thing is, Helen, you'd had way more to drink than you realised. I think the cocktails were strong, it had been a long night."

"Hang on," Helen interrupted. "Are you now trying to say I *was* drunk? After all this time? The CCTV is right?" Her head was spinning. She squeezed her eyes shut, desperately trying to remember.

"Yes," Mia sounded as if she was crying now. Helen wished she hadn't done this over the phone.

"I didn't want Simon to see you getting into the car," she sniffled. "He could see you were pissed. I know it was stupid of me, but I genuinely thought you'd be ok to drive. You go so slowly and carefully, and I knew the roads would be quiet. I didn't want Simon worrying, so I told him you were fine, it was just a bug and I would get you home. He didn't know about my driving ban, so I drove to the end of the road, and as soon as we were out of sight, we swapped seats.

"Hels, I just wanted to protect you. I know it was wrong to say you weren't drunk, but I made my statement and couldn't go back on it. I've wanted to tell you, honestly, I have. It's been awful, holding all of this," she let out a loud sob. When Helen didn't reply she continued, "I just didn't know what to do. I knew if I got stopped driving with the ban and no insurance and everything, I'd be in so much trouble."

"Mia, please don't cry," Helen began.

"I was terrified, Helen. It was stupid, I know that now."

"So that puts paid to the seatbelt theory," Helen said, thinking aloud.

"What?" Mia blew her nose.

"Remember that graze on my chest after the accident?" Helen replied.

"Yes?"

"It was just something Caroline said about you driving."

"Caroline? What are you involving her for?" There was an edge to Mia's voice now, and Helen immediately regretted mentioning her friend.

"I didn't involve her. She just came over last night, and we were discussing it. It turns out she knows Simon."

"Oh, how convenient," Mia snapped.

"It doesn't matter now anyway."

"No, go on, tell me."

"Really, Mia, it's irrelevant."

"It's not irrelevant if it involves me. Tell me."

"Fine. When Simon said I wasn't driving, I thought the graze must have been a result of the seatbelt tightening when we had the accident. Caroline said it wouldn't have been on that side of my body if I was driving."

There was a brief pause before Mia replied, her voice soft again, "Oh, well, now that you know the truth, I admit that that was down to me." Helen heard her take a deep breath. "When I pulled over for us to change seats, I slammed the brakes on. I hit them far too hard. I was just in such a panic having bumped into Simon, I nearly put us both through the windscreen. I had the same mark but on the other side." She sniffled. "I'm so sorry. I've just messed everything up again, as I always do. I was only trying to make things better. I wouldn't blame you if you never spoke to me again."

Helen was surprised her sister's tears were still flowing. It was so out of character.

"So that's it? All of it?" The whole story?"

"Yes, I've just told you."

"Adam wasn't there?" Helen asked quietly.

"What?"

"Was Adam with us, in the car?"

Mia hesitated.

"Mia?" Helen persisted

"He, er, he caught up with us when we were walking to the car."

"Was he WITH us Mia?" Helen shouted. "When we hit José Catrimano?"

Frustrated, Helen was shaking. She wished she'd gone to see her so she could look her in the eyes.

"Mia?"

Mia took a deep breath. "So… he was in the car *at first*, but not when you hit the motorcyclist. When I got out to swap the driving with you, he got out too. I'd wanted him to come back to the villa with me and that was the reason I didn't tell you about him being there. I knew you wouldn't approve. It was my last night. I'd had such a lovely time with Adam and didn't want it to end. You know I'd been so unhappy. I thought my marriage was finished. Anyway, he got cold feet and said he ought to spend the evening with the stag party and left. "

"I don't understand why you didn't tell the police this though. My disapproval was hardly relevant in the circumstances." Helen questioned.

"I know, I know. I was just so frightened and I panicked," Mia sniffed. "Being behind the wheel would have meant so much trouble for me. Even if it was for the shortest distance. It was stupid, of course I know that. And Adam being in the back of the car for a few minutes was hardly that important, was it? We made a pact to keep him out of it because it seemed to make the best of a bad situation."

"Oh how kind of you" Helen snapped. "I guess the truth might have led to his wife finding out he'd been on his way to stay the night with his girlfriend. I don't suppose Chris would have been delighted about that either." Helen heard Mia take a sharp intake of breath.

"Helen, don't. This isn't like you, please don't be mean to me. I stopped seeing him, just like I promised you."

Helen closed her eyes.

"So now you know the whole story, Hels and it doesn't change anything does it? Unless you want to tell the police I drove the car for a few yards, banned, under the influence and without insurance. Or maybe just tell Chris that Adam was with us. That would be super helpful wouldn't it" Her voice was dripping with sarcasm.

"Ok, Mia, there's no need for that."

"Please say you won't mention any of this? And you won't change your statement?"

Helen sighed. "If this really is it? The whole truth? I'm not going to discover anything else?"

"I swear to you Hels, I swear. This is the absolute truth. Please tell me you aren't going to say anything."

Helen closed her eyes as she contemplated their conversation. She was back to square one; the bare facts were still the same. She had killed the young man, everything else was likely to cause even more damage and heartache. She pictured her parents' faces. They'd been through enough already. What was the point in changing her story?

"Please Hels," Mia asked again.

"I guess not," Helen replied.

CHAPTER 40

As she said goodbye to her last patient for the morning, Caroline sat back and stretched. She was exhausted and it was only just lunchtime with a whole afternoon schedule ahead of her.

What a morning. Simon's dramatic revelation and then scraping into clinic with literally seconds to spare after getting stuck in traffic had not made for the most relaxing start to her day.

She could do with a walk after being at her desk for so long. Her next client was a tricky one. She was recovering from postpartum psychosis, and Caroline was concerned that her treatment plan wasn't working as well as expected. A young woman with her life ahead of her, who felt as if she had nothing to live for. Caroline was always good at drawing a line between work and her private life, but it was proving difficult today. Helen was occupying a lot of her headspace, and she was too close to the situation to be able to detach herself and assess it properly.

She changed into trainers and shoved her phone into her pocket. Stepping out into the busy Marylebone Street, she walked towards the park. A line of children were making their way along the pavement in identical school uniforms, chattering excitedly as they clutched little clipboards. A teacher led at the front with two more following at the rear. Caroline smiled as they passed.

She sighed as she thought of Helen. She must have spoken to her parents by now and could only imagine how they must all be feeling. It was going to get a whole lot worse.

She did a lap of the park – it was all she had time for – but it made a difference. The fresh scent of lime trees amongst newly mown grass was enough to lift anyone. On the way back, she picked up a sandwich from her favourite Italian deli. She would just have time to enjoy it before her afternoon's appointments.

As she walked through the main door, the receptionist caught her eye and pointed towards the phone she was holding.

"I'll just see if Dr Thomas is free." She muted the call, "It's Mia Carlyle. Do you want to take it?"

Caroline's pulse quickened. Had something happened to Helen? Mia never called her. She nodded eagerly and pointed to her office.

"I'll take it in there."

She picked up the handset before she'd even sat down.

"Mia?"

"How fucking dare you!" Mia's tone was guttural. Before Caroline had a chance to reply, she started again, "Who do you think you are? Interfering, brainwashing my sister into saying things she didn't need to. You're not helping anyone."

Caroline leant forward and activated the record switch. She'd usually go through the process of saying the conversation was being recorded. Not this time.

"I bet you've just loved this, haven't you?" Mia yelled. "Siding with your fucking friend to say I was driving. Well, let me tell you. I was *NOT*! There is nothing to prove that either. All I've been doing is looking after my sister, and if you wanted what was best for her, you'd be trying to do the same rather than filling her brain with poison. You've always been a grade-A bitch."

"Mia, you need to calm down. Of course I want the best for Helen. I want to ensure she—"

"Calm down? Would you feel like calming down if your sister's so-called friend, who wasn't even there, decides to rewrite history and drag anyone she can into backing her version of events? I'm not one of your fucking nut-job patients. You can't talk me into believing something that isn't true."

Helen had clearly spoken to Mia. Caroline shut her eyes as Mia ranted.

"For your information, *Car-o-line*," Mia spat, "all I have ever wanted was to make sure Hels was ok. Yes, your weird mate Simon might have seen me pull away, but she was driving when we hit that boy, make no mistake about it. But rather than running to the police and making everything worse, I have been trying to protect her. It was an accident. It won't bring him back. It won't stop her feeling guilty. What happened was a fucking accident!"

Caroline blinked as Mia screamed into the phone. Thank God she wasn't on loudspeaker. Caroline took a breath and changed tack with a softer tone, trying to sound calm, measured and reasonable, "Mia, listen. I know how much your sister means to you, and I know you'd do everything in your power to protect her, but don't you think you'd be doing best by her to simply tell the truth? This is a terrible situation, and I know how much it must be destroying your family but—"

"No! You listen to *me*!" she yelled. "I *am* telling the truth. Apart from her not being over the limit, because she probably was. She had been drinking, and you know what a lightweight she is. She'd only need a few to tip her over the edge, and she'd been on the cocktails that night, no matter what she might have said. But I have stood by her and backed her up when said she only had one small glass. Your mate Simon wasn't even at the party, so whatever bollocks he said is complete hearsay."

She wasn't going to give way; Mia was prepared to spin lie upon lie. Caroline needed to wrap the conversation up. She was going to be late for her next patient.

"Ok, fine. It'll be down to the court to decide."

"Except it won't, smart arse, because nothing's changed. Helen doesn't want this to go any further. She's not going to mention it to her lawyers. You need to butt out and mind your own business. Tell your little friend Simon to keep his opinions to himself too. She was my sister long before she was your friend, don't forget!"

Mia's possessiveness and egocentricity had never been more blatantly evident. The pathological lies, lack of remorse and even attempting to make out that she had been shielding Helen was unbelievable. Caroline decided to give it one last try.

"Mia, I am sure it was done for all the right intentions. You wanted to protect her, I totally get that, but this situation is far too serious to lie about. You've got to tell the truth. It was an accident, one with a dreadful, sad outcome but an accident nonetheless."

"She isn't changing her account. We aren't changing anything just because you say so. I'm actually doing you the courtesy of telling you that rather than doing it behind your back, which is clearly how you like to operate. My family does not need your interference," she snarled. "You think you're so bloody clever but—"

"I know you spiked her drink," Caroline said quickly, "and I know you panicked because she'd reacted badly and I know you got the GHB from the guy you had been seeing and I know you'd been seeing him long before Ibiza." Caroline hadn't drawn breath. She'd launched a full round of ammunition down the line, not stopping until she'd used every last bullet. Her words hung in the air, and she braced herself for a torrent of abuse.

But the reply, when it came, wasn't that at all. Her voice was different. She sounded more like the old Mia. Mia the innocent victim.

"You don't know that."

Just four words, a denial, but she sounded rattled.

"Mia, there will be an investigation. You can't hide from it." Caroline wasn't going to back off now.

"The guys on the stag night all know about the GHB. Adam told them. You may have kept it from the police up to this point, but not anymore. They'll have to give a statement."

"Hels hasn't mentioned anything to me about this. Why would Adam even say that?" Mia challenged.

"I don't know Mia. Why *would* he say something like that if it wasn't true? And the reason Helen hasn't mentioned it is because she doesn't know - yet. She doesn't know just how bad you really are. But she will. And believe me, the more pieces of this jigsaw we can put together for her, the more she will remember. And remember she will – it's just a case of when.

"How do you think she is going to feel when she realises you, of all people, spiked her drink? The little sister she has spent most of her life supporting and standing up for – and God knows she shouldn't have – has stood back and let her take the blame for a hideous accident. Something she didn't even do. If you really care anything for her, for God's sake, do the decent thing and confess."

"You've always been jealous of me, haven't you, Caroline?" Mia spat and hung up, leaving Caroline holding the phone.

CHAPTER 41

Caroline had barely a minute before her next appointment. It took all her professional expertise to divorce herself from the conversation with Mia and devote her attention to the young woman in front of her.

She saw patients back to back all afternoon, and when the last one finally left, she closed her eyes and allowed herself to think over Mia's call. She'd been cornered but clearly wasn't going to give up the fight. Caroline sighed. Helen was never going to stop protecting her sister. Despite their close friendship, Caroline knew she wouldn't be able to persuade Helen to change her attitude towards Mia. There was no point trying to convince her of Mia's classic psychopathic traits, that she was clearly damaged, that she didn't think or behave like most people. Helen already knew it, but she was too trauma-bonded to deal with her sister in a rational and logical way. Mia was a master of manipulation and knew exactly how to play her.

Armed with the recording of Mia's phone call, she decided to visit Meghan and Roger. It would be painful for them, and she was risking Helen's wrath by going behind her back. But she didn't have a choice.

She decided not to call ahead, gambling on them being at home as she drove the same long journey she'd made earlier that day, back down the M11. She needed to do this face to face and didn't want to risk giving Mia the heads up. When Meghan opened the door two hours later, Caroline couldn't hide her relief.

"Oh, Caroline, how lovely to see you, come in. Roger, look who's here. Sit down. Can I get you a—"

"Meghan, I've come to see you because there's something you need to know," Caroline couldn't contain herself. She was tentative at first as she outlined what she knew about Mia's relationship with Adam, the fact that she'd spiked Helen's drink and the ultimate betrayal of her sister. Meghan and Roger made it as easy as they could for her as they listened attentively. There were no tears, no recriminations, just passive acceptance.

"I know this must be so difficult for you," Caroline said once she'd finished. "I'm so sorry."

"No. I am very grateful for you coming to see us, dear. We both are," Meghan chimed in, taking control of the conversation. "I think we are beyond feeling shocked about Mia. You've known this family long enough to know Mia has had everything Helen had, maybe more, in fact, as we all kept making allowances for her. It's been like batting our heads against a brick wall. Helen went off to med school; Mia went off the rails. We've been used to the lies, jealousy and spite, but this… And against a sister who has done nothing but look out for her. She's evil! There was never any reason for her behaviour as far as we could see, and believe me, we have asked ourselves what was wrong, time and time again. But maybe it's been my fault."

"No!" Roger's voice was firm. He had been sitting quietly next to his wife. "No Meghan. It's not your fault."

Caroline looked from one to the other.

Meghan continued, "Yes, I think I always favoured Helen. No matter how hard I tried with Mia, I know I wasn't the same. Helen looked like me; we made her. But from a very early age, Mia was challenging. We all made allowances, but Helen made more than you and I did, Roger. She even tried to take the blame once when Mia lashed out at a friend and cut her eye. I should have been stronger. I know I wanted to be the same mother to both of them, but I don't think… I just don't think I was."

"Meghan, there is no blame here." It was Caroline's turn now.

Roger reached over and took his wife's hand. "I've told her that," he said. "When Mia was younger she could be so unkind, cruel even, and just didn't seem to understand how wrong it was, no matter how hard we tried to explain. Remember the rabbit at her birthday party?" Megan shuddered at the memory. "She's had so many chances. Far more than she ever should have and certainly more than we would ever have done with Helen. But we felt, that with her start in life, well, you know…"

Caroline nodded as he continued.

"Meghan saw it more than I did, of course," he said, rubbing his wife's hand. "She was at home with her more, so I probably don't even know the half of it. Helen cut Mia more slack than she ever deserved. I don't mean any disrespect here, but Mia played you both so well darling."

"I think we both knew she was more than just a rebellious younger sibling, but we didn't want to let her down," Meghan murmured.

"You didn't," Caroline interjected. "Professionally speaking, what Mia has, I suspect, is a personality disorder. It doesn't emerge out of nowhere. In my experience, all psychopathic adults show signs during adolescence or childhood. Mia would always have turned out like this, no matter who raised her."

"Psychopathic?" Megan repeated the term in a half-whisper.

"The layman's term for it, Meghan," Caroline continued. "It's a label, that's all. Greatly misused but it applies to her, for sure. She was born this way, not made. Nothing either of you have done has caused it. Just because someone is labelled a psychopath doesn't make them a serial killer!

"Children, even badly behaved ones, are viewed as maintaining some fundamental innocence, whereas psychopaths are seen as fundamentally depraved. Neither stereotype is absolutely true. Children, just like adults, are capable of cruelty and violence, and even highly psychopathic people are not cruel or violent all of the time. Mia shows narcissistic traits too – she probably always has." Caroline tried to spell it out for them as simply as she could.

"What she has done, how she is prepared to stand back and let Helen take the blame at the expense of her reputation, her career, maybe even her home, is incomprehensible to us, but it feels very different to someone like Mia. She's wired differently."

"Helen's going to take the blame, isn't she?" Meghan asked, looking directly at Caroline.

"Yes, I think she might."

"She's not!" Roger's tone was firm. "I'm calling her lawyer myself, right now."

CHAPTER 42

"I've got Belinda Stokes on the line for you."

Adam frowned, trying to recall the name. He'd just got back to his desk after a particularly boozy client lunch and was struggling to stay focused.

"From where?"

"She gave me the impression you knew her," the executive assistant sighed.

She was exasperated with him, as usual. He knew she was sick of him stumbling back into the office like this, but little did she know she wouldn't have to deal with it much longer – her P45 was waiting for her at the end of the month and he'd find another bimbo to take her place… one with a less condescending tone.

"Can you just take her details and I'll get back to her," he replied, unsuccessfully trying to stifle a hiccup. He needed another coffee. He really shouldn't have hit the red wine quite so hard. He had to be out again in a couple of hours. It was his wife's birthday, and they were meeting his in-laws for an early dinner before the theatre.

"She's already called once."

"Ok, ok, I'll call her back, just not right now."

"And did you see the message on your desk about Inspector Grayford?"

"Yes, I was just about to call him. I don't know him either. Did he say what it was about?"

"Something about working with Spanish police. He didn't go into specifics. It's too late to call him now, anyway. If you'd read the message, you'd have seen he was only available until three. He's back in the office from seven tomorrow morning."

Adam looked at his watch. It was 3.40 p.m. He went in search of a coffee, taking the long way round to the kitchen so he didn't pass his boss. He managed to get through the rest of the afternoon pretending to be absorbed in work. He surfed the internet, scrolled through his Instagram and sent a few emails. He'd catch up on the calls tomorrow. As soon as the clock showed 5.30, he picked up his bag and left for the day, going via the restroom to splash his face with cold water and gargle with mouthwash.

His wife was waiting for him in reception.

"Hello, gorgeous," he winked at her as she stood up. "All ready to celebrate your big day?"

"It looks like you might have started without me," she said, kissing him on the cheek. "Oh, for God's sake, you stink of booze."

"I had one beer at lunch with a client who insisted I join him."

"Of course he did," she shook her head. "Anyway, let's get going. I've been looking forward to this for ages."

"Me too," he lied. He'd rather be anywhere than squashed into theatre seats with his in-laws, watching some random performance he wouldn't understand a word of.

He slipped his arm around her waist as they left the building.

He almost didn't recognise the woman in front of him as he stepped out, blinking in the bright sunlight. The dark shadows under her eyes, unruly hair and casual clothes looked a world away from the polished appearance and fabulous lingerie he'd last seen her in when they'd shared a hotel room. He stopped dead.

"Hello, Adam."

"I, er… hi erm…"

"Hello, I'm Mia," she grinned at Adam's wife. "AKA Belinda Stokes or Maria Cline or various other names I've used to try and get through to you because you're a difficult man to get hold of. In fact, I wondered if you might be avoiding me." Mia tilted her head to one side and gave him a quizzical look.

"No, no, not at all. I've been out most of today, actually. Erm… look, can we pick this up tomorrow? As you can see, I'm just on my way out. I'll be back in the office first thing. You'll be my first call."

"But it's nothing to do with work, Adam, is it?" Mia cut in. She wasn't smiling now. Adam felt his wife stiffen next to him. He dropped his arm from her waist.

"What's going on?" she asked looking from Adam to Mia.

"Yes, what is going on, Adam?" Mia said. "And who's this? I don't think we've met? It's rude to not introduce us." Adam pulled at the collar of his shirt with two fingers. It suddenly felt extremely tight.

"This is Sian, my wife."

"Oh, your *w-i-f-e*!" Mia dragged the word as slowly as she could across her lips.

"Look, what is—" Sian began, but Mia interrupted her.

"Adam, I need a word with you. In private. Now."

"Listen, Mia, I can't do this right now. It's Sian's birthday. We're on our—"

"Or we can do it here, *now*, since you won't take my fucking calls!" She stepped forward, aggressively.

Adam glanced either side of him. A few of his colleagues had started to leave the office and were now staring at him. He noticed his boss and tried to smile, to reassure everyone watching that all was just fine. Nothing to see here, stand away. But his mouth didn't want to cooperate and remained frozen, half open in a small "O". His heart sank. He grabbed Mia's arm and pulled her towards him.

"Keep your voice down. This is my bloody office," he hissed into her ear before turning towards Sian. "Darling, do you think I could have a chat with Mia? We need to get something cleared up. I could meet you at the restaurant?"

Sian looked shocked, and there was something in her eyes that told him she knew. He wasn't going to be able to pass Mia off as just a disgruntled client. She shook her head, resolutely saying, "*No*, I'll wait."

He couldn't go back inside. He couldn't do this here. Whatever it was, he couldn't risk Sian hearing. Darling, please. This is er… sensitive information. It won't take long. Please, just go and meet your parents. I'll be there shortly." Sian was blinking back tears. For a second, he thought she was also going to make a scene, but she turned and walked away.

"Over there," Adam nodded towards the small churchyard ahead of them. Mia walked alongside him through the gate.

"What the fuck is going on?" he asked as soon as they were out of earshot.

"I've missed you too," Mia replied.

"Cut the act, Mia. What the hell do you want?"

"I just wanted to speak to you, but it's been a little tricky because you've blocked me."

"I blocked you because you wouldn't stop calling me. At home, at work. We're done. We had a great time, but it was always no strings attached. We both knew that."

"You fucking bastard. *You* were done, I had no say in the matter!"

"Mia, I told you, I've got kids. I've got to put them first. You have to understand that."

"No, Adam, your kids have nothing to do with this. You just started seeing someone else. I know all about that tramp Melissa. And your wife will know about her too – and us – if you don't help me out."

Adam hung his head. How the hell had she found out about Melissa? Mia was even more cunning than he had thought. Ever since he'd called time on their relationship, she'd been trouble.

"What do you want?" he asked.

"You told your mates Helen's drink was spiked at that boat party. Don't bother denying it." Adam shifted uncomfortably.

"You need to say you were lying."

"To whom?"

"To everyone and anyone. Just stop fucking opening your big mouth. And if anyone ever bring it up again, tell them you were wrong, say you were just talking shit. That shouldn't be difficult for them to believe," she added, her voice dripping with acid. Adam dropped his head and Mia moved closer towards him. He felt her breath against his face.

"Let's not forget the facts here. We dropped GHB into her drink. GHB that *you* got hold of. A young man *died*! We'll all be up against it if the police ever get wind of it. So, if you keep your mouth shut, I'll do the same."

Adam remembered Inspector Grayford.

"I think it might already be too late."

CHAPTER 43

Carrie Aulden pushed back her chair and stretched her arms above her head. It was dark outside, and apart from a couple of sub editors, the office was empty. Her lower back felt awful, her eyes were stinging and her shoulders tight. She felt a headache brewing but she'd never felt more alive. The adrenalin of writing up these notes fuelled her. She couldn't wait to see her editor's face in the morning when she presented him with the story. They wouldn't be able to publish yet, of course, but nonetheless, this was dynamite. Her dream of making tabloids front pages was getting closer.

Since her first tip-off she'd worked hard on the story of GP Helen Nash and the fatal hit-and-run, but from the outset she'd been suspicious about the doctor's account. Something didn't quite stack up. She'd spent months door-stepping friends and family but despite her dogged perseverance, she'd drawn a blank. Against her better judgement, but in the face of mounting demands on her time, she'd been about to give up. But then the breakthrough came.

Mike, her editor, might have raised an eyebrow when she wanted to travel to Ibiza 'on an educated hunch' but when she explained it might result in one of the paper's biggest ever scoops, he signed it off.

She met the interpreter at the airport and they drove straight to the remote finca, half an hour's drive away. Carrie had barely had time to freshen up when she heard a car outside. She was excited but resisted the temptation to rush to the door. Instead, she rearranged herself on the sofa, smoothing down her skirt and making sure for the fifth time that the voice recorder was working. The interpreter would handle it, as they'd agreed. She couldn't speak much Spanish anyway.

When she appeared in the doorway, the woman looked like a fifty's starlet, with huge dark sunglasses and headscarf. Carrie flashed a warm smile. "Buenos días."

Valentina nodded, giving a half-smile in return. She removed her glasses.

"Gracias," Carrie continued. "For coming, I mean" She looked at the translator.

"It's ok Miss Aulden. My English is good enough to understand most things," Valentina assured her.

"Um, er… excellent. Well let's make a start." Carrie gave the recorder one last glance.

It had taken months to get to this point although it had been a stroke of luck that she'd got the story in the first place. Bumping into her ex at a festival when he was home for the weekend was extremely fortuitous. He was clearly enjoying his secondment to the Spanish law firm and loved showing off to Carrie about some of the cases he was helping with. It hadn't taken long to find out where the British GP and her sister had been staying during their fateful trip to Ibiza.

Carrie had finally managed to persuade Valentina to talk following the recent death of her employer, famous photographer Victor Myers. Valentina had been his housekeeper for more than twenty years. The reclusive Myers had been passionate about his privacy and hadn't been seen in public since an awards ceremony over a decade ago. He had homes in London, San Diego and Ibiza, flitting between the three by private jet. Valentina had been reliable and trustworthy, making sure his celebrity friends were allowed to come and go at the Ibiza villa without harassment and organising Victor's life when he was on the island. When he died, she'd lost her regular source of income.

When Carrie first contacted Valentina she refused to talk. From her research, Carrie discovered that the housekeeper was no novice when it came to dealing with the press. When Myers' ex-partner had decided to go public with details of their affair, Myers fled to his Ibizan villa where he stayed, holed up, until attention died down. No one could get near him with Valentina at the helm. She was immensely loyal but now Myers had died, Carrie had tried one last time, hoping she may feel freer to talk, explaining there may be more to Dr Helen's story. What she discovered was more than she could possibly have dreamed of.

Carrie knew that Valentina hadn't been at the villa on the night of the accident. She was at her home half a mile away. However, Valentina admitted that she had seen the two women return. She had remote access on her phone to any unusual comings and goings via a security camera.

"If someone repeatedly enters the wrong code, I get an alert. It's not CCTV exactly, Victor hated that, but it did have a camera that allowed me to see who was trying to get in. It rarely happened. Victor never forgot his code and I'm always here for deliveries. But that night, the alert woke me, and I saw their car at the gate. Mia was leaning from the driver's side window, pressing the buttons. Helen was asleep."

"So Mia was in the driver's seat?" "Yes," replied Valentina confidently.

"And you didn't think about saying anything before?"

"I would never, ever bring scandal to Mr Victor's door," Valentina was defiant. "He didn't need any more unwanted attention." Carrie noticed the woman's eyes fill with tears. "But I want to make things right now. Mia, she is pécora," she spat the word.

Carrie guessed it wasn't a compliment. "And you'll be happy to speak to the police about this?"

"Of course. The police asked where I was on the night of the accident. When they learnt I was at home with my family they didn't bother me again. I had no idea about Helen until you called me."

CHAPTER 44

Helen felt exhausted. The dramatic highs and lows of adrenaline-fuelled emotion these past few days had been draining. She'd lurched between terror at incarceration, anguish over Mia's admission that she'd lied about Helen being sober and then relief at learning her sister hadn't committed the ultimate disloyalty after all.

Then the call came and it was almost too much to take in. She'd listened, shell shocked, before asking her lawyer to repeat it.

Afterwards, she tried to make sense of yet another version of events. She called Mia but she didn't pick up. She tried again and again but it always went to voicemail.

Instinctively she knew it made sense, no matter how much she didn't want to believe it. Her drink had been spiked. It accounted for the memory loss, her questioning herself about not drinking and of course the dreams and flashbacks. But Mia had been responsible. Valentina and Adam had corroborated it. Mia had been driving and had spun a whole web of lies, trying to cover her tracks. Caroline had been right all along – Mia was a pathological liar.

A loud knock broke through her thoughts. When she opened the door, she was shocked at Chris's appearance. He seemed to have aged dramatically since she saw him last.

"They're going to arrest her," he blurted out as she ushered him into the kitchen. "She's taken off, God knows where. She was hysterical. I take it you know?"

"I think so," Helen nodded.

"She's denying it," he went on. "Says she had only been lying to protect—"

"Let me guess, me?" Helen said. Chris started to weep.

"Look, Chris," she laid a hand on his shoulder. "Difficult though it is for us to understand, Mia isn't well. Of course she's denying it. She tells lies. She probably doesn't even know her own truth. I know that sounds harsh, but I've reached the end of the road with Mia." Chris looked confused.

"But she didn't say she was lying to protect you," he protested.

"I got Mickey to erm, keep an eye on her, remember?" Helen nodded, frowning.

"Well, she came clean about this bloke, Adam. Admitted they'd had a brief fling then completely by chance bumped into him again in Ibiza." Helen didn't comment, she wanted to hear what Mia had fabricated.

"It was all down to him! He spiked your drink; he drove the car." Helen raised her eyebrows as Chris carried on.

"Do you know Mia was seen driving away from the marina?" he asked. Helen nodded.

"So, a few minutes up the road this *Adam,*" Chris looked as if just saying his name was torturous, "complained that she was driving dangerously. He demanded she get out and let him drive. He was the one behind the wheel when you hit the motorcyclist!"

Helen noticed how dilated Chris's pupils were. He was trembling, hardly taking a breath, despite his racing speech. "She concocted the story about you driving to protect *him*. She knew it was stupid but agreed to it in the heat of the moment. She didn't want to jeopardise our marriage. Then the bastard fled the scene leaving her to drive home and you to take the blame." Helen took a deep breath.

"Chris, she's lying"

"That's what she told me,' Chris pulled out a chair and sat down heavily, his elbows on the table, head in his hands. Helen sat next to him.

"Chris, this is just the latest in a long line of Mia's lies."

"But why, why would she say that?" he started.

"Because she's cornered. She'll come out with anything to save her own skin."

"She swore it was true. She was intimidated by him and worried he'd tell me about the affair. She'd never have blamed you otherwise."

"Chris…" Helen didn't want to cause him any more pain but wondered if he really did believe Mia.

"She was so happy with you in Ibiza and said you'd really enjoyed yourselves," he continued. "She told me how Phil had always held you back as he wasn't overly keen on socialising so you were making up for lost time. And you were getting quite close to one of the guys in the group."

At the mention of Phil, Helen felt the heat prickling at the back of her neck. Something snapped inside of her.

"Chris, that is so not …Oh…!" Something caught her attention at the corner of her eye and she spun round to see Mia's face at the window. Chris leapt up and opened the door and Helen watched as she folded into his arms, sniffling.

Stung by the remark about Phil, Helen didn't hold back.

"Chris has been telling me how Phil didn't like me socialising, Mia. How lucky for me I had a great time in Ibiza making up for years of his controlling behaviour," she said coldly.

Mia's head snapped up from Chris's chest. Eyes wide, she opened her mouth to speak but Helen wasn't stopping.

"How dare you say that! Phil never, ever held me back from anything, he wouldn't and you know it."

"Hels, you're misinterpreting what I said. Chris has got the wrong end of the stick. Haven't you ?" She turned to him

"Erm no, you told me Helen had been unhappy before her husband died and that…" Chris began.

"ENOUGH! Helen yelled. You're a liar, a spiteful, narcissistic fucking liar, Mia !"

Stunned, Mia took a step backwards.

"Don't say something you might regret, Hels" Mia said.

"The only thing I regret is not waking up a long time ago. You need to too," Helen snapped, looking at Chris.

"One witness has her driving away from the marina, another sees her behind the wheel approaching the villa. Do you really believe she got out of the car just long enough for Adam to cause the accident and then calmly drive home? Come on!"

"Hels, please, what is this?" Mia asked.

"THIS," Helen said loudly, her arm sweeping a large arc, "is what I should have done a long time ago. You'll stop at nothing to get your own way."

Mia let out a little sob and moved back towards Chris.

"The truth is she's been seeing Adam for ages. That was no brief fling," Helen continued despite the pain and confusion in Chris's face. Mia gasped.

"She lied to me about *you*, Chris. Said *you* were the one having the affair. To get me to feel sorry for *her*. Lies, lies, all of it. Let me believe she'd met Adam for the first time in Ibiza. She's played me all along. And she's playing you!"

Mia stepped towards Helen, standing just inches in front of her.

"I am NOT lying!" she spat. Helen could feel Mia's breath on her face but held her ground.

"Of course you're not, Mia, you never are. But there's no getting away with it this time."

"Fuck you," Mia said and spun to walk out of the kitchen, without even glancing at Chris, slamming the door behind her

Chris and Helen stood in silence for a few moments. Helen's heart was pounding.

"I'm sorry you had to hear that," she said, bracing herself for his reply.

"I needed to." Chris's voice cracked. "She's lied about other stuff too."

Barely able to contain her surprise, Helen listened as Chris opened up. "She said so many things about my kids, and my ex-wife. Even friends of mine. Deep down, I kind of knew they weren't true but I always supported her. It's ruined my relationship with my kids but I was just head over heels for her, you know" A tear rolled down his cheek. "But that was small stuff, relatively. This is…" he faltered, "I just can't… can't… believe she would let you go to prison."

"She would because has no empathy and is incapable of understanding the feelings of others. Now she's trying to do the same to

Adam," said Helen. "And while I understand you don't care two hoots about him, he doesn't deserve it any more than I did. Mia's got to face the consequences herself and we have to accept that too."

As they both contemplated the situation, Percy took the opportunity to jump up onto Chris's lap, ignoring his attempts to push him off.

CHAPTER 45

Despite her best efforts, Mia couldn't keep a lid on it. Things moved quickly once the Spanish police were informed. Adam pleaded guilty of being in possession of GHB and got away with a fine. Simon's statement that Mia was driving was backed up by Valentina and the case was turned on its head as soon as the charges against Helen were dropped.

In the face of overwhelming evidence against her, Mia was forced to accept that she would never get away with it if it went to trial, and so reluctantly took her lawyer's advice and pleaded guilty to the charge of involuntary manslaughter. She received a sentence of three years plus a ban on using any type of motor vehicle for five years. She was also ordered to pay a sum ten times the average annual salary in compensation to José Catrimano's family.

By the time she was convicted, press intrusion had reached fever pitch, social media had gone into overdrive, and true crime content creators were going mad over it. It was one of the top-five news stories in the UK, both online and in print, for several days leading up to the end of her court appearance. The *Daily Express* claimed to have located Mia's birth mother and ran a story under the headline "Dr Helen's Spiteful Sister by the Mother She Never Knew" next to a photograph of a woman with her face obscured.

With the help of the best criminal legal team that money could buy, Mia's lawyers successfully campaigned for most of her sentence to be replaced by expulsion from Spanish territory. Almost as soon as she started her prison term, Chris filed for divorce. After serving just eighteen months, she was allowed to return home to the UK where she spent the rest of her sentence on licence.

Mia refused all communication with Helen and their parents, even denying them access when she was in jail. Helen thought about her all the time, wondering if she could possibly change. Was she receiving help? Would she ever admit the truth?

Helen visited the Catrimano family with Elisa Ramirez to pay her respects after Mia was convicted. She'd been overwhelmed by the kindness of José's mother who humbled Helen with her forgiveness. When Helen reached out to shake her hand, Mrs Catrimano hugged her tightly and the two women wept. Helen was keen to maintain contact with Chris. She'd always got on well with him and knew he shared her hurt. He told her he wanted a fresh start and put Oakley Hall on the market. He was moving to a penthouse apartment to be nearer his daughters. Helen had been delighted to hear he was trying to rebuild his relationship with them. He told her that Mia had asked for their house in Jersey as part of her divorce settlement.

Eventually it was a few column inches in the *Daily Mail* that alerted Helen to the fact that Mia was back in the UK. Accompanied by a grainy photograph, the bold headline read:

The Liar Who Framed Her Sister

Mia Carlyle, 38, tried to keep a low profile, wearing sunglasses and a baseball cap when she was seen out and about near Grouville, writes Will Charles.

This is the first time the disgraced former marketing executive has been spotted since being released on licence.

Carlyle served less than two thirds of her sentence in an Ibizan jail before being released back to the UK where she will complete the rest of her time on a tag as part of a Home Detention Curfew. She is banned from re-entering Spain for up to 10 years.

Her sister, Dr Helen Nash, who she had claimed was at the wheel at the time of the accident that killed a 20-year-old Spanish man, is also believed to have moved from her home village in Cambridgeshire. It is not known whether she is still in General Practice.

CHAPTER 46

Without a moment's hesitation, Helen dived into the pond and started to swim. Every nerve in her body jumped to attention as the cold water enveloped her. She'd soon tuned out the cold and was into a steady rhythm, matching her breath to her strokes, gliding steadily forward, feeling the pressure of the water as she lifted each arm out, up, over and back, out, up, over and back.

Helen had fulfilled a longstanding ambition to take up outdoor swimming more than a year ago when she'd moved to London. Reluctant at first, particularly on a grey, cold day, she soon discovered that whatever the weather, it was a great way of silencing the noisy chatter in her head. When she was swimming, she wasn't aware of the temperature, or even what the elements might be doing around her. It was just her and the water. Even on the chilliest days, the pond at Hampstead Heath felt like a treat. She'd often go early, before the rest of the world had started to stir, and loved the anonymity. Everyone looked the same in their swim caps. She had bought a season ticket and was soon a regular, swimming at least three times a week.

Once, when she had come to stay with her for a couple of days, she'd persuaded Meghan to join her. Helen couldn't stop laughing as her mum yelped when she first climbed in and the temperature took her breath away.

"Darling, this is more likely to give me a heart attack rather than boost my immune system," she'd howled. She'd done the swim, at a much slower speed than Helen, but insisted on completing the circuit.

They went for a hot drink afterwards, exhilarated as the endorphins coursed through their system. Meghan appeared happier than she had done for years, and regularly expressed her hope that Helen had turned a corner and was putting the past behind her.

Trading rural life for the city had been Caroline's suggestion. No one had ever really believed she would make the move, but once she had, it had allowed her to make a fresh start.

She had taken up a part-time position in a small practice in Highgate and had reverted to her maiden name of Alcott, which enabled her to reclaim a private life, something she thought the tabloids had robbed her of forever.

Today, after her swim, Helen luxuriated in the delightful tingling sensation of the towel against her skin as she dried herself. The temperature was dropping quickly these days. The sunsets came earlier, the nights were drawing in, and despite the pleasant daytime sunshine, they were hurtling towards autumn. It had always been her least favourite time of year.

As she made her way home through the leafy suburban streets of Highgate, Mia came into her mind. She thought about her less and less these days, but every now and again she would wonder what she was doing, how she was. Did she ever think about her too?

She had chatted to Caroline about her. Her friend had been key in helping her come to terms with the situation.

"So, you really think Mia couldn't help her behaviour?" she'd asked as they sat at a window table in Après.

"It's the million-dollar question, Helen. Classic nature vs nurture. A true case of what is commonly known as a psychopath is rare. In fact, only about one percent of suspected cases can be confidently diagnosed," Caroline answered knowledgeably. "There are those who are born with the genes and perhaps associated brain structures of a psychopath, but they're not guaranteed to become one. Likewise, those who suffer some form of childhood trauma or abuse are also not likely to become psychopaths. As far as Mia is concerned, we will never know."

Helen enjoyed being in London. The move had been a positive one for her. She saw more of Caroline these days; it was so much easier now they were just a cab ride apart. She missed her old patients sometimes, but her new ones were every bit as pleasant, and she'd made some new friends. She believed Phil would have been proud of her.

As she drove into the now-familiar street, she waved at the couple from number forty-four. They were tidying their already immaculate front garden and waved back. They'd enjoyed long conversations about magnolia trees, tulips and dahlias, plants which Helen had lost on a regular basis to the frosts or marauding rabbits, squirrels and deer when she lived in the countryside. The new garden here in Highgate was more sheltered and enclosed, it was a blank canvas for her to work on when she'd moved in. Helen had soon discovered that she could grow more or less what she liked and had thrown herself heart and soul into creating something beautiful. There was never a day when pottering in the garden that a passer-by wouldn't stop and comment on the transformation she had made. If anyone recognised her from the press coverage of a few years ago, they were too polite to mention it.

Even Percy seemed to have seamlessly adapted to the move. Initially, she'd been worried about him. He was getting old now, and although her street was very quiet, it was a world of hustle and bustle compared to what he'd been used to and where he'd spent the first three quarters of his life. But he'd been delighted to take up residency on the seat cushion in the box window of the handsome, double-fronted Edwardian villa. He would curl up in the sunshine, waiting for Helen's return. Now that her working hours were shorter, he saw a lot more of her.

Pulling into the driveway, she was surprised to see the car parked in front of the garage. She got out and made her way round to the front door, wondering why Percy wasn't in his usual spot at the window. Before she had a chance to put the key in the door, it swung open, and the cat's face loomed in front of her as he was held aloft.

Helen laughed as she gathered him from the outstretched hands and buried her face into his fur. He purred appreciatively.

"Did you have a good swim?"

"Lovely, thank you," she replied. "Not quite up to your marathon standards but fabulous, nonetheless. How was your day?"

"Tiring but interesting. I'm looking forward to a few days off, that's for sure."

"Oh, yes, and have you got any plans?" Helen put Percy down and wrapped her arms around Simon's neck as she leant in towards him.

"Nothing much – I've got an appointment at the registry office tomorrow. Just me and a few friends. It shouldn't take long, and then we are going for drinks and something to eat afterwards. Do you want to come?"

"Mmm, I might," she smiled up at him. "I'll see what my diary's like."

"I'll see what my diary's like," Simon repeated, mimicking her soft tone. "You'd better be there, Mrs March, I'll look pretty stupid if you don't turn up."

"Not *quite* Mrs March. I'm still Dr Alcott until then, remember," Helen replied.

Simon slipped his hands around her waist and pulled her close, pushing the front door shut with his foot.

EPILOGUE

He studied the photograph carefully. Squinting, he held the newspaper up to the light. He would never have recognised her. Thinner from what he could make out and it looked like she'd dyed her hair.

As he reread the article, he couldn't resist a smirk. '*...on a tag as part of a Home Detention Curfew.*' She'd find that a bit different to the designer clothes she was always banging on about.

What a grade-A bitch.

She might not have been the first fling he'd had over the course of his six-year marriage, but she was the reason it ended. If she hadn't turned up at his house that morning his wife would probably still be here. She'd been responsible for him losing his job too, he was convinced of it. They might have said it was part of a wider cost cutting exercise but he knew. That bimbo executive assistant had been far too eager to share his doctored expenses and time sheets with HR but it was Mia's repeated calls and messages, not to mention her turning up and creating a scene that had tipped it. She'd tried her very best to ruin his life as well as her own.

He thought he had it under control at first. After she'd accosted him outside the office on his wife's birthday, he'd just about managed to smooth things over. It hadn't been easy but he'd got away with it, convinced his wife they hadn't slept together, it had just been a drunken kiss, that she was mad; someone he'd met through work who'd got the hots for him. It would never happen again, he'd learnt his lesson. Blah blah blah…

It was when she realised the net was closing in on her that she really lost it and turned up at his home. His four bed, executive home with the double carport in the right catchment area – a far cry from the dump of this flat he had now. The one he could hardly afford the rent on since the divorce.

He shuddered as he thought back to that day. Her pulling up in her flash car, screaming at the top of her voice. He'd told her to keep it down but she was having none of it. Sian came out when she heard the commotion, the neighbours were watching. Even when she saw his kids on the doorstep, she kept yelling. Fucking lunatic.

She was hysterical, accusing him, screaming. He held her wrists as she tried to lash out. He was aware of more and more curtains twitching around them. Sian ushered the kids inside. She wasn't going to stop so he did the only thing he could think of; he pushed her away, just hard enough so she fell backwards. It gave him a chance to get to his car and he pulled away. Just like that. Drove off and left her, raging in the street and to everything she had coming to her.

He wondered how often she'd thought about him. As far as he was aware she hadn't made any attempt to contact him but then he had moved house and blocked her number. He'd done well to get away without a criminal record but as he'd told his lawyer, the drug had just been for personal use. He hadn't known she had dropped some into her sister's drink.

He'd followed the case in the papers, of course he had. The day she was sentenced he went out to the new rooftop bar and splashed the company credit card. When he woke the next morning with a stinking hangover, he knew she would be waking up to far worse, every day.

It was unfortunate her sister had reacted so badly. There had been such a small amount in there it should just have made her mellow. He was pissed off when she said they had to leave the party. He'd been having a blast. He'd thought about staying on his own but Mia had been begging him to spend the night at the villa. He decided to go after them and caught up near the car. They got her sister in the passenger seat and he climbed in the back.

Barely two minutes up the road and she'd already mounted the kerb once and was weaving all over the place. They were going to get stopped or she was going to get them all killed. He demanded she let him drive.

And then they hit the motorcyclist.

It was Mia's fault, really. She had been sitting behind him, messing about with his hair, stroking his neck, whispering in his fucking ear and distracting him. When he got out and saw how far the rider had plummeted, he panicked. In that split second he'd decided to get away. It was dark, the road was empty, there were no witnesses, he could walk back, staying out of sight. That stupid bitch didn't need convincing. She didn't want anything jeopardising her precious life-style. She might as well have been behind the wheel.

When he Googled Grouville he put two and two together. She must have got the house in Jersey when she divorced. The swanky architect- designed pad overlooking the bay. He remembered her showing him photographs – an amazing place, clearly worth a fortune. She must have had a chunky financial settlement too.

Standing up, he walked towards the window. He looked out onto a grubby patch of wasteland where unkempt grass and weeds competed with broken bottles and beer cans. In the centre, a derelict outbuilding plastered with graffiti was a magnet for local drug dealers.

He let his mind wander, imagining what her view would be. Sparkling blue water, sandy beaches and fancy yachts, no doubt. Even wearing a tag, her life would be the lap of luxury compared to this. He felt anger bubbling up inside of him. He'd lost everything – house, job, wife – and all because of her. Why the hell should she get away with it?

He took another long look at the newspaper photograph. While she was still on that curfew, he knew exactly where to find her.

THE END

ACKNOWLEDGEMENTS

Writing is a solitary business but by the time I got *The Little Sister* over the finishing line, it had involved a whole team. I'd like to thank my team mates.

Tom Drake Lee, for your patience and professionalism. You always made it fun.

To everyone involved at Lume Books for this exciting opportunity, including those I haven't even met yet. Aubrie Artiano, I know I was always pestering you, thank you for being so patient. Miranda Summers, what an added bonus to discover your book along the way. Carl Smith, you may have been a latecomer to The *Little Sister* party but your input has been enormous and much appreciated. Never have notes in the mark-up area made me sit up and notice so much.

If friends really are the family you choose for yourself, I count myself incredibly lucky to have some fabulous, supportive sisters. Tess, you've been my sounding board, life coach, agony aunt and much more. Just because the book is finished, please don't retire. Sharon, Tania, Elaine and Claire, I hope our N.A.R.B.C. continues forever.

Pen, such a wonderful marketing director for my first book, no matter where in the world you were. I'll always appreciate the confidence boost that gave me. Can you do it all over again?

Carolyn, you have been so generous with your insight and knowledge. Our genres couldn't be more different but our love of - and frustration at - the process is on the same page.

Monica, Rachel, Nicki and Di, great chat and good laughs are invaluable.

Bob and Lesley, your distraction from my book editing was as stylish as it gets. It was impossible to think about plot twists when May 21st was looming.

The serious crime officer who helped with research.

Percy Merrick, who has been inspirational. Not always in a good way but irresistible nonetheless.

There are really no words adequate enough to thank my husband, John, except to say that without your love, support and encouragement I wouldn't get any of it done.

Finally, to my amazing little brother, David. You are worth a million little sisters.

GLOSSARY OF ENGLISH USAGE FOR US READERS

A & E: accident and emergency department in a hospital

Aggro: violent behaviour, aggression

Air raid: attack in which bombs are dropped from aircraft on ground targets

Allotment: a plot of land rented by an individual for growing fruit, vegetables or flowers

Anorak: nerd (it also means a waterproof jacket)

Artex: textured plaster finish for walls and ceilings

A levels: exams taken between 16 and 18

Auld Reekie: Edinburgh

Au pair: live-in childcare helper, often a young woman

Barm: bread roll

Barney: argument

Beaker: glass or cup for holding liquids

Beemer: BMW car or motorcycle

Benefits: social security

Bent: corrupt

Bin: wastebasket (noun), or throw in rubbish (verb)
Biscuit: cookie
Blackpool Lights: gaudy illuminations in a seaside town
Bloke: guy
Blow: cocaine
Blower: telephone
Blues and twos: emergency vehicles
Bob: money, e.g. 'That must have cost a few bob.'
Bobby: policeman
Broadsheet: quality newspaper (*New York Times* would be a US example)
Brown bread: rhyming slang for dead
Bun: small cake
Bunk: escape, e.g. 'do a bunk'
Burger bar: hamburger fast-food restaurant
Buy-to-let: buying a house/apartment to rent it out for profit
Charity shop: thrift store
Carrier bag: plastic bag from supermarket
Care home: an institution where old people are cared for
Car park: parking lot
CBeebies: kids' TV
Chat-up: flirt, trying to pick up someone with witty banter or compliments
Chemist: pharmacy
Chinwag: conversation
Chippie: fast-food place selling chips, battered fish and other fried food
Chips: French fries but thicker
CID: Criminal Investigation Department
Civvy Street: civilian life (as opposed to army)

Clock: punch (in an altercation) or register
Cock-up: mess up, make a mistake
Cockney: a native of East London
Common: an area of park land or lower class
Comprehensive school (comp.): a public (state-run) high school
Cop hold of: grab
Copper: police officer
Coverall: coveralls, or boiler suit
CPS: Crown Prosecution Service, who decide whether police cases go forward
Childminder: someone paid to look after children
Council: local government
Dan Dare: hero from *Eagle* comic
DC: detective constable
Deck: one of the landings on a floor of a tower block
Deck: hit (verb)
Desperate Dan: very strong comic book character
DI: detective inspector
Digestive biscuit: plain cookie
Digs: student lodgings
Do a runner: disappear
Do one: go away
Doc Martens: heavy boots with an air-cushioned sole, also DMs, Docs
Donkey's years: long time
Drum: house
DS: detective sergeant
ED: emergency department of a hospital
***Eagle*:** children's comic, marketed at boys
Early dart: to leave work early

Eggy soldiers: strips of toast with a boiled, runny egg

Enforcer: police battering ram

Estate: public/social housing estate (similar to housing projects)

Estate agent: realtor

Falklands War: war between Britain and Argentina in 1982

Fag: cigarette

Father Christmas: Santa Claus

Filth: police (insulting)

Forces: army, navy and air force

FMO: force medical officer

Fried slice: fried bread

Fuzz: police

Garda: Irish police

GCSEs: exams taken between age 14 and 16, replaced O levels in 1988

Gendarmerie: French national police force

Geordie: from Newcastle

Garden centre: a business where plants and gardening equipment are sold

Gob: mouth, can also mean phlegm or spit

GP: general practitioner, a doctor based in the community

Graft: hard work

Gran: grandmother

Hancock: Tony Hancock, English comedian popular in 1950s

Hard nut: tough person

HGV: heavy goods vehicle, truck

HOLMES: UK police computer system used during investigation of major incidents

Home: care home for elderly or sick people

Hoover: vacuum cleaner

I'll be blowed: expression of surprise

In care: refers to a child taken away from their family by the social services

Inne: isn't he

Interpol: international police organisation

Iron Lady: Margaret Thatcher, applied to any strong woman

ITU: intensive therapy unit in hospital

Jane/John Doe: a person whose identity is unknown/anonymous

JCB: a manufacturer of construction machinery, like mechanical excavators

Jerry-built: badly made

Jungle: nickname given to migrant camp near Calais

Lad: young man

Lass: young woman

Lift: elevator

Lord Lucan: famous British aristocrat who allegedly killed his children's nanny and disappeared in 1974 and was never found

Lorry: truck

Lovely jubbly: said when someone is pleased

Luftwaffe: German air force

M&S: Marks and Spencer, a food and clothes shop

Miss Marple: detective in a series of books by Agatha Christie, often used to imply a busybody, especially of older women

MOD: Ministry of Defence

Mobile phone: cell phone

MP: Member of Parliament, politician representing an area

MRSA: A strain of antibiotic-resistant bacteria

Myra Hindley: famous British serial killer

Naff: tacky/corny, not cool

Naff all: none
National Service: compulsory military service, in the UK ended in 60s
Net curtains: a type of semi-transparent lace curtain
NHS: National Health Service, public health service of the UK
Nick: police station (as verb: to arrest)
Nowt: nothing
Nutter: insane person, can be used affectionately
Nursery: a place which grows plants, shrubs and trees for sale (often wholesale)
O levels: exams taken between age 14 and 16 until 1988 (replaced by GCSEs)
Old bag: old woman (insulting)
Old Bill: police
OTT: over the top
Owt: anything
Pants: noun: underwear, adjective: bad/rubbish/terrible
Para: paratrooper
Pay-as-you-go: a cell phone on which you pay for calls in advance
PC: police constable
Pear-shaped: gone wrong
Petrol: gasoline
Pictures: movie
Pillbox: a concrete building, partly underground, used as an outpost defence
Pillock: fool
Pips: police insignia indicating rank
Piss off: an exclamation meaning go away (rude), can also mean annoy
Pissing down: raining
Playing field: sports field

Pleb: ordinary person (often insulting)

Portakabin: portable building used as temporary office etc.

Post: mail

Planning Department: the local authority department that issues licences to build and develop property

PNC: police national computer

PSNI: Police Service of Northern Ireland

Prat: idiot, can be used affectionately

Premier League: top English soccer division

Proms: annual concerts held at the Albert Hall

Public analyst: scientists who perform chemical analysis for public protection purposes

RAF: Royal Air Force

Rag: newspaper

Ram-raiding: robbery where a vehicle is rammed through a shop window

Randy: horny

Recce: reconnaissance

Red Adair: famous oil well firefighter

Resus: resuscitation room

Right state: messy

Ring: telephone (verb)

Roadworks: repairs done to roads

Rozzers: police

RSPB: Royal Society for the Protection of Birds

RTC: road traffic collision

RV: rendezvous point

Royal Engineers: British army corps dealing with military engineering, etc.

Rugger: rugby (posh American football)

Sarge: sergeant

SCO19: Specialist Crime and Operations Specialist Firearms Command

Scrote: low life

Section: to have someone committed to a mental hospital under UK mental health laws

Semi: semi-detached house, a house with another house joined to it on one side only

Shedload: a large amount

Shop: store

Shout the odds: talk in a loud bossy way

Sickie: day off work pretending to be ill

Sixth-form college: where students study A levels

SIO: senior investigating officer

Skell: a homeless person, aka 'tramp' (insulting)

Skip: a large open container used for building waste

Slapper: used to label somebody as overtly sexual, typically a younger woman, aka 'skank' (insulting)

Smackhead: heroin addict (insulting)

Snout: police informer

SOCO: scene-of-crime officer

Sod: an annoying person

Sort: to do or make

Solicitor: lawyer

Sparky: electrician

Spook: spy

Spuds: potatoes

Squaddie: a soldier of low rank

Stunner: beautiful woman
Super: superintendent (police rank)
Surveyor: someone who examines land and buildings professionally
Sweeting: endearment, like sweetheart
Tabloid: newspaper, typically known for a sensationalist style of journalism
Tea: dinner (Northern English)
Tea towel: drying cloth
Till: cash register
Tip: a mess, e.g. 'This room is a tip', or a local garbage dump
Tipsy: a bit drunk
Top oneself: commit suicide
Torch: flashlight
Tutor: university teacher
Tower block: tall building containing apartments (usually social housing)
Twoc: steal a car, often just for joyriding (taking without owner's consent)
Upmarket: affluent or fancy
Wacky baccy: cannabis
Wally: silly person (can be used affectionately)
***War Cry*:** Salvation Army magazine
Wash: the washing machine
Water board: company supplying water to an area
White van man: typical working-class man who drives a small truck
WI: Women's Institute, organization of women in the UK for social/cultural activity
Widow's weeds: black clothes worn by a widow in mourning
Wilco: will comply, i.e. 'yes'

Wrinklies: old people

Yellowbelly: native of Lincolnshire (not to be confused with yellow-belly, meaning a coward)

Yob: a rude or aggressive youth or person

Yorkie: type of chocolate bar

Milton Keynes UK
Ingram Content Group UK Ltd.
UKHW041830130923
428631UK00004B/102

9 781839 015410